The elderly man who stayed at his window all night with a spyglass knew. So did the housewife who was having an illicit love affair. The town playboy knew. So did the spinster schoolteacher.

Everyone in the sleepy Southern town knew who the killer was. The problem was, everyone knew it was someone different...

SEASON OF THE STRANGLER

MADISON JONES

CHARTER BOOKS, NEW YORK

This Charter Book contains the complete
text of the original hardcover edition.

SEASON OF THE STRANGLER

A Charter Book / published by arrangement with
Doubleday & Company, Inc.

PRINTING HISTORY
Doubleday & Company edition / 1982
Charter edition / June 1983

ISBN: 0-441-75700-6

Charter Books are published by Charter Communications, Inc.
200 Madison Avenue, New York, N.Y. 10016.
PRINTED IN THE UNITED STATES OF AMERICA

For *Monroe Spears*
with respect and gratitude

Contents

SEASON OF THE STRANGLER

Prologue

The summer of 1969 was one that the people of Okaloosa, Alabama (pop. 38,400) are not likely to forget. There is more than a single reason. For one thing that summer produced the climax of racial unrest that had been visibly growing for at least a decade. It also, perhaps, witnessed the climax of a more general unrest of which the racial was only a part—the unrest that comes when old ways of being are rudely displaced by new ones. So, that summer would no doubt have been memorable in any case. But in fact there is a much more dramatic reason for why that one is remembered as different from all the others.

Beginning in May and ending in early September there was a series of five murders in Okaloosa. All the victims were women, all but one of them old women, each one strangled and sexually assaulted. The pattern was always about the same. The victims lived alone and were discovered hours or, in one case, a whole day later lying dead on their beds or on the floor close by. Always there was the gaping mouth, the throat discolored, the nightdress torn or ripped clean off the body. There would be a window or a door prized open but never any fingerprints. In fact the only piece of solid evidence the Strangler ever left on the scene, caught under a fingernail of one of his victims, was a strand of black human hair. That was all. Other evidence, of whatever kind, was seen at last to be no more than the fruit of somebody's fevered imaginings. It came to seem probable—the Strangler was so astute—that if he was ever to be caught it would have to come about through some unforeseeable stroke of luck.

Meanwhile there were a hundred different alarms, reports, rumors—enough to keep the police lunging here and there to check on a fact or to question still another victim of somebody's hysteria. People looked at their neighbors as they never had before. They went out of their houses with care at night, and windows rarely even locked in the past appeared with grilles or bars over them. At its worst, in August and September, hardly a night went by when *he*, the Strangler, was not *seen* among shadows out in a yard or peering in at a window.

CHAPTER ONE

A Strange Land

Suspicion was everywhere that summer, eating away. *Somebody* in Okaloosa had to be the Strangler and after those first two murders in May and June every week or so produced a new suspect who was taken more or less seriously for a while. One of those taken more seriously was Ragar Wells, the twenty-eight-year-old son of a fairly prosperous longtime widow. It was not only, as in some other cases, that Ragar was peculiar, or even that he had in fact when he was about twenty spent several months in the insane asylum at Reedville.

In this case the suspect fled and managed to elude the police
for almost five days. For that time at least, people thought
that the Strangler's identity was finally known. But Wiley
Brownlea, who lived next door to Ragar, did not have to
think: he knew. In fact he had known for many weeks that
Ragar was the Strangler.

Wiley Brownlea was a man up in his seventies and he had
been living in his son's home on Bass Street for a little over
two years. He had not wanted to come there. He had been a
farmer all his life and nothing short of permanent physical
disability could have made him yield to his son's insistence
that he sell his mortgaged farm and his cows and give away
his now-idle hunting dogs and come to live in town. It was his
hip. He had broken it a second time by falling off his tractor
and after that he could not do much more than hobble
around with a walking stick. This made Wiley bitter but it
was not the real cause of his bitterness. There was not any one
cause, except just the world, the way it had gone. How was it
that a man could work hard all his life growing the beef and
cotton people had to have and never get anywhere but back-
wards and end up without a pot to piss in? And his best son,
that boy he had loved and meant to carry his name on in the
world, dead long ago in that war over yonder. Then his wife
too, and finally a house with nobody but him to warm it. No
son at all, not really. Unless you could count a man who spent
his time between a country club and selling land he didn't
own to build those plywood houses on. It was no wonder that
Wiley's tongue had got rusty and his wit like an old file when
he didn't watch it.

By now he had almost learned to watch it. Glares and silences, including those of even his grandson Jimmy, had
finally taught him this much. They made him think of that
"home" where the corpses, still creeping or rolling around in

chairs, cackled at one another and sat by windows that looked out every way on a parking lot. That was Wiley's "option." "It's your only option, Daddy," James had said, and said in a way to show the old man how straitened he was in the world. What option, though, when even living under a roof with his son's wife Agnes beat it a country mile? The thought of it, because Wiley's tongue *would* break loose sometimes, was what finally made him choose to start eating in the kitchen by himself, where he couldn't hear what Agnes said or look up and see under the plucked arches of her eyebrows those eyes turned on him like a pair of beads. It was this that had made the food persist in falling off his fork.

As much as he could Wiley stayed clear of them all. The backyard was his solace but there was wintertime. At his insistence, in spite of his hip, he had his room upstairs and from there he could see down into the backyard and into the neighboring yard across the hedge. This was better than nothing, better than a parking lot, but it did not keep the winters from being hard. His eyes were still good and he read hunting and farming magazines and a little Civil War history. He sat by one or the other window and watched the rain fall and bare limbs over the house tops heave in the wind, and he would doze. Sometimes he waked up in alarm thinking he had overslept, that his cows were waiting to be fed, and he would be half out of his chair before he remembered. Then he would keep on remembering. In gray cloudlight and mist of rain his cows, with white faces, were standing around the hay shed lowing for him. Or he saw, from the narrow end, the long back pasture that was his favorite because it was surrounded everywhere by woods and because back there, concealed from eyes, deer came out to graze with the cows.

As soon as the spring weather allowed, Wiley spent his days in the backyard. He hobbled out early with his stick and first

tended his little patch of a vegetable garden near the high
back hedge. Close by was his chair, under a thick mimosa
tree. It was not a kind of tree he liked but it cast a good shade
and along with a fig bush gave him a certain remoteness from
the back of the house. Besides there was a gap through the
hedge here that opened into the alley beyond and once in a
while a friend came through the gap.

The friend's name was Tag, a man in his fifties. His
business was picking through garbage cans in alleys and what
he had to support was his habit. Squatting on his heels he
would always produce from somewhere among his ruined
clothes a pint bottle of clear whiskey. He handed it first to
Wiley, who took a drink, a small one. Then Tag would take
the bottle back and drink deep and set it on the ground in
front of him. He had a face—mottled red, with melted eyes
and stubble of gray whiskers—that Wiley might have known
his whole life long. And he brought the news. "Fight at the
swimming pool last week. Niggers started it." Tag would
shake his head and look up at the sky. Or he would say, "Fire
truck broke down. Hart's grocery burnt plumb to the ground.
Fire truck just set there."

Tag knew things that did not get in the newspaper, and all
the talk about everything, and he had a memory that seemed
to go back at least a generation before he was even born. He
knew what buildings used to stand where, and when they had
burned or were torn down. He knew the town's mayors clear
back to the turn of the century and he knew who had the first
motor car in the county. Tag's visits lasted as long as his whiskey did. When he left he was always richer by some change
that Wiley had fished from his pants pocket.

It was a disgrace. That old degenerate. Drinking with him
in the yard. This was what James, urged on by Agnes, finally
said to Wiley. The old man had been expecting it. His spot

under the tree was not remote enough and he had been conscious more than once of Agnes watching from a window of the house, watching from under those fake arches of what had been eyebrows once. In his defiance Wiley had said, "Well, anyhow he knows some things worth knowing. Ain't nobody else around here does."

"Yeah, learned them in garbage cans, I guess," James said.

"He never learned them at a country club."

This was a mistake. James' fat lips got tight and after a moment of cold silence he said, "Agnes wants it to stop. You've got to remember this is our house." He turned and walked away up the yard, the well-dieted shape of him trimly fitted into his blue sport coat.

That was his son, Wiley thought, a boy raised up to know the worth of a thing, prissing toward the house in his sport clothes to a diet supper where nobody who had a word to say that mattered could get it edgeways into the conversation. In fact Wiley had tried at first, before he began to notice in Agnes' eyes that flat or else that gimlet look and silences that grew more hostile with every word he said. Until he learned just to sit there and keep his mouth busy with nothing but his food. Who had got promoted to what or invited to somebody's house. The Gileses were tacky people, another threat to the club. And wrought-iron grille, like in New Orleans, that was the coming thing. This was how it went. At times, moments when fool excitement put a lilt in Agnes' voice, Wiley could almost see how it was she had got to the boy's sluggish heart. There were not many such times. Supper alone in the kitchen was a kind of reprieve for Wiley.

It was like a reprieve, maybe, but only a partial one. The kitchen was not far enough and even when the swinging door was shut her voice still reached him. Of course it reached him some of the time no matter where he happened to be, tran-

scending walls and distance. His room upstairs was no haven,
not when her voice took on the pitch it did in arguments or
when on the telephone down in the hall it rattled the hours
away. From a distance, Wiley thought, it had a quality like
some kind of a bird's voice and he finally remembered the
bedraggled and obscene mynah bird that had belonged to the
wife of one of his old neighbors. He was sorry he had remembered this. It made him hate the sound of her voice still more.
More, and also more often, he thought, because now there
were times he would hear her speaking when in fact there was
nothing to hear.

Fortunately the backyard was pretty much Wiley's private
preserve and even Agnes' voice did not often afflict him there.
He sat in his chair and read and napped, or painfully down
on his knees in the dirt picked every weed from his garden.
Most days he took a short walk in the alley, hobbling with his
cane between the rows of hedges and garbage cans down to
the street at one end or the other. Tag, just as if he had been
listening to James that time, never had appeared again. More
likely he was dead, though, likely poisoned. Or shut away in a
home someplace, for a nuisance. But Wiley still watched for
him. Even after the long confinement of his second winter at
James' house, his first day out, he went into the alley just to
see. Tag was not there but somebody else was, standing smoking a cigarette by a garbage can under the towering hedge.
That was the first time Wiley had ever seen Ragar Wells up
close.

It was the first and for many weeks the only time, yet the
face stayed clear in Wiley's memory. So did Ragar's manner,
hostile and defiant, like somebody caught in a criminal act by
a person whose proper business it was not. That was the way
he looked, defying an old man with a cane who hobbled past
him along the deserted alley. He made no response to Wiley's

nod or even his mumbled greeting. The uplifted hand with the cigarette, arrested at the level of the chin, never moved, and something about the gaunt face looking at him through the smoke made Wiley think somehow of a blunted hatchet. But this was the impression of an instant, gone the next. It was Ragar's eyes. They were like a hound's eyes, rusty like that—but a hound with the tables turned, itself at bay. There was something, like a little flash across his brain, that almost persuaded Wiley to stop and meet that curious gaze.

Wiley was not sure why, but afterward, and still after weeks had passed, he kept thinking about Ragar. The young man was like a puzzle he needed to solve or a secret hard to penetrate. But in all the weeks that followed, Wiley never saw him in the alley again. He had to be content with watching from his upstairs window or, at times when he heard Ragar's voice, approaching the thick dividing hedge to listen. He saw him much more often than he heard him, but all together, finally, it was enough. Wiley had his suspicions long before even the thought occurred to anybody else. In fact within a few days after the Strangler's first murder, in May, Wiley was already observing the young man with new intensity.

Until up in June, though, Wiley's suspicions never took on any real firmness. They were more nearly just thoughts that teased his mind, leading him on, renewing his watchfulness. Then two things happened. One was that second murder, the rape and strangling of old Mrs. Emma Quick. The other thing, though it had preceded this one by several days, leaped into Wiley's mind as if it too had been described there on the front page of the newspaper. He saw it happen all over again and heard Mrs. Wells' voice, though not very clearly, just as he had heard it from his bedroom window that morning. He could see the gray head on top of her stiff figure ducking and bobbing and hear her tone of rage. "Nothing," she said. "You

didn't even . . . the weeds . . . from morning till night, nothing." And Ragar standing there in front of her like a post in a
gale, though he did once lift a hand.

But what had happened happened after Ragar's mother
turned her back on him and with a slap of the screen door
behind her went into the house. Ragar just stood there, still
like a post, for at least a couple of minutes. The distance was
too great but Wiley imagined he could see in the face the
hound eyes and the look of being at bay. Then Ragar turned
around and started walking.

At the back of the yard by the hedge was a little house not
much bigger than a child's playhouse where Ragar seemed to
spend most of his time both day and night. Not far from the
door was a slim magnolia tree maybe ten feet tall. When
Ragar got to it he suddenly stopped and confronted the tree
as if it might have spoken to him, insulted him. Then with a
sort of lunge through the foliage he seized it by the trunk. He
began to shake the tree. He shook it so hard that the big green
leaves fell reeling onto the ground around him, the top heaving, until it seemed sure the little trunk would snap off in his
hands. It never did. Ragar let go all at once and looked toward the back of the house. Then bending to pass through the
door he went into the little house by the hedge and did not
come out again. Or did not in the hour while Wiley sat
watching from his high bedroom window.

That, or rather, a few days later, the recollection of it, was
the real beginning for Wiley. On the front porch in the afternoon, as he hurried his slow eyes down the columns of news-
print, it ran in his head like a part of the story his eyes had
not got to yet. Of course that part was not in the paper. He
knew this well enough and yet, reading those columns over
again, coming a second time to the end, he still imagined that
somehow his eyes had skipped it. No, no, he had skipped

nothing. There was a car, a shiny one, approaching along the street, slowing down as it passed in front of him. Inside was a woman's head—the gray oblivious head of Ragar's mother. This was the way it came to Wiley, suddenly, like a thought sneaked into his mind. Watching that oblivious head, watching her turn and pass from sight beyond the curtain of hedge, he felt his heartbeats falling one by one.

Recovering his cane from the floor Wiley went into the house. Except for the slow distinct one his heart made in his ears there was not any sound. He paused in the living room, among the too-much furniture, all spidery, all gleaming with the fakery of wax he could smell on the air. Poor stuff, pitiful stuff, that would not survive one solid kick of his foot. Lifting his cane he rapped a chair and went on back to the kitchen. He spilled a little coffee when he poured it, and did not care. When he sat down at the kitchen table with the paper and started to read it over yet again, there was another difference. This knowledge that was his alone gave him new eyes to read with.

Wiley did not hear the car stop in the carport or Agnes until she opened the kitchen door. It would be unpleasant, he knew this instantly. But he knew it with a difference this time, as if from across a distance his secret made. She entered on spikes like a balancing act and stopping to look down at him pinched her lips together. There was a burnt smell about her. It was the hair, piled up in a heap of twists and rolls that would have inspired, two years ago, a crusty mockery on Wiley's part. He was tempted again. But Agnes, in a tone that was not quite severity, said, "I thought you would be outside this nice day."

She did not notice that this got no reply. She was already looking around for damage he might have done and he saw her see the coffee spill on the stove. Her thin breast lifted.

With a thump she put her purse on the counter. Taking a cloth from over the sink she wiped the spill with twice the strength it needed. "Couldn't you be a little more careful, please, Papa?"

It was like what he was waiting for. "You see this?" Wiley said, putting a finger on the headline of the outspread newspaper.

Agnes glanced around at him, looked at his hand, stared for a moment from under the fake eyebrows. "Yes." And then, "Horrible," she said and resumed wiping the yellow top of the stove. It was wasted motion and Wiley's blue eyes followed it back and forth.

"That's two, now," he said. "Same fellow. *Police* ain't got a notion."

Agnes went to the sink. She rinsed the cloth, wrung it dry, arranged it precisely on the rack.

"Paper says that kind, you never know . . ."

"Let's not talk about it," Agnes said. She finished drying her hands. To clear the kitchen of him she said, "It's time I started supper now."

Wiley decided on one more shot. Reaching for his cane he said, "And niggers raising hell, too. This town . . ."

"Do you have to talk so rough?" She picked up her purse and left the kitchen. When Wiley went out a minute later into the backyard it was to stand for a while beside the hedge at the closest point to Ragar's little house.

The third of the murders happened not quite two weeks later. Miss Marilyn Barfield, alone in the house, must have waked up too late to scream or even to struggle much, with hands already tight around her frail old stalk of a neck. The same hands too, no question about it now. Somebody with those white or black hands was walking around town like any other man, meeting people, living next door to somebody.

Many a person tried to remember all the hands he had shaken in these last few months and also thought about his neighbors up and down the street, whether any one might be the one. This was when the whispering about Ragar Wells got started. But these were whispers, doubtfully passed. Wiley knew. All his watchful intentness over these past weeks had put the answer beyond doubt in his mind. With some trouble, secretly, he had got hold of a spyglass—a child's toy but good enough—and by the hour in his upstairs room he would sit at his window and watch. He could see the face, just a little blurred, up close, and see the hands, that they were strong. When this last murder occurred Wiley realized that he had already been expecting it.

His life was changed. A part of the difference was obvious, because now instead of out in the backyard under the mimosa tree Wiley spent hours of every day in his hot bedroom upstairs. Even his night routine was changed. Instead of just until twilight he was likely now to stay outside for a long time after dark and at ten or eleven o'clock come hobbling into the house. Or even later sometimes. Agnes especially did not like it. For one thing he might fall. Besides there was that madman, that Strangler out there someplace—who knew where? She had another reason. Often there were guests in the living room, and Wiley, a goblin with a walking stick and a black felt hat on his head, would delay at the foot of the stairs and look in at the company. He had a way of looking, as if what he saw vaguely alarmed but mostly filled him with loathing.

The deeper change in Wiley was not so obvious, but it was felt. At least Agnes felt it. He was reverting, she thought at first, going back to the way he had been when he came to live in her house. No, it was more than that, or worse. She never had liked that look he would fasten on her sometimes. She liked it a good deal less now. It was not only hostile, it was veiled, like a secret, and alone in a room with him she was likely to surprise the look if she turned around suddenly. Something else different was the number of times she found herself alone with him. These had been rare in the past. Not anymore. It was not uncommon now for him to enter the kitchen where she was and without apparent reason sit down at the table. Finally, twice, he even came into the little parlor where she had her afternoon hours to sit and sew or read her fashion magazines. This much by itself would have made her nervous but there was more. There was his fixation on that awful Strangler, and he would say, maybe, repeating himself, "Liable to be anybody, you can't tell. Crazy like a fox. Liable to be . . ."

"Let's *not* talk about it."

Then Wiley might sit there for long minutes without speaking again, and Agnes, nervous, might suddenly glance at him and catch that look of his. It got to the point that before she entered the kitchen or the parlor either one she always scouted ahead of herself. Finally she complained to James, insisting he speak to Wiley. She also insisted that he put new locks on all the outside doors. Wiley had got her thinking more than ever about the Strangler, and especially about that Ragar Wells next door.

That was mid-July, with days not much hotter than the nights and continuous flickers of dry lightning in the sky north of town. One of those nights, right after dark, was the night when James, coming out into the backyard to do it, spoke his piece to his father. He was very vexed. The flickers of lightning revealed this in his face, and so did his tone, as if that bird voice of hers was speaking out of James' mouth. "Isn't it bad enough," he said, "without you scaring her more?" Was it on purpose? A little consideration, please, in her own house. Then he was gone, flickering toward *her* house.

Except a grunt or two Wiley had made no answer. It had not been easy. There had been a moment when the words crowding into his throat felt like a shout he had stifled there, while he heard, distantly, that rattling bird voice coming at him. He heard it still in his mind, even minutes later, imagined it running and then shut off in a hard wet gasp of breath. Wiley got to his feet and leaning on his stick waited out the interval while his stroking blood subsided.

He went through the gap in the hedge. The flicker of lightning showed him down the alley nothing except the intermittent silver gleam of the ashcans. He went a dozen careful steps and stopped for a while. Another few and he stopped again. He was in back of the little house and through the density of hedge he could see glowing eyelets and tatters of a lighted window. Except for the quiet of crickets and a dog somewhere and the far-off fading whine of a semitruck Wiley could not hear anything. But Ragar was in that house, sitting, just sitting with open eyes staring. There was that look, a cornered hound's, baffled and desperate. And his strong hands lay open on his knees. He never moved or made any sound but breathing, the lonely resonance of breath rising and falling in the room. Night after night, a familiar sound. It was his own breath that Wiley was hearing. He stood there for a long time.

On into August there was lightning almost every night and Ragar's yard and his little house at the back were visible in the flashes. Now there were whole nights when Wiley did not leave the chair he had placed by the window. At times he would fall asleep but he would wake again to see it all stripped of darkness, all detailed in the stark shuddering light of a moment or two. And twice, at some hour very late, he had seen Ragar. The second time, when Ragar was standing not far from the boundary hedge, Wiley imagined that Ragar

was looking up, looking back at him. Later he was convinced
of it, even if this conviction did seem to have come upon him
in one of his fits of sleep. Then he thought it was more than
just a look. Something, like words shaped on a silent mouth,
had passed into his mind. At any rate that moment made a
difference in Wiley's vigils. There would be, next time, no
need for him to draw back into the dark. Maybe in fact he
would answer, lift his hand, stand up to make himself plainly
seen at the window. And then, what? This thought made his
heart beat. It also made some nights when Wiley's vigils went
almost unbroken by intervals of sleep.

Then James went out of town on a three-day business trip
and Agnes was left alone in the house with Wiley. Her strong
protest had been in vain. What, she complained to James, if
six weeks *had* gone by since that last murder? He, the
Strangler, was still out there someplace, was he not? With all
the rumors, suspicions, alarms, what woman could help but
be afraid? And right next door that Ragar Wells, and all the
whispers about him. She sniffed at the mention of Wiley. In
fact he was the opposite of a comfort. She saw to it that Wiley
got still another warning before James left.

Afterward Agnes wished she had seen to it that the warning be made much stronger. Almost from the moment of
James' departure she felt the old man watching her. She tried
to ignore it and could not. Several times she tried facing him
down, deliberately turning to meet the gaze she could not
help but feel. It would skitter away from her then and fasten
somewhere, the carport door or the window. But only until
she was back at her business again.

For the first time in quite a while she took full notice of
Wiley. She was surprised. At first she thought that suddenly,
as often happened with old men, he had reached the point of
getting onto his last legs. He had that appearance—abruptly

thinner, more sallow, forgetful of his clothes and the white stubble on his face. He even moved slower, with a new deliberateness. And that look, maybe feverish, in his eyes could be read this way. But soon Agnes thought not.

She could not decide what it was about her that Wiley kept looking at. There was the old hostility, or worse, in his expression, but also, as she now imagined, there was more. It was a kind of curiosity, a kind she could only think to call detached or speculative, as if something might be about to happen in connection with whatever part of her he was scrutinizing. Anyway at this time, when there were already enough things she did not want to think about, it made Agnes more than just uneasy. In the first two days of James' absence she went out at least a dozen different times to shop or visit friends or sit by the pool at the country club. The second night she even went to a movie by herself. It was that night, while she was in the movie, that the Strangler got his fourth victim, Ernestine Bell.

By ten o'clock next morning the news was out and running everywhere. Agnes, who knew or had known Ernestine Bell, heard it in town and because of Wiley went to a friend's house instead of home. So, until up in the afternoon when the newspaper came, Wiley had not heard anything. He had seen something, though. He had seen two men in street clothes get out of a police car and go into the Wellses' house and a little while later come out with Ragar and drive away with him. After that, waiting and waiting, Wiley stayed at his window. An appeal, he thought: that was what it was when Ragar, just before he stooped to enter the car, had lifted his eyes and looked at Wiley. "Help!" he seemed to say, and Wiley, too late, had nodded his head. Why hadn't he been quicker? And raised a hand besides? After all these nights, these secret nights between the two of them, it was like a betrayal that he had not. He cursed himself. "Help!" Ragar had said, and Wiley cast about in his mind for a way.

But they brought Ragar back in the afternoon. They let him out on the street and drove away and it was all over. Ragar went straight into the house and stayed. It was all right now.

Half an hour later, though, when Wiley got up from his chair, he was still nervous. That was why his sudden thought about the newspaper sent him hurrying as best he could down the stairs and out to the front porch. The paper was there. For half a minute the headline held his eyes. Then his eyes were scanning, hastening down the page. Once he was sure that Ragar's name was not there he folded the paper and took it inside with him to read.

Later, in his room, he heard the bird voice call him to supper. The second time she called he answered something, but he did not go down, not yet. In fact it was whole hours after that, while Ragar's little window burned like a steady eye looking back at him, before he so much as remembered her call again. The window had seemed to blink and then to flicker and this was what reminded him that he had not eaten all day. Even so he waited longer, watching that steady eye. Wiley got stiffly onto his feet and went downstairs to the kitchen.

Because of the silence he had thought Agnes was not even in the house any longer. Then there were her footsteps, intruding, coming toward the kitchen. There she was, in street clothes even now, with something in her hand. Her face was different. It was pale, a pallor that darkened her eyes and made them look uncertain. Her voice was uncertain. "I could . . . warm that up."

His food, she meant. From over the plate where his head was bowed a little, he just watched her. He saw her swallow.

He saw her give up and, hesitating, move across to where a stool stood by the kitchen counter. That was sewing in her hand and she put it on her knee. She did not start to sew. There was no sound at all but a dripping of water into the sink.

"It's just so horrible." Her hand moved, drew the needle out of the cloth. It was trembling. "I tried to call James . . ." Her voice died away but it came back after a moment. "Ernestine . . . she was just forty-seven. Just a few years older than me."

Getting closer, then. The tightness in Wiley's throat was like a bubble of laughter about to come and he thought about speaking the words, thinking how her face would look. At last it was enough to see that her lips would not stay quite together. She drew a breath.

"What kind of a person would do such a thing?" she said, above a whisper though not by much. She was facing the carport door, watching it now, and still in that secret voice she said, "Such a horrible thing."

Wiley opened his mouth and said, too loud, making Agnes jump, "Be anybody, you can't tell. On this street, maybe . . ."

It had not only been too loud, it was too much. He saw this at once in Agnes' face and he cast about for words to repair his blunder. Fool. It was too late.

"That Ragar Wells," Agnes murmured, watching the door. "They questioned him today. They still don't know. They still think maybe . . ."

Wiley watched her, hating her face. Suddenly he said, "It ain't him."

"They say . . . Somebody thinks they saw him last night. Up that way, where Ernestine . . . He was in the asylum, you know."

Wiley's movement made his chair creak. "Somebody lying. Making that up." He tried to pause but the words came rushing. "He was home last night, I seen him. See him all the time. Some liar making that up . . . Goddamn liar! I'll tell them!"

In the hushed aftermath with Agnes' head bent and motionless over the sewing in her lap Wiley could hear still echoing the sound of his own harsh voice. Fool, damn fool. What could he say? He mumbled something that did not make good sense and, a little later, saw the tremulous hand with the needle slowly begin to sew. Now his eyes followed but his mind did not. His mind was running, running. "Help!" the boy had said to him. Wiley was startled when Agnes said something faint about bedtime and got up off the stool with her back toward him.

It was after midnight when Wiley, in slippers, one slow step at a time, moved like a thief down the stairs and out of the house. The flickers of lightning that he had to wait for guided him to the gap through the hedge. He stumbled once in the alley, and once when his stick struck something, a can, the clatter stopped him cold. Where Ragar's lighted window appeared through the hedge he stopped again, preparing himself, thinking what he would say. "Boy . . ." he would say. There was no sound but crickets and a motor in the distance. There was a confusion in his mind. It seemed he had made an obscure mistake somewhere, one that now had set his heart pumping, and for a space he could only stand there waiting for it to come to him.

What came to him, though—it seemed straight into his ear—was a sudden voice. Only his stick saved Wiley from a fall and when he got his balance back he was looking into a dark face thrust up close to his own, saying, for the second, the third time, "Old man . . ." That was what Ragar said, in a voice that sounded as if it had been snatched out of his throat. For what seemed a whole empty minute that was all he said, and Wiley, casting in his mind, could not come up with a single word of the many he had planned. The lightning flickered. The face, so close to his, seemed in that brief light drawn up like a whitened fist around the blunted nose.

"Old man . . ." The same snatched-out voice said it again. "Spying on me, all the time, spying on me. You're the one told them!"

Wiley found he could shake his head. Then he had a voice but it was too small.

"You told them, goddamnit! Lies. Old man . . ."

Wiley saw Ragar's hand. Recoiling he made a backward step, and stumbled. An ashcan saved him but still the face was there, pursuing, as close as ever. It flickered out of the dark.

"Listen, Son . . ."

"It wasn't me! It wasn't me, goddamnit, *goddamnit!* You're the one needs choking!"

This last was a kind of shriek and then Wiley saw the hand, both hands. But what they seized was his walking stick that he had lifted against them. They tore it violently out of his grip and, all in an instant, he saw it poised arm's-length high in a tremulous flash of light. The next flash happened inside his skull. After that, for some indefinite time, there were no more flickerings or cricket sounds in the dark.

A little more than a week later Agnes received a telephone call from the county home for the aged. A vacancy, the voice told her, had developed unexpectedly and Mr. Brownlea could come the next day, if he wanted to. It was all news to Agnes, who thought at first that it must have been James' doing. There was good reason. Over the past few days they had both come to the conclusion that, whatever the whole story might be, something had affected the old man's mind. To say the least he was like a different person. In the first place he rarely came out of his room anymore except to eat, and that was never at mealtimes. Now Agnes always left his food out on the kitchen table knowing that in an hour or two, when and if the house got quiet, he would come hobbling down in a way that made her think of a decrepit thief. It was like that, stealthy. When surprised he would mumble something and turn his face away and go on into the kitchen. He might eat half the food on his plate. Then he would go back up to his room, where he kept the window shades drawn almost down to the sill. He was like a man in hiding.

Right at first Agnes had supposed that the whole trouble with Wiley was the fall he had had. That was what he told her that night when, roused by sounds in the house, she had got out of bed and, terrified, switched the hall light on. He was on the stairs, both hands on the railing, with blood on the side of his face. She also noticed that one of his feet was bare. He had been for a walk, he said, and had a fall. That was all he said. He would not let Agnes come near him and he would not hear of a doctor. At the time she had believed him.

She did not keep on believing him for very long. First, the next morning, there was the news that Ragar Wells had run away and that the police, more suspicious than ever, were looking for him. This made Agnes think about last night and what Wiley had said to her in the kitchen. Then, that evening, there was the matter of the walking stick and also the slipper. James, who had got home in the afternoon, went on a little search. He found them in the alley lying among rubble from an overturned ashcan, the slipper and both pieces of the broken walking stick. He did not know what to think. And his

visit upstairs in the near-dark room left him no better in-
structed. What he got out of the old man lying with his face
turned to the wall was not a word more than Agnes had got.
It was nothing that James could or would have gone to the
police with.

So it was a great relief for both of them when Agnes got
that call from the home, and a still greater relief the next day
when they left him there. Through the whole trip Wiley said
nothing to them. Just before they left him in the little white
room he did ask one question. He wanted to know if Ragar
Wells had been found. The answer was yes, two days ago,
and after a long grilling had been released again. But before
James had got half through with this answer Wiley had already turned his back and was on his way to the window to
let the shade down. It looked as though he was not even listening. If he did listen he soon forgot, because he asked the
same question over again the next day when James and Agnes
came to see him. It was almost the only time he spoke. And in
fact this was to be the pattern. They would come once a week
or so and answer his question and watch him fall back into silence again. They were never sure he even heard most of the
things they said to him.

This silence was just part of the reason that James and
Agnes all but stopped coming to see him. Half the time he
would not even open his door to them. The nurses told them
that pretty often it was the same way in their own case. And
when the nurses did get in and tried to brighten up the place
by raising the shade, Wiley would get off the bed and draw it
down again. Of course with only a parking lot to look out on,
there was nothing lost except a little daylight in the room.

CHAPTER TWO

Loss

Myra Nettles' feeling that she was somebody else, somebody different from herself, had been with her from the very instant she opened her eyes that morning. That had been back in May, about the time the stranglings started, but she still could recall those moments in every detail. The sunlight in her room, streaming from her east window and reflected in her dressing table mirror, was not different from yesterday's light—and yet it was not the same. Around her in the room, wherever she glanced, things looked that way, distant and strange somehow. It had taken her a little space to think why, and when the reason came it was one she all but flatly rejected at first. Because it was a dream, imaginary, and could not have happened. But it had happened. It was there solid, still warm in her mind, a thing just hours old. Myra Nettles, forty, mother of Louise and wife of trusting Baxter Nettles, was a brand-new adulteress.

There was not any sense of guilt, not then, even though she had got into this same bed last night, mere hours ago, feeling sick clear to her heart, feeling as if her body must soil these freshly laundered sheets. That had passed off in her sleep, though, somehow, and what awakened in its place was this astonishing sense of her own newness. Like a fresh body given to her. It was something that did not pass off, either, the way her guilt had done in the night. All day and then for many days she kept being dogged by the notion that just such another reversal, the guilt coming back, would seize her and plunge her into despair. It did not happen. The passing weeks and, now, several repetitions of her adultery still did not make it happen. She was free, a person merely in the disguise of a cast-off former self.

Before that first day was over, Myra had discovered that her new condition, behind her disguise, afforded her a kind of pleasure she had not at all anticipated. She did not see her husband until suppertime that evening. Baxter Nettles was an agent with Dale & Arnold, the busiest real estate company in Okaloosa, and he had just got home from one of the business trips that took him out of town fairly often for two or three days. He arrived just in time to wash up and almost his first words to Myra were spoken across the supper table. "Anything new?"

This stopped her hard, almost like a blow. In the act of reaching for the plate Louise was passing down, Myra's hand

paused and she could not make her tongue speak the word
No. This lasted a second or two. What she said, to her own
consternation, was "Yes," and with something like an alarm
running in her head took the plate and began to serve it from
the bowl of stew.

"Aren't you going to tell me what?"

Myra risked a glance at his face then. It looked a little
tired, barely interested. A little dumb, too. To her surprise
again, she said, "Very exciting." The surprise this time was
not much, though. She handed the plate of stew to Louise
and then looked up at Baxter, looked squarely at him.

"Have I got to guess?" Baxter said, taking the plate from
Louise. He was not looking at Myra but at his food.

And suddenly it was easy for her. "You'd never guess," she
said. "A little party at the club last night. The usual." Baxter
was deep in his stew already and Myra, seeing how perfect
was her disguise, felt her new boldness rising. It prompted her
to say, with only the smallest catch of her breath as she spoke,
"There was somebody new, though. A man . . . named
Gude. Henry Gude." Out of a full mouth Baxter made a
noise like "Uhmn," an acknowledging noise, and nothing
more. Myra added, "A very nice man." And then, "Very
amusing." Immediately she felt as if she might be about to
blush and she lowered her face. No, she was safe. It was not
alarm that had set the blood skipping in her veins.

This was the kind of pleasure she learned, on that first evening, to awaken in herself. It was only the first of her small
discreet jokes, with one meaning for Baxter and quite another
one for herself. Her pleasure in them increased, too, even to
the point where her daughter's presence added something to
the spice. It was Baxter she observed, though, watching the
gaunt face that yet was fleshy, puffed under the eyes, that beneath a thatch of randomly graying hair was not handsome

any longer and that registered nothing at all when she made her jokes. This, his blankness, was part of the pleasure. There was no other time when she felt so completely the newness of herself, as if she was placed at such a distance that neither Baxter's puffy eyes nor Louise's brightly blue ones could make out the least difference in her. That was another woman there at the table under the small crystal chandelier she had bought two years ago at Dobey's Antique Shoppe, seated among the blue hand-painted china her mother had left her, backed up to the massive sideboard that she had brought from a cousin's old home in Montgomery. Those were all things that belonged to that woman, pieces of *her* self, just as were that careless man and that frivolous teenage daughter. But she, the new, the real Myra now, sat here across a distance they had no inkling of, content in the thought that at last she belonged all to her very own self. Though not quite *all,* she reflected, thinking of Henry Gude.

Hadn't she made it too easy for him? He had asked her to dance. Her body had fitted his and his breath smelled not of cigar smoke but pleasantly of something that was not quite mint. He made her laugh. And he was a stranger, a little of a mystery even though he told her that he had been in Oka-loosa six months working in the textile mill as a sort of direc-tor. Before he had even proposed it to her, that they meet for a drink at a motel bar safely out of town, there was something of the sort, and more, already on her mind. They met and he was charming. Then they were in bed and she, amazed, felt that old self of hers split and sundered and falling from her as if it had been a shell.

Too easy for him. At first, when she supposed it had been a one-time thing, she had not worried about this. When, not wanting to, she found that she wanted him again, and after that again, then the worrying started. She tried a little

coolness, and once, for no other reason, turned him down. She
also began to take a kind of pains that she had neglected for
several years, with her looks. She went secretly on a diet and
she spent much time at her dressing table. What she saw at
first in her mirror was like news that is not very good. It was a
wonder, though, what a little attention could do. She had
thick brown hair with hardly a strand of gray and now, with
help from the shampoo she had had to shop for all over town,
the luster came back. Searching a beauty magazine she discovered a treatment with whole cream that really did wake
up her skin. And presently her hazel eyes, that she had used to
be rather vain about, seemed, under the tended lashes and
softened lids, to regain old depths they had lost. Or to gain
new ones—a birth instead of a rebirth. And that was how it
should be: a face to go with the newness inside of her. Henry
noticed, too, because he told her, and also because, if anything, he grew more ardent each time.

There were of course, as Myra knew, all the routine dangers. Even Baxter might happen to notice and wonder at least
about these outward changes. Or other people might. Some
accident, some small unlikely thing, might bring it all into the
light of day. But she almost never worried about such matters,
not in this town now, when old women were strangled in their
beds and scandals were all but the common fare and changes
followed changes faster than memory could record. She
looked ahead to that next call from Henry, to that next meeting with him. She looked in the mirror and watched her
newness find its way into her face.

So things went on through the summer. In July, Louise
went to stay with a cousin in Birmingham, a welcome change
because it gave Myra more freedom. Much less welcome was
the prospect of Baxter's vacation in August, when she would
have to go with him to the beach for at least one tedious

week. There was nothing she could do about it. They went, and added to the tedium of her days was an uneasiness lest her absence in some way make a change in Henry's feelings. As it turned out, Myra's uneasiness was, if ironically, justified.

The change in Henry was one that at the same time excited and disturbed Myra. Her first meeting with him, at noon of the day that followed her return, was ardent as none had ever been till now. He touched her in ways he never had before and the black eyes fastened on hers had the shrouded look of eyes blind with desire. There was violence in the way he seized her at last. It took her breath and for a few moments really frightened her—enough in fact to make her, later, look at Henry with something like bewilderment, as if she was not quite sure she knew who he was. With his dark head on the pillow beside her he smiled, showing his clean white teeth. "What's the matter, kitten?" He had not called her this before. Kitten. She hated it. Then, "Hunh?" he murmured and put a hand on her cheek, caressing it, and finally let the hand come to rest on her neck. Somehow it troubled her resting there. She removed it. She said, "You were so . . ." and broke off. He smiled again and kissed her on the mouth.

Myra both wanted and did not want it to be that way again, and both with the same intensity. The conflict kept her awake that night, stewing inside her, with lust displacing nameless fear and being displaced in turn. Fear of what, though? She could not tell. Once, late in the night, she got up quietly and went to the open window and looked out into the backyard. Half of a waning moon cast mingled light and shadows of trees across the lawn. The pale shadows seemed to change, patterns slowly melding and crossing one another, confusing vision. Later, before she went to sleep, she had her feelings in order once more. The stewing was all to no purpose. For that had happened one time, once only, and only because of her long week's absence from him. Now it would be the same again.

Myra was wrong. The next time was all but identical, and so was the next and also the time after that. "Please. Don't . . ." she cried out in those moments. But it was as if his violence made him deaf, as if his craving was less for her than for her destruction. Until he was all spent and lay with his dark head on the pillow languidly smiling at her. "I'm sorry, kitten." Kitten again, though she had more than once protested. "It's just that you take me out of myself." She lay there afraid and also wanting him.

Her nights were restless. She kept the windows shut and locked, which made Baxter complain about the heat. "Hadn't you just as soon be strangled as suffocated?" he would say. "You think he's coming for you with me here?" And Baxter started sleeping in the guest bedroom. Often Myra would get up in the dark and stand at the back window looking out. There was no moon now, only starlight, and nothing was really visible but the spectral shapes of the trees. She had bad dreams. One of them was recurrent. In this dream she saw herself, though not very clearly, lying here in her black, her sexy nightgown and looking oddly small and still. There was a sound of whispering in the room, but very dim, with no words audible. One night in this same dream there was a new development. She saw that she was covered, face and all, by the bedsheet. She approached and lifted the sheet from her face and saw that she had been strangled.

That dream jarred her awake in panic and her hand reached out in vain for Baxter beside her. Switching on the bed light she got up and, her blood still pounding, checked the windows she had locked. Her image in the mirror stopped her. The face that looked back was very pale, almost deathly so, like a face close-masked in a tissue of skin soon to shed away. She left her light on and went about the house checking windows. In the end she found herself standing outside the door of the guest bedroom where Baxter wheezed in his sleep. She never did go in, though.

But when Henry called her the next day she turned him down, with only a flimsy lie. She heard his anger and heard her own hesitant and frightened voice. After that for two days she refused to answer the telephone. She would hear it ringing and turn her back or else go out of the house until it stopped. Because it was all over with, Myra told herself, lying to herself, knowing that finally in one of her vulnerable moments it would ring and she would go and answer . . . Unless she had luck, help from somewhere. But where? Stepping back into her Sunday school days she tried praying—brief prayers because they went out of her head before she could finish them. In any case they would have been no help. Fate was against her.

At least it seemed like fate when, after those two days of abstention, Baxter told her his news. He had to go on one of his trips again, suddenly. Myra's only luck was that when he said this her back was to him, because she was chopping celery at the kitchen counter. Three days, and Louise absent too. Her heart was pounding. Then it was pounding for a different reason, from fear, and she had to master herself before she could speak. Gazing down at her still hands she said, "Couldn't Amon go this time, instead of you?" But no, they were both going, it was important. She did not stir for a moment. Meaning it she said, "Couldn't I go with you?" She heard him move, his step just behind her, and felt his hand come to rest on her shoulder. "You can stay with Anne and Ryder. They'd be glad to have you. I'll call Anne right now." His voice was gentle. Myra knew that his face, close to her head, was also gentle and that if she were to turn now he would take her in his arms and kiss her and tell her she could go with him. Safe, safe with him. She almost did turn. It seemed as if she had been fated not to, against her will.

She refused to stay with Anne and Ryder. It was foolishness. She would keep the windows locked and bring Bugs into the house. Besides, the police were everywhere these days and also she would alert them. But, Myra thought, it was not for the sake of Henry Gude that she would remain at home. When she kissed Baxter goodbye next morning she put into her kiss a warmth she did not have to feign, a warmth she had not felt toward him in such a very long time. After that her waiting for the telephone to ring was a waiting only to ignore it. But it did not ring. All day it did not ring and her restlessness in the silent house that night fed solely upon her aching sense of loss.

It did ring the next day at noon. Hesitant and trembling she at last picked up the phone. And there like a muted violence in her ear was Henry's voice. She meant, tried to say no and managed only to sound evasive, holding him off, thinking how she could end it all by simply hanging up in his face. But his voice, tender and violent at once somehow, kept pouring into her ear. It flooded her senses, took her strength, and wrested from her finally the thing she had been determined not to reveal. Then the last ground was gone from under her feet. "You're by yourself, then, huh?" he said. "Then why don't I just come there? Late tonight?" Myra said no. She said it repeatedly, in a voice that she thought must have sounded loud over the phone. And yet, somehow, in the end it had come out yes. Holding the dead receiver in her hand she stood there in astonishment.

Myra tried to call him back and was told he had left the office. A little later she tried his apartment and the office again and then again an hour after that. At suppertime, calling his apartment, she got a busy signal, but when she tried once more five minutes later she still could get no answer. At nine that night she gave up. When he came she would not be here. He would come, at eleven, through the backyard and see the house all dark and find when he put his hand on the knob that the door was firmly locked. Maybe with his lips close to the glass he would call softly to her. Maybe he would come to her bedroom window and tap at the pane and maybe give the window a try. She shuddered, thinking of herself in the bed seeing the dark shape of him, his dark hands at her window. Like a dream, and she could not cry out, watching the hands come closer . . . But she would not be here when he came.

Myra meant to leave. She took her purse and sweater and went as far as the kitchen door. But she stopped there in the door. Out in his pen, invisible in the dark under the trees, Bugs barked twice, then hushed. She shut the door. No need yet: she had two hours still. There on the kitchen counter was the celery she had not chopped for the meal she had forgotten about. Forcing herself to make another try she took up the knife and began to cut the celery, cutting and cutting, the whole package finally, as if there had been some purpose in it. She put the knife down and turned to look at the clock. Ten past nine. She would leave now. But she did not, she decided to take a bath first.

After that, as she stood in her dressing robe, the little green clock on her night table said a quarter till ten. She would dress now and leave . . . Why leave, though? She could put out all the lights and go to bed and when he came and found the house dark and no answer to his knock he would go away. Simple. She took her nightgown from the closet. She had started to put it on before she realized that it was her black one and she quickly put it back and took another. The phone rang, a violent ring, a bolt in the stillness. It rang again, then again. She was naked. But the ringing compelled her finally and holding the nightgown to her breast she stepped out into the hall to the telephone.

The voice was Baxter's. It took Myra a little while to be certain of this, because of the bad connection and also because of the blood thrumming in her ears. Remote. Baxter might have been speaking from another continent, repeating questions to which she repeated half-distracted answers. Naked in the hall. And also, as she now discovered, visible through the panes of the back kitchen door. From out of the distance Baxter's voice said something final and the click of the phone cut dead an answer that was already there like a cry swelling in her throat. No sound came from her open mouth and the dead wire hummed in her ear. It was as if she stood naked in a place no longer familiar to her, and no longer safe.

Quickly Myra shut the bedroom door. Lifting the gown to put it on she got a glimpse of herself, herself and the lighted room behind her in stark mirror-image—but only a glimpse, refusing to look. She wanted everything dark. The bedroom lights first and then the kitchen and then the living room. She came back in a darkness that twice caused her to blunder into walls.

It was too hot in the room. Soon, unwillingly, she put off the coverlet she had drawn up to her chin. Then she lay vulnerable in the dark holding her eyes shut, trying to make a blankness of her mind. But the stillness of things kept creeping in and presently also the shape of that pale window, just as if her eyes had been wide open. Once her eyes were startled open. There was bright light in the yard and she sat up and knew that it was the beam from a police car out on the street. It cut like a scythe through the shadows and the moment was like a small bright island of safety. Then it was gone.

Myra could not really have dozed, not with her blood throbbing and hot that way. It was more like an interlude of absence from herself, in which though wide awake she was conscious of nothing except her abandoned body throbbing there on the bed. Anyway it was like that when, with a jolt, as if she had come violently back to herself, her eyes flew open. What she at first saw was a man at her window, but this was an illusion, quickly gone. He was out there, though: Bugs was barking. A thing, rushing in with panic, was suddenly clear to her. She had not locked that door.

For some seconds, because of the panic in her, Myra could not move. Then she was up, off-balance, and with her head struck the doorjamb hard enough to make her stagger. She lunged for the door to the kitchen across the hall and found herself as in a strange dark room not knowing where the door was that she sought and turning and turning to search it out. She bumped into the table. Then she saw the door. It was partly open and there was a man standing in it. Myra screamed.

That was only the first of her screams. It was as if her own screaming blurred her mind and exactly what happened was not very clear to her for nearly a whole day afterward. When he started toward her with his hands out and words uttered in the hard vehement tones of a threat, Myra could think of nothing except that he was attacking her. Then he had hold of her and his hand that was trying to stop her mouth seemed to be groping for her neck. That was when she lunged back, screaming, and fell across the counter with her arm in the heap of chopped celery, and that was when the knife got into her hand. She struck blindly. She heard the grunt he gave and saw him recoil backward to the wall beside the door. His voice made a hissing noise, as if air was escaping from him, and then, just before she screamed again, she heard him say,

"Bitch . . . crazy bitch!" When the screams kept on he made his way out the door and disappeared.

By then there were lights on in the house next door and only a minute or two later Jeff Rains, her neighbor, rushed in. He found her on the floor sitting propped against the counter, not screaming any longer, only moaning, crying. She had blood on her forehead and the knife was lying there. The police were not far behind Jeff Rains. But all Myra could do was point, moaning, to the back door where the man had gone out. They gave up trying to question her that night. They took her next door and left her in the care of Helen Rains and a doctor who came and gave her something to make her sleep.

The police had Henry Gude before the night was over. He had got to his car, parked a couple of blocks away, and had got home all right, thinking that the wound under his ribs was something he could take care of himself. But he was wrong and, still bleeding, he barely made it to the hospital. He was able to talk to the police, though. Even after getting what he had got that night from Myra he tried at first to clear both her and himself by lying about the wound. But when he saw clearly what he was suspected of he came out with the whole story. To support it he named two friends who had known all along about his affair with Myra, and one of these he had even told about his plans for tonight. There was a clerk, too, at the motel where he and Myra usually met, who would vouch for him. The police checked and before Myra had even waked up the next day they were already convinced.

Of course the *Okaloosa News* ran a story the next day, a premature and garbled version of what had happened. After that the story was killed entirely. It made no difference in this case, though: the story, all revised, went faster and to more places than any newspaper could have carried it. Baxter, who could not at first be located and did not arrive until afternoon, was one of the late ones to hear the more accurate version.

He did not hear it from Myra. When finally, with his gaunt face haggard and his lips set together like the two halves of a dough biscuit, he managed to drag himself into her presence, what he got was last night's unrevised horror story. While she told it to him the tears ran down her face and her whole body shivered. From the bed where in her nightgown she sat propped against the headboard, she kept reaching her hands out to him, inviting him to come and embrace and comfort her. Finally she got up and, all tearful, came to him. With Baxter standing like a post she leaned herself against him, crying on his neck, her brown hair in disarray falling over his shoulder. For a while there he actually believed her. It was due to some curious mix-up, that version he had got from the policeman an hour ago. All wrong, all crazy.

Myra's act was so good because it was not really an act. Somehow, ever since last night's event and right on up through her encounter with Baxter, she really had managed to keep her mind shrouded in this illusory version of the thing. She *was* attacked and it *was* the Strangler: Henry Gude was the Strangler. She wanted him charged, imprisoned, hanged by the neck. She said this to Baxter, meaning it, in real forgetfulness of the times she had slept with Henry Gude. Not exactly forgetfulness maybe. It was more as if her recollections were of some not quite familiar woman whose performance with that man in a motel bed she herself had merely observed. So her heart *was* in the show she put on for Baxter.

This state of things could not last long, of course. There were too many facts, hard ones that kept intruding. Baxter's impulse to faith in her did not survive the afternoon, and the curious illusion that had sustained her act and made it so elo-

quent could not sustain it any longer. For a while, in desperation, she kept it up, watching her pratfalls follow one another.
Baxter, with a suitcase, left the house. Except he paused at
the door before he left and looked squarely at her one last
time. "I'll leave you to your 'conscience,'" he said. "Or to
that Gude bastard, in case you haven't got one."

Possibly if Baxter had not said this, if he had left her in silence, it might have made some difference. At least it might
have postponed things for a while. Those words, intended to
give pain to Myra, had, very soon, another kind of effect. For
a little while they gave pain, all right, made her look inward
at her sinful self. But the more she looked the dimmer that
self became. It was gone, trailing off like a phantom in possession of this house. She was not that Myra. She was the Myra
with Henry Gude cavorting in a motel bed.

The next morning Myra opened a pair of cold eyes on her
bedroom. She packed her things, all she could get into three
suitcases and a paper bag. She drove out of town to the familiar motel and settled in. She was there for a couple of days.
The next thing anybody heard about her she was in Birmingham. Later on, rumor had it that Henry Gude, who had lost
his job because of the scandal, was there also and that they
were living together. Anyway after a few months she was gone
from Birmingham too and nobody had any real idea where
she went. Or Henry Gude either. There continued to be people in Okaloosa who, in spite of everything, still suspected that
he was the Strangler. That was how they explained the fact
of Myra's final and apparently complete disappearance.

CHAPTER THREE

Faith

The Reverend Harold Gates had served as Pastor of the Calvary Presbyterian Church for eighteen years, ever since he came to Okaloosa as a young man of twenty-seven. By the time he reached his forties he was half bald—exactly half bald in fact, because his thick black hair, combed rigorously sideways, lay like an abbreviated monk's cowl straight across the high crown of his head. From that point down to his eyebrows there was not one hair and his long arching forehead gleamed impressively in the light that fell over the pulpit from above. His vigorous body had fattened a little by this time, too, though the only plain evidence of it was the dewlaps that had formed underneath his jaw. But these only added to his impressiveness in the pulpit. In his moments of strong feeling the dewlaps quivered visibly, as if little currents of electricity were passing through his body. Small children hard to keep quiet in church always fell silent at those times.

Reverend Gates had come naturally by his strong moral feelings. His father before him had been a preacher too, of the strictest sort, and in the home where Harold Gates grew up all infractions of God's Law, even the rumored infractions, were subjects for indignation and prayer. It was no wonder that Okaloosa, so different from the farming community where he had been raised, was something of a shock to him. But he was a disciplined man and he had the Bible always to remind him what must be expected of human nature. If he never quite got used to the town, at least he learned to live in it with as much serenity as a pilgrim ought to feel. And the sense of shock that he never entirely got over served him well as a preacher. It was this that carried his words to his congregation and made even the small children appear to listen.

So for at least a dozen years things went smoothly enough in Reverend Gates' life. Sunday morning and night and Wednesday night he preached. In times of trouble for members of his congregation he was always on hand, consoling, advising, praying. All the many duties of a good pastor he performed with an energy that amounted to zeal, including the part he took in public matters. He was pretty often present, and outspokenly so, at meetings of the City Board and the Board of Education and at least three or four times a year he felt morally obligated to deliver his opinion in a letter to the *Okaloosa News*. That his public efforts were for the most part in vain did not discourage him too much. He had recognized how the world was going and that all a Christian could hope to do was his best. Meanwhile there were God's promises, and His blessings. There, the greatest of all his blessings, was the home God had given him, the good wife Leah and the boy and the girl God had entrusted to him. There was comfort when nothing else was, in the white frame house next door to the church on Orchard Street.

The change that eventually came over Reverend Gates did not happen all at once or even in a single year or two. It was gradual enough to be undramatic and those in the congregation who knew him best and noticed early had little trouble understanding the new intensity in him. There had been so many things, happenings in the town—wicked or disorderly things that in some measure had touched or shaken almost everybody. One of these things, the biggest, was the new racial conflict. Reverend Gates was no liberal but for several years there he was considered to be one. When there was occasion, any incident of violence against a Negro, he spoke out from the pulpit and in other places. One of his sermons, with the text "Even unto the least of these, my bretheren," almost cost him his job. His congregation thinned out a little and the Board of Elders, in a threatening mood, met with him. He rode it out and never did back down.

This was only one of the things. Another one was the new textile mill that brought in so many new faces and strange ways and immoralities on a scale not known before. It also brought the drugs, or seemed to, and with these the long hair and the boys and girls that even the best of parents could do nothing about except pray. For Reverend Gates, even if all this had not touched him in his family life, the new shape of things would have been burden enough. But it did touch him there. His son Paul and, later on, even his daughter Martha became a part of all that. To people who knew something of his intimate life it was no wonder that at last, facing his congregation from the pulpit, he sometimes had the look of a man fiercely and defiantly at bay.

Still, up until the time when the stranglings began the difference in Reverend Gates was by no means striking. Even on that Sunday morning after the day his seventeen-year-old son was arrested for possession of narcotics he stood before the silent scrutiny of his congregation and delivered his prepared sermon on God's justice with a composure that astonished everybody. He knew perfectly well also that there was talk, whispering, about his daughter. However great the pain, he kept the evidences of it locked up in the privacy of his soul. Except sometimes, when those small lapses offered just a glimpse of what was passing in him. Then the stranglings started.

The first victim, on a night early in May, was a seventy-eight-year-old widow named Rosa Callahan, raped and strangled in her bed. She lay there through the rest of the night and all the next long day before she was discovered and it was bedtime when Reverend Gates got the news. When he came back into the bedroom Leah saw how white his face was. He would not answer her question at first. He was fully dressed and had paused at the door when, with his back turned, he finally told her what the call had said. Then he walked the four half-lighted blocks to the house where Rosa Callahan had lived.

There was no real point in it. Reverend Gates had barely known Miss Rosa anyway and by the time he got to her house the body had long since been removed. There were still people standing around in muted clusters under the streetlamp, but no family, no kin for him to comfort. In fact, though he did not realize it for a while, this was not why he had come. He stood on the sidewalk for nearly an hour listening to the talk, moving nearer to this little group or that one, until at last there was nobody left except him. Still he did not leave. He entered the little yard and walked around to a side window where, as he understood, the killer and rapist had got in. It was dark there in the shadow of trees. A scented darkness, because some of those trees were locusts full of blooms, white blooms like stars sweetening the air. Appalling, a rotten sweetness. He thought of her lying there through that night and day. At last he said something out loud, not hearing it then but hearing it later, as if the words still floated close by in the sweet appalling dark. "What kind of a man . . . ?"

This was the first time. The four other murders that followed in the summer and early fall were for Reverend Gates almost like replays of this one, different mainly in their different settings. In the empty wake of each one he was there, staring at a window, imagining he could smell a scent of star-like locust blooms. He imagined something else too, repeatedly. It was the shape of a man in the window creeping through, only the back of him visible. He imagined this at the time and also afterward in his memories of each occasion. The day came when he had to remind himself that in fact, however familiar the shape of that man's back, he never had seen anyone in any of those windows. No one had. For all that had been discovered about the man it might have been an evil spirit entering at those windows.

This was the period, in the middle of that summer, when the change in Reverend Gates began to be marked. It showed itself mainly in a kind of withdrawal, a kind of retreat inward upon himself. Not that this caused him to neglect any of those activities that he considered to be his duty. He never slighted a sermon or became a whit less mindful of the sick. People noticed the difference, though, the impression of enveloping silence that even his most public voice did not quite dispel. It was as if behind his words and gestures there was another self

that thought and watched. Now his sermons, though not
changed in their real substance, made his congregation feel
uneasy. It seemed to be the sermons, the words probing their
hearts. In fact it was the sense of being watched, all watched
at the same time, as if he meant to fathom all secrets masked
behind their faces. In the light from over the pulpit the long
arch of his forehead gleamed. This of course was nothing new
but people noticed it more. There were some now who were
hard put to keep from staring at it.

Of course it was Reverend Gates' wife Leah who more
than anybody else noticed the change in him. She was a small
timid woman somehow still in awe of her husband and she
never was one to pry. Once in a while that summer, though, as
she watched the silence gathering over his life, she ventured a
soft and deferential question. "Is something the matter,
dear?" She would get no answer, or almost none, only a shake
of his head. Except once, when she got a sort of an answer.
He shook his head this time too, though with passion, so that
the dewlaps quivered. "This world . . . When will His justice
come?" This was all. There were times when Leah was
shocked to see how dark was the gaze that he turned upon the
one child still left at his table, as if his own daughter had been
his enemy. It was the same gaze Leah saw at other times
when she walked along the street with him and followed the
direction of his eyes to some innocent or unfamiliar person
walking ahead of them. There were his nightmares, too, ac-
companied by outcries, but never any words she could inter-
pret. Afterward he would usually wake up and lie there silent,
his open eyes defined sometimes by the flickering of heat lightning at the windows.

Toward the end of the summer Leah began to notice something else. It was the amount of time her husband was spending in and around the church building next door when there

was no good reason for him to be there. She never had any idea what was happening, though.

Earlier that summer the deacons had hired a new janitor, a Negro who was a deaf-mute. They had hired this man mainly for reasons of charity but he was also an excellent janitor and scrupulous about keeping the building clean and the yard neatly trimmed. He always came early, before people got up, and if need be worked clear through until suppertime. No bossing was necessary. When there was something hard to communicate by signs Earl (Earl Banks was his name) could read the notes handed to him. But he never smiled. Also, unusual in a Negro, he had very green, almost gem-like eyes. This, the eyes, was the first thing Reverend Gates noticed about him. Not long afterward he noticed also that Earl was much younger than he appeared to be: his stoop had belied his age. In fact he was probably not over thirty, and quick and sure with his hands. This made two surprises. Together they suggested yet-unreadable depths in Earl, and these were what prepared Reverend Gates' mind for the teeth of obsession waiting to fasten there. This obsession came later, in August of that drawn-out brooding summer.

The reason for it was Earl's back. Reverend Gates, who at dusk came over to fetch a Bible he had left in the Sunday school room, had thought he was alone in the building. When he opened the door to the room the first thing he saw in the twilight was Earl standing at a window. Of course Earl had not heard him. He went on standing there, looking out, in the characteristic stoop that all of a sudden put a thought in Reverend Gates' mind. The thought was that Earl was about to crawl through that window. For what must have been quite a while, a space without sound or movement, Reverend Gates stood there staring at him. He never did turn on the light or in any way make his presence known. What he did do, finally, was reach behind him for the door and back out of the room and leave without a thought of the Bible he had come to get.

That same night Earl with his gem-like eyes and stooping posture appeared in Reverend Gates' dream, making a nightmare of it. This was only the first time and the nightmares grew worse. But worse still was the fact that in the daytime also he could never get Earl out of his mind, that between himself and the sermon he was composing, the food he ate, the face he was looking into, Earl or the ghost of him was there, always there. And now something new had caught Reverend Gates' attention. Barely visible in the black forehead was a mark, a faint discoloration, as if maybe, long ago, a thumb of fire had laid its imprint in the skin. Or was this just an illusion? There were times when, however hard he looked, Reverend Gates could see no trace of the mark.

Not a day, hardly even a stretch of hours passed when he did not make one of his visits to the church. They were all for the same purpose, to spy on Earl. Sometimes from hidden places, through the crack of a door, he would watch Earl at his work of sweeping or mopping or washing a window, observing every motion of the stooped body, the sinewy arms. Or, approaching him to order some little task just now devised, Reverend Gates would glance into the unreadable face, looking for the mark, or gaze searchingly at the hands that he saw were lithe and powerful. Once, forgetting himself, he became so much absorbed in looking at the hands that Earl finally put them out of sight behind his back. More and more Reverend Gates made him nervous.

Of course there was not one shred of real evidence and Reverend Gates kept telling himself this. However certain he might feel, however much confirmed in this certainty by his daily observations of the man, he knew that after all even the truest human heart was full of error. He prayed about it, praying that God would enlighten his heart, would cleanse it of any self-deceit and by some revelation wipe away all reason for questioning.

The fifth of the stranglings took place on a night in early September. Because the victim, old Mrs. Gladys Stallworth, had been a member of his congregation, Reverend Gates was notified quickly. The body was still there when he arrived at the house and was admitted into the small living room where the middle-aged son and two or three other people stood in benumbed silence. Reverend Gates did his duty, tried to give comfort. He did not know whether any coherent words came out of his mouth. In his breast there was something like a fire raging. It drove him finally, just before he left the house, past a reluctant policeman and into the room where the victim lay on her bed. Her head was covered but he uncovered it. He saw the purplish tongue between her lips and the strutted discolored face that had been the face of gentle old Mrs. Stallworth. He saw also the bruises on her neck and the shoulders naked, stripped naked. For the minute or two while he stood by the bed he could not even in his mind give shape to words of prayer.

Later he could pray and that night on his knees at his bedside he prayed with a fervor that amounted nearly to rage. His voice that kept erupting out of the silence in which he was accustomed to pray wakened Leah and made her lift her head from the pillow. All she could see at first was his half-bald head gleaming under the bedlamp. Suddenly he stopped praying and looked straight up into her face. After a moment he said, "How long will God stand for these abominations?"

It was like an accusation and Leah did not dare even try to answer him in his wrath.

Reverend Gates got his answer in the night. Late, just at daybreak, Leah heard him get out of bed and, without turning on a light, dress and leave the house. Through the window she watched him cross the stretch of lawn to the church and enter at the back door. Still for a little while no light came on. Then, at ground level, a small basement window suddenly was lighted. It was the janitor's room. Seconds later she saw just above the level of the sill what clearly was the crown of her husband's head under the light bulb. It stayed there perfectly motionless for a long time, so long that before it disappeared from her sight she had begun to think it must be something else, some unguessable shiny object placed on the window ledge.

What had stopped Reverend Gates and held him transfixed there in the middle of the closet-like room was an odor. It had been faint to start with: slowly it defined itself, grew unmistakable. Now he knew why he had been wakened as by a voice out of his sleep thinking of this room. The window was shut. This scent of locust, like a pale sweet stink of corrupting flesh, had its source here in the room with him. It made him afraid at first and after that a little sick. Soon he mastered himself. There was something to be found. Trying not to breathe the air to the bottom of his lungs he set about it.

There were not many hiding places. A jacket of drab olive cloth hung on a nail. He handled it with loathing and found the pockets empty. There was a paint-blotched desk with drawers. A pause and then with a jerk he opened the drawer at the top. Loose tacks, a hammer, a stiffened paintbrush. In the second drawer there was nothing. The bottom and last one waited for him. Knowing that whatever it was he looked for would be in this drawer he put his fingers on the handle and slowly pulled it open. Reverend Gates' first response was a blankness across his mind, like the shock of a betrayal discovered suddenly. Near the back, the only thing in the drawer, was a single glove.

That blankness still across his mind he stood for a while looking down at the glove. One glove. As if by direction his mind started to work again. He remembered about the gloves, that the Strangler must have worn gloves because he never left fingerprints. One glove. Then where was the other one? At last he bent over and, conscious of that scent in his nostrils again, reluctantly took the glove from the drawer. There was white paint on it. Its fellow, then, lying somewhere, would also have white paint. Lying where? Like a sudden gift the answer was in his mind.

Reverend Gates, when he heard the footsteps, had already made a first move toward the door. The shock was such that it stopped him there, the glove still dangling from his hand like a thing he was about to present to the now-visible figure across the threshold. Earl was staring at it. Except for just an instant when his lidded eyes glanced up and blinked, he kept on staring at the glove. That mark in his forehead was visible, pale, like the ghostly imprint of a thumb placed there long ago. Suddenly one of Earl's hands moved as if to reach out. It never completed the movement, fell back to his side, but the moment was enough to set Reverend Gates' blood stroking in a different way. One little shudder, though, and he had mastered his fear. Because this too, Earl's appearance this way, was surely of God's doing. And except for that one upward glance the lidded eyes had never left the glove.

"Yours?" Reverend Gates said uselessly. He pointed to the glove and then to Earl.

The barely perceptible nod said yes and, for a moment, the green eyes bared themselves. Wasn't that in his eyes the flicker of fear? Reverend Gates held out the glove.

"Where is the other one?" Reverend Gates held up two fingers, then pointed to the glove. "Where?"

The eyes flickered. The shake of the head was to say he did not know.

Reverend Gates stood waiting, but waiting for a sign, or maybe a voice. There was something, he did not know what, but it caused him to move. Crushing the glove in his hand he stepped toward Earl, through the door and past the retreating figure. The gesture of his hand meant that Earl was to follow him. It was not until now that Reverend Gates clearly understood the plan that had come so suddenly into his mind.

The sun was coming up and a milk truck went by on the street. Earl trailed behind him, reluctant, eyeing the stiff figure striding on ahead. His face was not expressionless anymore. His green eyes stood wide open, showing the whites, glancing as if to search out dangers lurking under the shade trees and the hedges. Three blocks and they turned, one block and they turned again. The silent housefronts were like masks through which the windows peered at them.

Reverend Gates stopped where a walkway, leading to a roofed front porch, passed between clipped hedges. A cord was stretched across, on which a sign hung that said: NO TRESPASSING POLICE DEPT. Reverend Gates ducked under the cord. For the first time since leaving the church basement he turned and looked at Earl. He saw the face he had expected, the eyes wide and bright, evading his gaze. "Come on," he said and made his summoning gesture. Earl did not move. In sudden rage Reverend Gates felt his jaw tighten, locking his teeth. He gestured again, harshly. This time Earl responded, though very slowly, bending as low as if he believed the cord he passed under carried a deadly charge. "Come on," Reverend Gates said. He had to make his fierce gesture again.

The Strangler had entered through a kitchen window at the back of the house, that overlooked a small hedge-enclosed backyard. Reverend Gates did not stop until he stood under that window. When he turned he saw that Earl, standing barely a step beyond the house corner, was looking at him with a face the color of ashes. "What are you afraid of?" It seemed as if the fist in which all this while he had held the glove was locked shut in a cramp. He had to force it open. Then he pointed to the glove and then to Earl and then to the dense camellia shrubs crowded along the house foundation. "Find it."

Earl did not move. His wide eyes, glaring green, were fastened on Reverend Gates' face.

"Find it." Reverend Gates' voice had risen. "Find it, you . . ."

Reverend Gates did not know exactly what he had meant to do but he made a sudden move toward Earl. There came a muted cry, Earl's cry, like an animal's voice out of a human mouth. Earl wheeled and fled, plunged staggering through the hedge and disappeared beyond a garage next door.

Reverend Gates had pursued him as far as the hedge. What was the use? Where could the man go anyway, or hide for very long? For another minute or two Reverend Gates stood undecided. Turning abruptly he hurried back and began to search among the shrubs along the back wall of the house.

He searched for an hour and more. He pushed his way among the shrubs and shook the branches and crouched down on his haunches to look. Time and again, feverishly at last, he circled the house peering along the foundation. He traced and retraced his steps across the yard and combed every foot of the boundary hedge. He found no glove. There was no glove here but the one still gripped in his hand. But neither was there any doubt.

Finally Reverend Gates went and stood under that kitchen window. Something came into his face, stirring his lips, and passed and came again. He shut his eyes. His lips moved silently for a while and then he bent down and thrust the glove deep into an azalea bush beside him. He left the premises. A while later he went to the police station.

That night at his aunt's house out near the city limits Earl Banks was shot by the police. The bullet hit him in the back and the next day in the hospital, without ever having regained consciousness, he died. It was Earl's own fault, or so the police considered it. In spite of having had to track him down they had not approached the place with any idea except to capture him. When they found him hiding in the woodshed in back of the house they had a fight on their hands. Earl knocked one of the officers down and lit out running. The young officer, new on the force and raw, had drawn his gun and fired—almost at random but he hit Earl.

By that time the news had already gone around that they knew who the Strangler was and were looking for him. The town had heard such news before and most people were pretty skeptical at first. That night when the report of the actual shooting got around, when they had a real man in the hospital wounded, nearly everybody except the Negroes believed it and believed that the months of nightmare were finally over. A long sigh of relief went through the white community. The Negroes not only remained skeptical, they protested at once. Early the next morning Hershel Rawls, the black leader, was in Mayor Duncan's office. The day after that he led a march, in which several hundred participated, to the courthouse, and for the next couple of days the disorders and lootings in and around the Creektown section fell just short of becoming a serious riot. This kind of thing of course was almost to be expected. It was all the more reassuring to the white people that a respected preacher, a conscientious

man sympathetic toward Negroes, was the one who had put
the finger on Earl Banks.

This time, though, it turned out uncomfortably for the
white community. Not only did several Negroes swear as to
the whereabouts of Earl on that night of Gladys Stallworth's
murder: their testimony was confirmed by Ella Peden, a responsible white nurse at the hospital who said that Earl had
spent almost the whole of that night sleeping in a chair in the
room of his sick nephew. So it seemed practically foolproof. A
poor frightened deaf and dumb Negro had been shot and
killed for no reason. If there was any reason to doubt, it lay
only in the fact of Reverend Gates' unruffled conviction that
he had not been mistaken. For most of Reverend Gates' congregation at least, this was enough. For a while it was enough.
But most other white people, not to mention black ones, were
a good deal less than convinced.

There was a glove in the azalea bush, though, just as Reverend Gates had told the police there was, and the glove
evidently was Earl's, just as Reverend Gates had sworn. As to
what he was doing there, with Earl, so early in the morning,
Reverend Gates had a credible answer. People, he said, might
call it a hunch, a hunch he had had about Earl for a long
time. He called it God's intervention. God gave him the plan
and it had worked. Earl, seeing the glove, seeing himself
known, in his fear had revealed his guilt. So Reverend Gates
testified without a bobble, with all the serenity of assurance
and a conscience perfectly clear. And why not? What motive
could such a man have had that he needed to lie about.

So the matter stood. Bad feeling lingered on in the black
community and for weeks there were racial episodes, small
outbursts of violence. Reverend Gates, as he had from the first,
looked on with sympathy. He wrote a letter to the *Okaloosa
News* in which he spoke of the necessity for faith, because

from faith and only faith would flow God's peace and justice. For four Sundays in a row this was his text in the pulpit. He spoke with remarkable fervor, the light gleaming on his forehead, and his congregation thought these sermons the most powerful he had ever preached. How could they doubt such a man? If there had been nothing for witness but those sermons alone it might have been possible. But how, when they felt in his daily life, and this increasingly, a fervor which if anything surpassed that of his eloquence from the pulpit? They not only felt, they saw it—made visible in his deeds and also, they imagined, in the face that had grown less fleshy, more spiritual than before. Among his congregation, anyway, last doubts were all but forgotten. In fact as the weeks and then two and then three months went by and still no other murder took place, there ceased to be very much doubt in any quarter except the black one.

Then, just after Christmas, after a ministry of eighteen years at the Calvary Presbyterian Church, Reverend Gates suddenly resigned. He offered no good reason, even to personal friends—just a few words about having heard God's call to go out and seek new vineyards. In two weeks he was gone. He went back to the county where he had come from and for a while, not very long, preached at a Church of God. Then he resigned from that church too. The report, from the daughter who was eighteen now and came back by herself to Okaloosa, was that he had joined some kind of a Holiness church, one that nobody in Okaloosa had ever even heard of. When the daughter had left there Reverend Gates, and of course his ever-faithful wife, was on his way to some place out West. In that place, he said, was a true vineyard. There people would listen to the message of faith, of faith and faith alone.

CHAPTER FOUR

Sim Denny

The death of Earl Banks had consequences that went beyond the near-riot it caused and the bitter feeling that lingered for a long time in Okaloosa's black community. One of the people affected, in a different way, was Sim Denny.

Sim Denny was a Negro with skin about the color of an eggplant. He was a tall man though stooped a little now, after sixty-six years of which at least fifty had been years of hard work. It was not just the years that had bent him, though. Partly it was a shortness of breath that had come on him: it

seemed he could breathe easier when he bent over a little. His
heart, he reckoned, and did not inquire any further. He just
went a bit slower at his job of cement finisher and occasionally thought about hiring a helper to take some of the
load off of him. He had used to employ two helpers. But that
was before his wife died, six years ago, and before everything
got so different. Since then working, and being, alone had got
to be a habit. It was a hard habit to break, even when finally
his lonesomeness began to frighten him.

Sim had never been very talkative but there had not been
any reason except that he was quiet by nature. When there
started to be another reason to keep quiet he hardly even
minded, at first. He went on with his cement finishing, working almost always for white people, proud when he pleased
them and made them acknowledge his mastery, the finish like
glass he could put on a cement surface. He went on showing
respect, even when he did not feel it, saying Yas Sah to them
—Yas Sah this and Yas Sah that. And he went on making
three or four visits a year, for old time's sake, to the home of
Mr. Will Cottrell over there in the hill section where the class
white folks lived. In those days Sim did not mind a bit breaking his accustomed quiet to give a piece of his mind to offend-
ing black people. "What you want go to school with them
for?" he would say. "Ain't black folks good enough for you?"
Or, "You behave yoself, they treat you awright." And that
first march, about the schools, had made him sneer. "Crazy
niggers. Making trouble for ev'ybody."

That was how it went, back then. Sim was the aggressor
and half the people he confronted like this were silent in ways
that meant they agreed with him. Soon, though, there were
not so many. In time there were almost none at all, or none
who would admit it. That was when his remarks began to be
answered not with silences anymore but with open scorn and

ridicule. There were some people who now called him, right
to his face, Uncle Tom or Rastus or White Man's Nigger.
Even his own daughter Maybelle sometimes did, though this
was mostly because of her husband.

They lived in Sim's house, in the Creektown district of
Okaloosa. It was a nice house, small but of clean sound
white-painted frame, on a street where now the rest of the
houses resembled beehives made of red brick. In back of the
house was a little outbuilding where Sim had used to keep his
tools but where, nowadays, he spent most of his time when he
was at home, sleeping on a cot he had put there. There were
two big shade trees, a black oak and a chinaberry, and between the house and the street a decent stretch of yard that
Sim, until lately, had always insisted be kept swept bare. Just
like a nigger. That was what Maybelle had said to him, more
than once, quoting her husband Herman. From the very first
Sim had been more than half afraid of Herman.

It was not so much a physical fear, though there was some
of that. Herman had bad light eyes and an ugly razor scar
like a worm on his neck. He was not big, he was just too
quick. He moved around like a nervous cat, especially when
he was angry, and he seemed to be always angry, seething.
But Sim might have lived with this. What made him really
afraid was something else about Herman. He could see it
reflected—more than a reflection—in his own daughter, who
had gone off to Birmingham one kind of a girl and come back
another kind, pretty near as much of a stranger as that one
she brought with her. Right here was the trouble, though. All
of a sudden it was like Sim was the stranger, in his own
house. Maybelle said things to him, hushed him up. Herman
with those bad light eyes just looked at him. Then there
started to be meetings in Sim's house, people he had known
since they were children who looked at him now almost the

way Herman did, as if Sim was something between a joke and a threat. Things he heard said in his own house gave the same kind of hitch to his breathing that hard work did sometimes. By now Sim had all but stopped saying the kind of things he used to say.

He moved out, into the toolhouse. "It make a fine room," he said to Maybelle. "Mo private. Won't be no bother to you."

"You don't have to." Maybelle's underlip was out, purple-looking, and her voice was flat. "This here yo house."

It did not seem like it. "It's awright," he said. "Make a fine room."

"We be out of here fo long." She kept on mopping the floor, with long hard thrusts of the mop. "Soon's Herman make them white people at the mill pay him mo money."

Once Sim would have said, "It's plenty good jobs for maids you could get." Now he said, "It's awright. You welcome here."

It was all right in the toolhouse, with his bed and cabinet and chairs and his wife's picture on the board wall. Except at breakfast and supper he rarely had to see Herman at all and he could not hear the voices when the meetings took place in the house. It seemed like his thoughts went better too, as if they had got almost free of spying eyes. He could drop back unseen to his childhood days on old Mr. Will Cottrell's farm, to young Mr. Will and himself, naked as a pair of snakes, diving off the sycamore tree into the blue creek pool. And the billy goat Sam they used to bait, making him hit the fence like a cannonball. Riding on top of the cotton wagons, deep in cotton, on gold late October afternoons. Mr. Will. Months since Sim had gone to visit, to sit on the back stoop or in the kitchen with him and call up those old things and talk about these new times and shake their heads and have a drink together. Lean Mr. Will now, rheumy in his eyes. And months had gone by. This thought was like a heavy weight riding on Sim's chest.

There was another weight riding on him, one that was more constant and growing heavier week by week. There were times when he felt like somebody in enemy country, a spy who people knew was a spy and who, since he was not a very dangerous one, they simply let be. At the start of that big mess about the schools, when the black people made that first march up to City Hall, Sim had watched from the sidewalk and sneered and said things to the people around him. When almost a year later the second march happened he watched it too, but in silence now, the sneer locked up in his breast. Standing mute on the sidewalk with a little space between him and the others, he watched, knowing many or most of the marchers, the sullen black faces passing by in ranks, and watched their mouths stretch open when they started to sing like they were walking into a church about how they were going to overcome. Overcome. He shook his head. It was a gesture nobody noticed. He went home feeling lonely.

That was the same week when Sim decided he would not go to church anymore, not until they stopped all that and got back to the Bible. He stuck to it. Sunday mornings he slept and read his Bible and let his mind drop back, dreaming. He began to work harder at his job, even if it did make his breath come short, and down on his knees stroking wide with his float he put finishes on cement floors that a person could see his face in. Then winter came on, a wet winter with skies dripping all the time and the earth a slush to walk on and there was not much work for him. Most of the day he was in his little room out back and when he did not turn on his lamp the light was like a desolate leaden-colored pall. That was when Sim started to be afraid.

His dreams seemed to be the cause. He was now in the
habit of lying on his bed and, between sleeping and waking,
letting his mind drop back to the old time, the childhood
time. But so often now something would happen that he
could not control. Suddenly, back there in the middle of one
of those bright memories, he would look around and not be
able to find Mr. Will, no matter how hard he looked—or anybody else either. He would be, maybe, out in the big pasture
behind the house and, looking around for Mr. Will, discover
also that the house was gone and the land was not green
anymore and the sky gave no light except this desolate leaden
one. It was a winter place, without any motion or voices or
any landmark to guide him out of it.

Sim thought it would be better when spring came and sunlight and hard work again. But the bad weather kept on into
April and then, when May came, that first strangling happened. The event did not seem at first to mean anything special for Sim. An old white lady strangled in her home on the
other side of town: Mrs. Rosa Callahan. Sim had known the
family long ago. He silently shook his head. Such a time. But
there was more to it than he had foreseen. Within a few days
there was a tale, a rumor going around. Sim was late to hear
it. People, even Maybelle, did not tell him things anymore
and because Herman had been absent for a couple of days
there had been no talk at the supper table for Herman to listen in on. So the rumor was already at full flower on the night
Sim first heard Herman talking in his bitterest voice to
Maybelle about it.

"Nigger hair. Yeah. They knows nigger hair when they sees
it . . . ev'y time. Yeah."

Afraid to ask, afraid of drawing Herman's anger, Sim had
to listen a while before he could get it straight. Hair. They

had found it under one of the dead lady's fingernails: black hair, nigger hair. So it was a black man that had done it to her. Bent over his plate Sim kept on making his hand lift the food to his mouth.

"So a nigger done it. That's all they need, a little black hair. If it's bad, a nigger done it."

Without looking Sim could see those light eyes on fire. He could actually see, obliquely, Herman's knotted brown hand holding the dinner fork as if for a weapon, making it shimmer under the bright light bulb.

"Got to get 'em one, now. They be down here to get 'em one. Anybody do fine. Might be me."

Bowed, Sim kept working his jaw. Then he felt the eyes and suddenly could not swallow what he had chewed.

"Won't be you, Uncle. You got white folks. They takes care of *their* niggers."

"Lay off him," Maybelle said, but not with much force.

Sim managed to swallow the food but he could not meet the eyes, the anger coming straight at him.

"He one of their pets. He ain't got no worries."

"Ain't nobody's pet," Sim said gruffly.

"Lay off him, Herman," Maybelle said.

Herman withdrew his gaze, let it pass carelessly across Maybelle's face and settle on his half-eaten plate of food. He speared a carrot with the fork. "All the same, I wouldn't feel easy if Uncle thought *I* was the one done it."

Sim drew a breath, drew hard to fill his lungs. "Ain't nobody's pet. I'm a black man same as you."

Herman bit off the carrot. Chewing he said, "On the outside, awright. But just only yo hide, is all." Still chewing he got up from the table and went into the living room and then out the front door, letting the screen bang shut.

"Eat yo supper now, Daddy."

He could not eat. He pretended to, hiding the crisis of breath that had come on him, until it was possible to escape.

The next Sunday, after more than six months, Sim went to church. Somebody was there already sitting in the place up front that used to be always saved for him and he had to sit near the back close under the white-painted wall where hung the picture of Jesus making the waters be still. It was like Sim was not noticed, had not even been missed. His nods and his smiles drew nothing but the slightest kind of answers and he sat there under the picture feeling like somebody invisible, too still to be noticed. When the singing swelled he tried to join in but his breath was short. It seemed like the River Jordan was rolling over his head. When Brother Dick in the pulpit got going, lacing the Pharisees and the Sadducees and the white people all at once, with his voice coming like waves cresting and breaking and his strong young spade-like hands shaping out the rhythm of it; when the groans and the Amens started and the heads began to pitch and sway as if a big wind was blowing through the church; then Sim felt like somebody struck dumb and stiff and cold, unable even to stir in his pew. He kept trying, as if it was a tight shell of ice he had to break, to shatter. Finally he could move his head and then his lips and could shape the word Amen and utter it. The word came out wrong, off-key, missing the beat of things—like a tune he had failed to catch. He did not risk another try. He nodded his head, moved his lips, and hoped it would be enough for the eyes around him.

That was Sim's first effort to get back in and in a way the result frightened him more than any of his dreams had. This setback only drove him the harder, though. He not only kept on going to church, he also began to make efforts in other directions. For one thing he hired a boy, Tod Nells, to help him

with his cement finishing. For another he changed his manner
with white people. Or he tried to, for he only succeeded in
part: his old nigger courtesy would too often come back on
him, defeating the impression he meant to give. Still there
were unexpected things he said and expected things he did
not say that put a look of surprise on the white faces. It was
pain for him, but with Tod behind him he stood it. Also he
was not so scrupulous about his work now. In fact, on purpose he would sometimes leave a whorl or a nick in a cement
floor and then turn sullen if there was a complaint. Shoddy
work was pain too, though. He had moments in his room
when it felt as if those whorls and nicks were graven on his
soul.

It seemed when it was black people Sim talked to that he
could not say those things rightly. Always there was that note
like a cracked bell, ringing false. It was not only too plain to
him, it also made people's eyes look at him with second sight.
His one and only try with Herman, a remark about "Whitey"
he had overheard somewhere, brought that look and more besides into Herman's face. "Look out now, Uncle," he said,
showing his yellow teeth. "What yo white folks gon think
about that kind of talk?" Sim learned not to say those things
except when he had to and then he studied about each one,
figured how to say it. Most of the time he settled for just
agreeing with what he heard said, nodding, and poking his lip
out.

They did not believe him, though. It did not seem to matter how often he went to church or how many people he nodded his agreement with or how painfully rude he made himself act with white people sometimes. Because it was an act.
You had to be what you pretended or people saw through it,
heard it in your voice. To say a thing right you had to be it.
And this meant you had to give up things. Like Mr. Will,

thinking about him. Like letting your mind drop back, too. Now Sim tried not to think about those old things anymore. And finally he got another idea. But that was not till September, after that fifth white woman got strangled and the police killed poor old deaf and dumb Earl Banks for it.

The night after that happened there was a big meeting outside the Baptist Church, with people crowded in the churchyard and the whole street too, singing, and Brother Dick and Hershel Rawls on the church steps shouting and praying and waving their arms. Some gangs of black boys went uptown on Cotton Street and broke windows and yelled at the police and got, a lot of them, put in jail. The day after that there was a march, to City Hall, and a meeting on the steps between the mayor and Hershel Rawls. In those days Creektown was like a place on fire, except there were not any flames or smoke. The nights were noisy, broken with sudden outcries and cars going by faster than usual and people talking in the streets. Nobody talked about anything else. And Sim was afraid.

It was, when he could think clearly about it, not a fear that any personal violence might be done to him. And yet to make himself come out of his little room in the backyard was all Sim's strength could manage. It was as if outside there were howling winds with fierce eddies that would seize and twist his body and cruelly wrench his limbs out of their sockets. He lay on his bed straining for breath. And yet he went out. He was at the meeting at the church that night. The next day with everybody else he marched to City Hall and stood there in the crowd, standing so far back that he could see nothing except, now and then, the bald head of the mayor and the agitated black one of Hershel Rawls. Of what they were saying, of their voices even, he could not hear anything. What were they saying, talking about? Suddenly, like a dream coming on, he could not even imagine what, any more than he

could think why he and all this listening murmurous crowd
of black people were standing here in the town square in the
harsh sun of early September. But that moment grew from
dream to nightmare, in which it seemed to him that he stood
here alone of all this crowd in helpless ignorance, among all
these black heads filled with a knowledge he could not even
conceive of and that he would have given everything he had
in the world to share. The sweat ran down his body, his breath
came hard. His head was as light as an empty shell set on top
of his neck.

But out of that terrified and confused moment Sim got his
idea. He had a savings account at the bank that came to over
fourteen hundred dollars. He had been building it for a good
many years, putting in a little bit almost every month, and
once it got past a thousand it began to be a considerable thing
in his mind. He read his statements every month and thought
about the money lying there in one big pile that nobody but
him could lay a hand on. He had no idea of spending it, ever,
he meant to leave it. There was a sort of awe in the thought
of a man, a colored man anyway, having that much money to
leave behind him when he died. The thought he had in bed
that night after the march was still more awesome: it left him
stunned. By morning, though, he had made up his mind to it
and he was uptown waiting outside the door of the bank at
least an hour before opening time.

That was such a day. Leaving the bank with that sealed
envelope full of green money clutched tight in his hand he
walked as he had used to walk thirty years ago—straight-up,
long-stepping, with easy breaths of the morning air swelling,
gorging his chest. Walked better in fact, as if he had grown
taller and need not look any way but down into the black
faces he greeted along the way. Up Cotton Street and across,
ignoring traffic, down Willow Street to Bean and into Creek-

town he never once broke his stride or felt one lapse of this new power trilling in his blood. Children watched him as if they knew, could see it, and so, now, did the men and the women he passed by. He slowed his steps to savor it. Even so he got there too soon and, to let it build, he paused for a minute or two outside the door. It was a rectangular brick building, once a grocery, and a sign on the wall said: OKALOOSA IMPROVEMENT ASSOCIATION.

It did not go as Sim expected, all complete in one triumphant stroke. Hershel Rawls was not there. A secretary in the small front office, in front of a shut door with a glass pane you could not see through, told him to try again in an hour. He would not state his business. He went outside and paced the street and never for long let his eyes wander from the front of that building. He was not at all crestfallen, not yet. The envelope full of green money went on ticking away like something alive between his tight thumb and fingers. An hour would make it better, the greater for being put off. The astonished smile, the welcome, on Hershel Rawls' stern face.

Sim was not to see it, though. Every hour when like clockwork he entered the building again he was met with just such another disappointment. One time, when he went in right at noon, he had thought it was about to happen for sure, because the woman told him Hershel Rawls was back there, in conference, behind that pane of glass you could not see through. But he never came out. There must have been a back door and Hershel Rawls came and went by it. At five o'clock when the whistle blew and Sim walked out of the building for the eighth and last time he felt almost as if the whole thing had been spoiled. He had not wanted to do what he finally did. It was that woman's impatience, wanting to know his business, and her face nearly as light as a white woman's. She got it out of him finally and got the envelope out of his hand. He stopped her from dropping it into a box that was there. "You give hit to him, yoself. You tell him who. You tell him Sim Denny."

She said she would, not to worry, and gave him a smile that reassured him a little.

"He got a surprise coming. When you gon give hit to him?"

She said maybe even tonight, if she saw him. Then she said, "And I know he'll be wanting to get in touch with you, to thank you."

That was most of the comfort Sim took home with him that evening. Hershel Rawls would get in touch with him, to thank him. He would send for him, or maybe even come by the house, come out back to Sim's room. And anyhow there would be that smile when he opened Sim's envelope. This thought kept coming back and growing in Sim's mind, shading out his long day's disappointment. By suppertime it had raised him almost to the pitch of this morning's elation.

He was too full to eat but he ate a little, waiting for his moment. He would have liked, to launch him, some little break in the silence over the table. But it did not come, forbidden by Herman's sullen face, his look as if it was anger alone that drove him at his food. Tonight, though, this was not enough, not for Sim. He said, "Old Hershel Rawls got him a surprise coming."

"What you talkin bout?" Maybelle said. Herman went on eating.

"When he op'm that *en*velope I left for him." Sim looked straight ahead of him at the green plaster wall.

"What *en*velope? What you talkin bout?"

"That'n I left for him." He paused. "Got foteen hundert and twenty-seb'm dollar in it."

Even Herman stopped eating. Maybelle said, "Of *yo* money?"

"Ev'y penny."

It took Maybelle a moment, with her mouth open, to digest the fact. "You done gone crazy?"

"For the Move*ment*," Sim said. "Hershel Rawls be in touch with me." He put a bite of something in his mouth, started chewing. His head felt light with triumph.

"You gone plumb ravin crazy," Maybelle said.

"Naw." This was Herman. His bad light eyes were looking at Maybelle. "He just think he can buy his self black." Now he was looking at Sim. "Ain't that right, Uncle?"

At first somehow this shot was more confusing than painful to Sim. All he could think to say was, "I ain't 'Uncle.' "

Herman made a small derisive noise with his tongue. "Come on, Uncle. What you care bout the Move*ment?* Yo white folks is what you care bout." Herman suddenly put his head back. "Hey, wait a minute." He got up and stepped through the living room door and came back immediately with a letter. "From yo white folks, Uncle." He placed it on the table beside Sim's plate.

It was hard to see but Sim could see this much—in print up in the left-hand corner. William Cottrell. And Sim's own name in the middle, shakily written with ink. He could do nothing but stare at the letter.

"Better open it. He might need you to come shine his shoes."

"Don't shine no shoes," Sim faintly said.

"Lay off him, Herman," Maybelle said.

Herman went on standing there. He said, "I'll thow it away for you, Uncle, if you don't want to read it."

Now Sim lifted his eyes, slowly bringing Herman into focus.

"Want me to thow it away for you?"

"Lay off him."

"It don't matter," Sim murmured. "Be awright."

"Okay, Uncle," Herman said and picked up the letter and flipped it into the trash box by the stove. "So long Mr. Will." Then with a toss of his head he left the kitchen.

"Finish yo supper, Daddy."

Sim just managed to eat a little more. He would not think about it. He would not wonder what it said inside, in that shaky handwriting, and he would not let his mind drop back. If a dream tricked him in the night he would wake up and think about the next day and Hershel Rawls being in touch with him. But he had to walk a long time in the streets before he was tired enough to go to bed.

The next day was Friday but Sim did not go to work, he waited. He waited on the front porch, in the swing, watching every car approach and keep on past his house. The mailman did not even stop at his box and all day long the telephone was silent. At nearly four o'clock he set out walking. He walked to the Association office and after a little pause outside went straight in, straight up to the desk and the woman who had skin like a white woman. She gave him the smile that somehow had been more comfort to him yesterday and said Yes, Mr. Rawls would have it by now, because she had put it in the safe last night. That was not what she had said she would do. "How he gon know who hit come from?" Sim said. That smile again. Because she had written it on the envelope, in big letters: Mr. Sam Denny. "Hit's Sim," Sim said. "*Sim* Denny." She was sorry, she would fix that. And Mr. Rawls would be in touch with him. Behind her that door with the pane of glass you could not see through looked as if it might have been nailed shut.

It did not happen the next day either but the day after that

would be Sunday. By Saturday night he had got it in his head
that Sunday would be the day. It would be at church, maybe,
and people would know and maybe, just maybe, when the
time came for announcements Brother Dick would speak it
out from the pulpit. Then Sunday and meeting in the morning and evening both went by and it did not happen. He went
back to work on Monday.

Something did happen on Monday night but it was not at
all what Sim was waiting for. It was in the newspaper that
Maybelle showed him. "Yo white folks done died, Daddy."
He stared at it for a couple of minutes at least, though he
never got past understanding that it had happened last night
at the hospital. At the hospital. It was like his mind had got
stuck on this fact—this and the thought that he never had
been to a hospital and never would go to one. He kept thinking this, just this one thing, on until he finally went to sleep
that night.

Such as it was, what Sim had been waiting for came to
him on Wednesday, after a long day in which he had put on a
cement floor a surface like a pool of water that mirrored a
clouded sky. It was a letter and Hershel Rawls' name was
signed. ". . . your generous gift . . . men like you . . ." it
said. He showed it to Maybelle, who only shook her head and
gave a sigh. He did not show it or even mention it to Herman. He put it in his pocket. When he got to his room after
supper he read the letter again and put it in his cabinet
drawer. Then, conscious how his body ached, he lay down on
his bed without undressing and went to sleep.

The next afternoon while Sim was down on his knees
drawing his float with long sweeping strokes across the wet cement his breath stopped on him. He had to fight to get it
back. It came with pain and then he lost it again. This kept
on until Tod Nells, alarmed, led him off to the car and drove

him home. Sim was better by then. He made Tod go away and went around the house to his room and got on his bed.

Maybelle appeared half an hour later (Tod had found her at a neighbor's down the street) and wanted Sim to go to the hospital. He said he wasn't going to no hospital, that he was all right now, but Maybelle called them anyway. They came and took him, over his protests, by force really, and carried him on a stretcher into an elevator and up and into one of those windowless dim-yellow hospital rooms.

Sim died on the night of the next day. They had thought he was much better, out of the woods now, and just an hour before he died said it would be all right for him to have a visitor or two, if he wanted. A little later Brother Dick appeared and the nurse went into Sim's room ahead of him. Sim was lying on his back with his face turned the other way, toward the wall. He seemed not to hear the nurse the first time she spoke to him. "Mr. Denny, it's Brother Dick," she repeated. "He's come to visit you."

Still there was silence for a few more seconds. "Mr. Denny." The nurse could see that his eyes were open.

"Tell him go way." Nothing but his lips moved.

The nurse was surprised and made another brief try. She got the same answer, spoken exactly as before, and she had to go out and send Brother Dick away with a little bit of a lie.

Half an hour later the nurse was in Sim's room again, to check on him. He was still lying with his face to the wall. She heard him say faintly again, "Tell him go way."

"He left a long time ago, Mr. Denny."

"He out there. Got a letter fo me. Don't want to see no white folks." There was a pause. "Don't want to see no kind of folks."

He said nothing else, would not answer the nurse, and about twenty minutes later she found him dead.

CHAPTER FIVE

A Worldly Man

Okaloosa still had a few families that were generally regarded as "aristocratic," old families that for three or four generations had held on to a measure of prosperity and power and, it was believed, certain of the old values. One of these, though dwindled now to only two members, was the Carney family. There was Dr. Charles Carney, who at fifty was already practically retired from his medical practice, and his nineteen-year-old son Bruce who was a student at the junior college. Of course there had been a Mrs. Carney and in fact a woman of that name—or what was left of her—still survived. She seemed very remote, though, at least in the town's eyes. Not only had she been separated from Charles for almost fourteen years, but she had spent the greater part of those years in and out of the insane asylum down at Reedville. And many people, when they did think about her at all, remembered only, or at least best, the unlikeliness of that marriage between Charles Carney and the daughter of a fundamentalist preacher.

The bad marriage did not leave any observable scars on Charles. Shortly after his wife's mental breakdown, which happened only weeks after she left him, he got the boy back and then, it seemed, the divorce had made not even a ripple on the face of his contentment. That was the kind of man he was, content, at ease in the world, the aristocrat who knew how to live a life. And besides the disposition he had the means for it, both earned and inherited. A year before his marriage the original family house had burned, but Charles, without so much as a pause, had built another one on its ashes—a smaller version but like the old house otherwise, classically elegant and with front and back verandas connected by a central hall. It sat on six hedged-in, clipped and shaded acres at the extreme edge of town and had behind it a long view of open bottom land, always in corn, and the hills on the other side of Okaloosa Creek. The whole place in its look of insulated and well-groomed serenity seemed like a kind of portrait of its owner. It was hard to imagine that either the one or the other could be in any way vulnerable to the town's discords or the growing threat of the Strangler.

Such a portrait, as far as it went, was fairly accurate and was not inconsistent with some qualities in Charles that made him a good deal less than admired in all quarters. One of these qualities was an aloofness that his screen of immaculate

manners did not quite hide. People, or most people, felt him
looking down at them. To more puritanical types this was especially galling in light of another fact about Charles. He was
a man of dissolute morals, a rake. The word was maybe
a little strong. He was anything but gross with women and he
was marvelously discreet. In fact it was not until after his divorce that the reputation of philanderer got fastened on him
and even then, because of the family name, there were many
who refused to believe it. Charles himself made no great effort
to quash this reputation. Either way, believed or not, it did
not much concern him. Or at least it concerned him only as it
might affect his friendship with his son.

This with his son was a small worry for Charles. Bruce had
a puritanical streak, not big but still detectable, that Charles
never had been quite able to stamp out. It was a heritage
from his mother, or by way of his mother from that bellowing
old Jehovah of a grandfather. Every thought of Ira Bledsoe
made a pause in Charles' serenity. And so did Bruce's visits
—rare, thank God—even when the visits took him only to see
his mother at the asylum. Those other visits, to his grandfather's house in the country where his mother stayed during
her better intervals, were worst of all. Old Ira standing by.
Prognathous jaw, gunman's eyes, voice of Lazarus from the
tomb. It was during these visits, while waiting for Bruce to
come home, that Charles always planned his most eloquent
counterattacks.

Except indirectly, though, Charles never said the things he
had planned. With the boy present his confidence came back
and it was enough for Charles to follow, only with variations,
his old pattern. This was the story of his marriage, his mistake, with suitable reflections on his own and the world's
follies, and almost without his accustomed tone of irony. "I
was a fool," he said. "An impassioned fool. I supposed people

could just slough off the kind of raising she'd had. Your mother thought so too. We were both wrong, it went too deep. And besides, there was old Ira still back there in the wings prompting her with that crazy stuff. Blasphemer. That's just one of the things I was. He could make a pathology case out of a Greek philosopher. Even in this benighted region he's an outrage."

Bruce listened. If he had heard all this too many times his intent face did not show it. Intent and a little sad, while Charles went on with his story. If the weather allowed they would be on the back veranda seated in deck chairs, each with a drink of Scotch in his hand. (For a little Scotch, Charles liked to say, had never yet done harm to a sensible boy.) It would be evening and, often, the veranda dappled with spills of sunset light through the cedar trees. Always, even on these occasions when he had to choose his words by design, this was the day's best hour for Charles. Lucky, he thought, resting his eyes on the clear handsome face in the other chair. A body to match, too, a supple runner's body with flawless skin almost the hue of corn syrup where the sun touched it. His mother's skin, that much was hers. Charles quickly put this thought away, and thought how the boy's eyes and the spirit behind them were his own eyes and spirit. Their intentness now was like a proof of it and Charles would go on with his story to the end. "So, not being a natural fanatic, there was nothing I could do. So she went back to the arms of Jesus. And then to the insane asylum, of course . . . Which Jesus, stay clear of, my boy, is my advice to you."

And Bruce's smile, just a little wan, would bring the conclusion Charles had been eager for.

Charles was proud of his friendship with his son and he thought he could without vanity congratulate himself for this achievement. A clear head and respect for a boy, these were all that was needed. And openness, the hardest thing. In one realm of his private life, his love affairs, this had taken a little doing on Charles' part. His solution was typical. It was simply to steer a course somewhere between concealment and display, answering only but frankly those questions that happened up in his path. There were few enough such questions. Bruce was a tactful boy and occasions that touched upon these matters were the rarest of accidents between him and his father. Did he disapprove? For their friendship, best felt in those warm evening hours of talk on the back veranda, it did not seem to matter if he did.

Maybe in those years Bruce, insofar as he was aware of things, really did not disapprove—or did not know that he did. His father was not only best friend but mentor to him and had set out by design, subtly, to implant in his son what he saw as wisdom. He thought of it, too, as a means of defense, like conferring a shield on the boy, not only against the follies of the town but also, and mainly, against the boy's mother and that equally insane old man. So, in those easy evening conversations, one of his favorite topics had long been religion and its follies. It was usual for him to let his irony play through the discussion, but not always. At times he could be as flatly dispassionate as the surgeon he had started out to become.

"Of course so much of it's just fakery and self-deception. Because they don't want to face up to our mortal lot. They think they're too important to come to a real end."

Bruce was interested. A ray of sunset light put a luster on his clear cheek and forehead. He said, "It's not that way with all of them, though, it looks like. Some of them really do get struck down."

"In a way. I guess you're about right." The way Charles held his glass with just the tips of his fingers gripping the bottom made it almost a balancing act. Between the lapels of his white knit shirt the hair like that on his head had tufts of gray. "And most of the time it's no different from real insanity, either. Except that you can't get them committed for it. Wrong kind of insanity." Charles paused, drank from his glass. His eyes rested with pleasure for a moment on his son's glowing cheek. "Self-induced. It's their mortality, it stinks for them. They've got to be lifted out of it, away from the smell."

Bruce was silent, listening, his drink untouched. To lighten the tone Charles said, "Well, I'm glad I haven't had much trouble accepting mine. On the whole I've even found mortality fairly satisfactory, so far." And then, "I would judge you have too, pretty well. Aren't I right?"

"I guess I have," Bruce said and smiled and took a drink.

Until that summer when Charles was fifty people were right to say about him, except in different words, that he found his mortality satisfactory. Despite being a doctor he was careful not to strain it and even from the very outset of his practice he had made himself more difficult than easy of access. He was successful, though, because he was good and also because his name in the town held him up. At nearly forty he took two young doctors into practice with him and after that he worked less than ever, appearing at his office about three times a week to minister to stomach aches and ringing ears and streptococcic throats. At forty-nine he began to experience a slight heart murmur. It was not much, with care it was not even dangerous, but he made the most of his opportunity. Except for mainly token appearances at his office he retired. He rested a little more now and stopped smoking and drank less, but the biggest difference was that he went oftener to the country club. As to his love life, that did not change at all. Or at least it did not change right away, and when it did the fact had nothing to do with his heart murmur.

In the past the country club had furnished, among other things, a hunting ground for Charles. Except for one or two his affairs had all originated there. It was by design. Charles did not like to take chances, not big ones anyway, and the women at the club were in general the "safest" women. Not only were they married and therefore more discreet, but they were also of the class least likely to make a row. Such, anyway, had been Charles' luck. Even on occasions when he knew with certainty that he had been a cause of domestic discord, nothing public or even very trying for him had ever been made of the fact. So it was a kind of an aberration when in mature middle age he broke with his proven pattern.

It was a keen stab of desire such as Charles had not felt in a good many years. It happened in his office, on one of those now-infrequent occasions when, just to keep his hand in, he spent a half day seeing patients. A cow, he thought at first, five-nine at the least and big all over and sulky-looking. But the sulky look was the pain of walking with the sprained knee and, all but the little pout hanging on her lips, went away when she sat down. It was the shape of the leg and the white firm texture of the flesh in his hands that, as he bent close to her mysteries, sent that first stab through him. Lorraine Williams was her name. She was, as Charles' friendly questions revealed, the wife of a bricklayer and mother of a thirteen-year-old girl. Already he was thinking, though a little hectically, that Lorraine had a knowing look and that a pubescent daughter was a powerful warden on discretion.

It was another mistake, though really, Charles reflected, only his second one. He was a good while realizing his mistake. There was so much daytime fun of an intensity that made him occasionally fear for his murmuring heart, there was so much of her. And Lorraine understood and accepted his intentions: he was never vague about these. Besides, as she confessed, she was several times not a virgin. So, at peace with himself, Charles burrowed in for the winter. To his surprise he was still there when spring was in full blossom and it was not until the beginning of summer that he looked up one day and saw that he was tired of her. He also saw that she was emphatically not tired of him.

That was the summer of the Strangler and especially after the third of those murders, in June, the muted though general disquiet that had got loose in the town began to touch even Charles. As the summer wore on he found himself checking to see that all the downstairs windows were locked for the night. And that bottom field close behind his house where the corn grew denser every day was less and less a comfortable resting place for his eyes.

It was not really the Strangler that Charles was afraid of. In that quarter, anyway, afraid was too strong a word. There, he was just uneasy, jumpy, and that figure of the Strangler had become a sort of focal point for his nerves. It was a new kind of experience for him, this nervousness, but so were the causes new. He often thought, recalling that winter day in the office, that putting his hand on Lorraine's swollen knee had been the first move in opening not just hers but also Pandora's box. Irrational or not, that was how it seemed—as if directly out of that his other troubles, and troubles not even peculiarly his, had been born. It was the nervousness of course, spurring fantasies. Nevertheless, and especially after that next murder in August, he kept having to reject the notion that what he had engendered on Lorraine's big lustful body was, like some inscrutable contagion, at the root of everything that preyed upon him.

One of Charles' troubles of course was clearly his own doing. It had been dumb of him to suppose, even on the basis of a wide experience, that he could count on a woman's lust

to cool off just because his own did—stupid, in fact. What in
his mistake did not appear so stupid was his failure to have
imagined how far her lust would finally bring her. It brought
Charles to the telephone more times than he could count and
also, when he could no longer put her off, to the Starlight
Motel where already half undressed she would be waiting to
devour him. "Do you love me, Charlie?" And he would say
yes, caught and held against that breast where the fierce heart
extinguished the sound of his own murmuring one. She was
the one he was afraid of and it was not for his heart's sake.
There was too much of her, no limit to her hunger. So he told
her yes when he had to, planning how he would slowly wean
her until he had starved her out.

Lorraine by herself would have been trial enough, but
there, all at the same time, were his other troubles. It was this
coincidence of things, Charles reflected, that made them seem
all like parts of one evil brew set going by his own hand that
winter day in the office. Even that lethal madman out there
whom Charles locked his windows against. Even the racial
strife, which in the form of his black maid had entered his
kitchen now. He avoided her, skirted the kitchen and overlooked the slighting of even his most venerable wishes. For
this one was the smallest of his troubles. The greatest of them
was his son.

Charles could not recall exactly when it had started,
though it was sometime early in the summer. Reflecting back
he could see now that the hints had been there; silences
that should not have fallen and looks that rested a little too
long on Charles' face. Until one day Charles noticed, beginning with the ritual drink that Bruce left sitting untouched on
the floor beside him. The same thing next evening too, and
after that it was water or lemonade Bruce fixed for himself in

the kitchen. In his brow was a crease, plain when the sun touched it, like a small bloodless cleavage in the skin. When had it come there?

Now their evenings on the veranda, even when the sun broke through the cedar trees, passed as though in a kind of shadow light. Topics kept failing them, growing thin, and the long spells of uncertain quiet seemed harder to break each day. That little crease in the boy's brow, what was behind it? Some painful cleaving thing inside the skull, Charles thought, gazing secretly, meeting Bruce's eyes sometimes with a faint shock like that from a collision. Yet he kept on holding back. That was his style, not to pry, a part of his tact with his son. So he told himself. It was no use finally. He could not any longer hide from himself a foreknowledge of what he did not want to know, and one evening, in a voice that ruptured the hush between them, Charles asked his question. It drew a nod from Bruce but this was all.

"I thought maybe you hadn't seen her this summer," Charles said. The thing was launched now. "You usually mention it."

"I saw her today."

And other times this summer? How many? "How's she doing?"

Bruce was not looking at him. That crease, deepened by the ray of sun on his face, looked more than ever like a wound, like pain. "Not so good."

"Oh?" Charles said. "She's at the asylum, then?"

"No. She's at home."

"Then it's no wonder she's not so good," Charles said and drank from his glass. He waited. Nothing came. When the cedars stirred in a sudden breeze and made the ray of sunlight flicker in his face, Bruce did not even blink. Finally, trying for

his most casual voice, Charles said, "Was there something spe-
cially unpleasant?"

Charles was surprised. He was more than surprised. The
look he drew not only baffled but in some obscure way appalled him. He had to hide his confusion in another swallow
and afterward wait until the whiskey had got settled and warm
in his belly before he could get his thoughts together. Even
then he did not speak, not for a little while. At last he said,
"Was it something about me?"

Bruce had turned his eyes away. He was gazing, it seemed,
straight into the sun. Then he nodded.

"What?" Charles said.

The lips parted, then shut, then parted again. "She says
you tried to choke her to death."

Charles had to breathe once. "For God's sake!" Bruce was
still gazing at the sun when Charles added, "They'd better
take her back to the asylum. She tell you that today?"

Bruce nodded. "She's been saying it a long time, though
. . . She even says you're the Strangler."

"Oh my God! They'd really better take her back. She
oughtn't to even hear about things like that. And she oughtn't
to be around old Ira, either . . . for sure. Among other
things, I'm sure he's what keeps her hating me after all these
years."

Charles drank again, a little interruption before he looked
back at Bruce. Then he was conscious that Bruce was still
looking away from him, gazing as if blind at the sun, and
now, for a second time, Charles felt that stroke of dismay. He
managed to say, "You don't believe that, surely?"

"Of course not."

"I mean, about me trying to choke her to death?"

"No." It was not strong enough and did not interrupt that
blind gaze at the sun.

"She's insane, you know. And hates me . . . For God's sake!"

"I said I didn't believe it."

Charles' mouth was open to speak again, because he was not satisfied with the limp and distant tone of that answer. But he closed it and said nothing. And that was right. Without seeming to protest too much, what more could he have said?

Afterward, after days when Charles could not bring himself to mention it again, he wished he had taken the chance he let escape, wished he had squashed and stomped out of that crazy lie the last small germ of anything credible. Why not now? Watching Bruce and the distance that had not stopped growing between them, Charles kept asking himself this. Why not, when just a little strategy could make it all seem natural? Yet he kept postponing it. Day after day he postponed it and what finally happened seemed, somehow, by a kind of nightmarish logic, to have been all along the reason he had not spoken.

What happened was the murder of Ernestine Bell, strangled and assaulted. Charles first heard about it around noon at the country club and came home not long after. Ernestine. Given that Charles had known her it was natural he should be shaken. That lethal madman. Who was safe? The other women had been old but this one was not, whose birthday Charles remembered, whom he knew to be forty-seven. A break of pattern, then, so what now could be counted on? He kept remembering, more often as the afternoon wore past, that on her forty-fifth in a motel up at Colburn he had put a gold-filled chain around that neck.

Charles' effort at a nap was a failure and along in the afternoon he went down to the kitchen for a drink. He was taken aback. The maid, Cassie, was still there, and not only

there but seated at the table reading the newspaper. It was
the front page and except that she looked up at him, just
briefly with her yellow eyes, he would have retreated. He entered, got a glass, took his whiskey out of the cabinet. This silence was only her black defiance and the pressure of eyes
heavy on his back was his own imagining. He made careful
haste and with some mumbled pleasantry went out onto the
veranda. It was not far enough. He went into the backyard,
out of her sight, to a stone bench under the largest of the
cedar trees. He was glad that nowadays she always left by the
front door.

It was hot with the sun slanting under the tree and not a
breath to stir a bough or a leaf of the man-tall corn in the
field down there. Once the thought that Bruce had come up
behind him made Charles, with a sudden stroke of his heart,
turn his head around. It would be that hour soon. But he,
Charles, would not be here when it came and leaving his glass
on the bench he got up and walked to the garage. He never
got in the cár, though. He thought of Ollie Bell, Ernestine's
ex-husband, who was so often at the club, and so often drunk.

Charles was still there at five o'clock, on the veranda with a
drink that was his third. But the whiskey did not quiet his
heart. What did finally bring him some ease was a glance at
the hand on his wristwatch. It was past time now and today,
maybe, Bruce would not appear. He counted the minutes on
his watch. Then he was almost sure and closing his eyes, resting his head, he managed for a little while to stop his pulse
from stroking. The thought that made his lids spring open
also caused the glass to slip from his hand. It was as though
an obscure alarm had reached him from somewhere out in
the sun-glazed corn.

It was foolish, though, the way he had let that thought take hold. It was foolish of him to be where he found himself not twenty minutes later, in his car driving all these miles to check on whether his thought had been right or not. Still he drove on, through countryside he had not seen in years, and spied just before sunset the familiar unpainted barn close to the road. Beyond it was the house, also unchanged—small, peeled white-frame, with a front porch under the roof like a thousand others. Driving slowly he approached and he was almost squarely in front of the house when he saw that she was on the porch, seated in the swing. More, her face distinct in the shadow under the roof, she was watching him pass by. He ducked his head.

Had she known him? The after-image of her face had a startled whiteness. Then he saw that this was partly caused by the black hair framing it, still black, unaltered by all these years. Beyond a curve Charles had stopped his car and, hands on the wheel, sat gazing at an inflamed cloud just above the skyline. No Bruce, no car in the yard—alone. This thought came slowly, somehow, but with an effect that set the wheel pulsing in the grip of his hands. When he finally moved one hand away, that cloud at the horizon had lost its flame.

Nothing had changed except the light. She was still there in the swing exactly as before, watching him as he approached and stopped his car in front of the gate. Her motionless face, still watching and watching him through a whole minute, seemed in the growing dusk only the whiter. It was a moment when Charles almost relented and even moved his hand back to the switch again. What could he say? Irene, he would say, gently, the old gentle voice that had charmed her once. Words would be given to him. Charles opened the door and got out.

He heard a chicken somewhere clucking but not any other

sound and when he opened his mouth to speak, nothing came. Her head and pale face where the eyes were like dark bruises in the twilight never yet had stirred. Some gift: why hadn't he some gift, flowers, that would have made her eyes brighten? He drew a breath. "Irene. It's me. You know me, don't you?" The face said nothing. He was able to move now and a few deliberate strides brought him up to the porch steps. "Bruce said . . ." A porch post was between them. He climbed the first two steps, all except the last one, and stopped. Her face! It was creased and ravaged, a desolate hag's face only the more for that shocking black black hair. And the eyes, all melted, staring at him from some unbridgeable distance. Words, Charles thought, even if he had been able to speak, would have been nothing else but waste of breath.

She had moved some way, some way Charles had missed. A hand? Then one of her hands did move. It moved from its resting place on the swing beside her and, outspread, hesitating, came up and touched her breast and then her throat. Her mouth opened. In the shock of that scream it was as if her face had come at him through the dusk, close to his eyes, afloat in its own ravaged and screaming desperation. Charles stumbled backward and fell.

It did not seem to have been the fall, the impact with the ground at the foot of the steps, that made him unable to get up for a little while. It seemed to be the screams, confusing his movements, making it hard to get his hands placed between him and the ground. This was at first. After that it seemed to be the figure at the top of the steps standing, leaning with all its massive weight, as if it would topple and fall upon him. He heard the harsh voice, Ira's, but the words were not clear. By the time he got on his feet the porch was deserted and the cries, muted now, came from inside beyond the shut front door. Then Charles was back in his car and driving fast toward home.

Something had happened to Charles that evening. He told himself at first that it was an effect of the fall he had had, the slight concussion that had put his faculties a little bit askew. Hadn't he, approaching home on a street tediously familiar to him, taken that wrong turn? Then it was no mystery why, with his foot on the threshold, he had got this feeling that something was wrong, strange about the house—as if he had been not an old inhabitant but somebody, like an accustomed visitor, who was merely well acquainted with its details. So this apprehensiveness that at times amounted to real fear. A good night's sleep would mend it all.

Charles was wrong. A night did not mend it and neither did two nor a whole week of nights. It was not, then, the fault of that blow to his head. Nerves, Charles told himself, and took barbiturates and finally whiskey. Except to retard things and bring them late like afterthoughts to his mind, these made no difference, though. In fact some of his most uncomfortable moments were those when he was drinking and seemed to discover too late, in a flash of perception, that somebody had been in the room with him. Of course he did not even have to turn his head to know, almost always, that these were illusions. What disturbed him more, and more and more often, was the thought that what caused him to have these illusions might possibly be real. It might be that his senses were *not* playing tricks and that somebody who was not Bruce really was using his house at night. He kept dismissing this thought. It would not stay dismissed.

Another presence, or the threat of it, was much more certainly real. For three days after that evening Charles refused to answer the telephone, though it rang and rang like screams assaulting his nerves. He would disconnect it, he always thought and never did, stopped maybe with his fingers already on the plug. More than once it rang in the night and one time, that second night, he dreamed he answered it. He went out into the dark hall and lifting the receiver to his ear heard a voice so throttled and faint that he could not recognize it or the words it spoke. Then he knew the voice. It was Ernestine's.

Finally, the third night, Charles did answer. Lorraine's voice was quiet at first, while he told her lies, evading her, straining to shape and soften the tones of his voice. Soon, in her voice, he heard that note again. It made him think of a tendon stretched too tight or a vein about to rupture and he was afraid. He said yes, only putting off the day, agreeing at last to the Friday four days from now. Of course he could not, would not be there. When the phone was back on the hook he said this out loud, imagining someone somewhere in reach of his voice.

And there was Bruce, a Bruce who seemed every day a little more like somebody Charles did not know very well. Not that Bruce was present much, even for that once-accustomed evening hour on the veranda. He blamed Charles, that was more than clear, and in a way that went beyond all reason. "It was . . . It was awful of you." There was something in his voice that Charles had never heard there before.

"But I didn't do anything," Charles said. "I just thought if I could talk to her . . . I didn't even get close to her." He was glad he could not see into Bruce's eyes.

"She thinks you tried to strangle her again."

An oath and then a denial died on Charles' tongue,

though his mouth stayed open. "Again." He had need of the drink in his hand and he lifted the glass and swallowed. He swallowed too much. It hung in his throat, made him cough. When the little spasm was over he saw Bruce, the sun on his face and the crease like a bloodless wound in his forehead, looking at him. Bruce said, "They took her back yesterday. She's in bad shape. The worst she's ever been. They have to keep her from . . . hurting herself."

Charles started to say he was sorry, and could not. What he finally said was, "You couldn't think . . ." and did not finish, stuck on the words.

Even this much, coming as it did, where it did, ought to have been enough to get an answer. It got nothing. Gazing at the sun again, Bruce might not have heard him speak at all. And he got up and left without saying anything more.

Charles tried going to the club once and then again. He never saw Ollie Bell but the chance he might was what kept him so painfully restless, watching the doors, looking behind him from the bar. And just as at home, whiskey did not help. He went to his office several times, thereby astonishing the nurses and his two younger partners who asked him pleasantly what was wrong and looked him over with a certain attentiveness. He stayed in his office, maybe saw a patient. He never stayed long. A curious feeling of urgency always took hold of him at last. It was as if he had a compelling reason to go home, as if in his absence he might somehow lose out and find the doors locked against him when he arrived. There was no use shaking his head, no shaking the notion out. He went home. Except for these few outings there was hardly an hour that whole week when he was not in the house or close by in the yard.

Friday morning out of a thin drugged sleep Charles waked up conscious how his heart was beating. His dream had caused it, he thought—or rather his dreams, for there had been more than one. Lying stretched out on the ground in the wake of that blow he could not get up because of Ira's voice. It was too loud, obscuring the words, and heavy with a resonance Charles' strength was not equal to. The dream, lasting moments, ending in despair, came back several times. But it was another dream that waked him, in which somebody, somebody stealthy but all the same assured, was making free with his house. His tread went past Charles' door repeatedly, while Charles, not daring a breath, lay stiff in his bed. This was why he waked up with his heart stroking but it was not why, after many minutes, the stroking continued just about as before. Charles had remembered that today was Friday.

It was the same all morning. He paced, went into the yard, came back and took up a magazine in which the pages looked all alike to him. When he saw noon coming on he got in his car and drove, but not toward that motel where Lorraine would be arriving now. Already undressing maybe, listening for him. He drove to the grocery and then to the drugstore and finally to a shop where he ended up buying a tweed sport coat that he did not like much. At nearly four when he entered the house the telephone was ringing. After it stopped he pulled the plug and did the same to the phone upstairs.

Bruce did not come and finally, on the veranda drinking, Charles felt an evening lull set in. Sunset flamed in a bank of clouds and below him, beyond the cedars, not one leaf in the glazed-green cornfield stirred. Then the sun went down. When he looked again the field was all in shadow and suddenly he heard the telephone ringing.

It might as well have been real. When darkness came he was pacing again. He puttered at making supper in the kitchen and did not eat. It seemed to be the telephone. He turned on the light in the hall and checked the plug. This did not help, he kept on listening. About eight-thirty, leaving only the hall light on, he locked the back door behind him and started toward his car in the garage. Charles was too late.

Another step or two and he would have come out in plain sight beyond the big camellia bush. As it was he ducked back, hid himself. She had stopped in the drive. There was only a little starlight, just enough to make her visible in a ghostly kind of way, and for a few seconds Charles was able to hope that his senses had played another trick on him. Lorraine moved again and a few uncertain steps brought her where he could plainly see that she was no illusion. The shape of her big cow's body standing planted on his grass was all but defined in the starlight now, and her face, a sort of discolored pallor, was lifted slightly to search his upstairs windows. Bruce: he thought of Bruce arriving. He clenched a fist.

Once more she moved, walked slowly past the bush and him into the cedar shade and paused at the veranda steps. It was just a pause, just long enough for Charles to have spoken to her, but he did not. For all his rising anger he could not and he watched her climb the steps and at the door lift her hand and knock. A timid knock, three times, just audible. She knocked again, a little louder, and after a moment, shocked, he heard her voice. "Charles. Charles. Please, Charles . . . Please!" Shuddering and shrill that way, it was not even like her voice. And somehow this, for a moment or two, stifled his anger.

Charles saw her move again, walking slowly back to the steps, descending to the ground. Leaving. Charles held to his bush, holding his breath. Instead of leaving she sank down onto the bottom step and folded her head in her arms. He heard her sob, and then another sob that visibly shook her body. He thought of Bruce. A pulse of anger turning to rage brought Charles out from his bush with words already in his mouth.

"Goddamnit, get up, Lorraine, come on."

She had jumped. Now there was only the stillness of her night-darkened face looking up at him.

"Come on!"

"He followed me . . ."

"Come on!" Charles reached out, seized her arm.

"Frank did. I let him in, I thought it was you . . . I didn't have any clothes on."

This made a stop, with Charles' hands gripped fiercely tight on her arm. "Your husband? For God's sake!"

"He said . . . He said never . . ."

Charles let go of her arm, stood there above her clenching and unclenching his hands. Fool, he was a fool. Bitch!

"I didn't tell him. I didn't tell him who. He . . ."

"God," Charles said between his teeth. Then, "Come on, get up!" He seized her arm again and pulled her to her feet, like lifting a dumb insensate animal's body.

There was sound and then a sweeping beam of light: impossible. Charles swung her around, as if to thrust her into some near hiding place. There was none. "Quick!" he said and had nothing to follow it with. The car appeared, turned into the parking space, and Charles, letting go of her arm, stood there in the full blast of the headlights.

"He'll kill me."

The voice came as from a distance and Charles saw that she was on the ground, on her knees. Her head was up and the glare of the lights detailed a bruised disfigured face he would not have recognized. For a moment that seemed much longer, standing fixed in the glare of eyes from the car, Charles could do nothing except look down into the battered face. "It's not your husband," he finally said, or thought he said. The lights went out.

He heard the car door and suddenly Bruce was beside her, bending down where she knelt sobbing. "Here," Bruce said, "let me help you," and gently lifted her onto her feet. Charles made some gesture, extended a hand. "Let her alone," Bruce said and steered her off toward his car. Charles tried to speak: his throat was too tight. All he could do was follow along and watch Bruce put her gently into the car.

Bruce did speak to him again. After he walked around to the other side of the car he paused with his hand on the door. In a perfectly flat voice he said, "I think she's dying."

Charles opened his mouth. Nothing would come out.

"My mother, I mean," Bruce said. He got into the car and the headlights suddenly blazed in Charles' face, his open mouth. Then the car backed up and drove away.

Charles' heart stopped in the night. He felt it stop and gasping for breath lay there afloat in a black and limitless terror. It started again but it labored, sputtering, and a long helpless interval passed before he felt its measured beating resume. An hour later he dared to creep, with pain in his chest, out to the telephone and call the hospital.

The next day in his hospital bed he remembered what had caused his heart to stop. The person in his house, or in his dream, had entered his room and in darkness that was not quite black had leaned over Charles' bed with his hands extended. It was not to choke, it was to embrace Charles. And this, the pressure of the embrace, was what had stopped Charles' heart. At least that was the way he always remembered the event.

Charles was in the hospital for three weeks, walking around

sometimes, always carefully, as if he was glass that might break. He had to be careful now. They told him this but he knew it anyway—very careful—and he started early training himself to avoid all occasions of stress. This was why he never inquired of Bruce, who came twice to visit him at the hospital, about his ex-wife or even about Lorraine. He avoided topics that so much as might lead to these disclosures, and Bruce, when he did break his usual silence, talked only about trivial matters. In the end Charles learned purely by accident, not through Bruce, that Irene had died and he never did learn how or exactly when it had happened. He never learned anything at all about Lorraine.

By the time he left the hospital Charles already had himself well trained and at home he perfected his training. Or almost perfected it. Avoiding physical strain came easy for him and after he converted the parlor downstairs into a bedroom he had no reason to climb steps. There was not much he had to do. Even more than in the past he left Cassie in charge of the house and if there was a little dirt and disorder they were not worth an upsetting confrontation with her. Besides, with Bruce gone, transferred to the University, there was really nobody except him to mess up things. And Charles now was care itself.

Giving up whiskey was hard, though not so hard when he remembered how whiskey would stir his fancy. The harder things were things of the mind and heart. Old lust seemed gone by itself. As for the memory and the imagination there were strategies and tricks. There were magazines and television and hours in the kitchen preparing a healthful but delicate snack. There was keeping up with his weight on the balance scales he had bought and little trips to the drugstore and the grocery. There were even strategies for sleep at night. He slept with his bedlight on and his radio, tuned to an all-night station out of town, softly playing. These were the least successful, though. There were still times when he waked in the night afraid for his beating heart, from a dream of himself with his hands reached out to seize a woman's throat.

CHAPTER SIX

Aspiration

His name was Junior C. Moss. The C did not stand for anything but it did supply the first letter of the name he gave as his own when he enrolled at Okaloosa High School that fall. He thought that nobody, no white person, had Junior for a real name—not here in Okaloosa anyway. He had never known anybody named Carl and when he saw the name on the Confederate monument on the town square he seized it. He was Carl Moss. The name made him feel new at first, even though at home he was still Junior.

This was only one of his lies. In fact he was seventeen though he told them he was sixteen, and he also told them that he belonged in the tenth grade instead of the eleventh. He had done all right at school in Stone County and, though thin, he was plenty tall enough for his age. He was afraid here: he had to have an advantage. This far he was successful. For some reason the school principal never saw his record. And so he was Carl Moss, sixteen and taller than his classmates, in the tenth grade where he was able, if just barely, to keep up with the work.

It was a sort of accident that he, Junior-Carl Moss, was enrolled at the city instead of the county high school out near the textile mill. When his father had sold their little mortgaged farm the spring before and moved the family up here he had planned to live in the mill village. He had not liked the looks of the place. Right away he had what he regarded as luck, though the house he found was, if anything, worse than the one he had left behind in Stone County. It was on the other side of Okaloosa Creek and isolated, from the town and everything else, but because recently the city limits had been extended the house was technically in town. So Carl's assignment. At least, though, the house was isolated—by trees and the creek and a good stretch of dirt road off the highway. The lies that Carl was forced to tell about his family were a lot less likely to blow up in his face.

The lies, though, did not get Carl anywhere, even during the interlude before it was discovered that they were lies. These town kids were a different breed from him and all his timid advances seemed to meet with a casual or else a vaguely hostile indifference. He stood close by, in range, hoping for the occasion that would bring him into one of those clusters of clowning boys and scrubbed-looking pretty girls. After the first week he had clothes like theirs. He put all of his hard-

earned little hoard into jeans with colored patches on them
and embossed T-shirts and sneakers with thick crepe soles. It
was no use. It was as if he had been a prowler looking in unseen through a pane of glass.

Of course he was not unseen, however quickly the eyes
passed over and beyond him. They saw a tall boy, thin and
getting thinner, with straw-white hair and glass-pale country
eyes—a goose's eyes. They also saw the expression on his face.
It was a little stupid. The reason was his broken tooth. A cow
had once kicked him in the mouth and almost half of an
upper front tooth was gone. He had not thought much about
it before. But when he started to school at Okaloosa he
quickly developed the habit of hiding the tooth under his
upper lip, holding the lip stretched down even when he spoke.
His classmates soon said it was because he kept his mouth full
of snuff.

Besides the black students there were, as always, a couple of
other outsiders in the class and Carl might have made friends
with them. He did not, he rejected their overtures. He continued, and that increasingly, to haunt the outskirts, hoping and
half-expecting that soon now a hand from one of those clusters would reach out and draw him in. It was only a short
time before he knew every name and who was who among
them and even where some of them lived and what their
houses looked like. He knew how their houses looked because
he had followed them home, trailing at a careful distance like
a scout or else pretending that he himself lived farther on beyond them in one of those blocks of shaded brick or stone
houses.

Above all the rest there was one boy who captured Carl's
attention. The boy's name was Phillip Woodrow. Even the
name sounded special, and the more so when Carl discovered
that there was a Woodrow Street in town. It was not just the

name, though. Neither was it that Phillip was impressive to look at, being smaller than most, nor that he was in any way especially athletic. But there was something about his small dark proud head and about his eyes, level eyes that measured everything. They seemed to say that he was worthy to assess any and all creatures and to set their value in the most rigid mind. It was like some special grace he had. It was like some spirit power standing by to hand him just the word he wanted and exactly the right gesture and the sureness that left him no need ever to hesitate one jot. And all his classmates saw it. To Carl the boy was like a prince, watched by everybody around him for the marks of his approval.

But what could Carl find to say to him? Chance encounters froze the tongue in his mouth. Even in his desk by the window, clear across the room from him, Carl felt the blush rise in his face when Phillip looked his way. There had to be some right word, right words, winged transforming words. He thought about it in his desk, covertly tracing the clean proud line of Phillip's head in profile. He thought about it in his bed at night, his narrow cot in the room where his small brother and sister snuffled and wheezed the night away. At meals too. He would forget to eat, sitting there with fork in hand and lips moving in search of some clever phrase, something casual and gallant.

"What's the trouble with you?" his mother said. "Talking to his self. Don't eat enough to keep a bird alive."

His mother had a snouted face and she was fat and wore a stained apron over the bulge of her belly. But his father was fatter, obese in fact—"Fats" Moss, with cotton lint in his hair. It was not always that Carl forgot to eat. He did not want to eat. He wanted a body so different from theirs that it would seem they had no blood in common. To watch his father working his fork like a shovel feeding a dark furnace door made him physically sick sometimes. So did the food that all of them spilled on the oilcloth and so did the grease on the once-white stove in the corner. These were among the times when he longed for Stone County again. There were no eyes there to look in through the windows. Here the threat of eyes was as constant as the going and coming of breath.

One night he found the words. It was so simple, so obvious when he recalled that every day for weeks he had watched Phillip enter and leave the school parking lot in the little thundering gold MG. "Say, Woodrow." Not Phillip, Woodrow. "That's a cool little machine you got out there." He rehearsed in the dark, shaping his face in a look of casual admiration, just lifting a thumb to point "out there." It would go on from this, could go many ways. Tomorrow. He would wait for the time and follow Phillip alone into the bathroom.

And the very next morning he had luck. Except that he felt his face was on fire and his tongue turned to stone at the root. A step away at the second urinal Phillip was already zipping up before Carl could utter the words—strange words in a strange broken voice. They fell into silence, silence except for a sound of water dripping.

"Yeah, thanks." Phillip was carefully tucking in his shirt.

On a deep breath Carl said, "I'm looking at one kind of like it for myself." Then, "Not as good as yours, though. A little older."

Then Phillip looked at him. His eyes were dark and did not seem to be quite focused on Carl's face. "Yeah? Where?"

Carl could not think where, and panic came. It seemed he could not think of anything except that his fly was still unzipped though his fingers rested there on the zipper handle. And the half-focused eyes were still looking at him—or looking past him. He had his mouth open but no idea what the words would be, when Phillip said, "See ya'," and passed behind him and went out through the door.

His chance was gone! After a wooden minute or two of standing there unzipped Carl felt the spirit in him come to life again. The question went unanswered still and Phillip, leaving, had said to him, "See ya'." Not unfriendly. Carl had his answer shaped on his tongue before he left the bathroom.

He had bungled his one rare chance, though, and all the rest of that day at school he could never catch Phillip alone. When school let out he hurried to the parking lot, toward Phillip's car. He had failed again. There was a boy, Reed, with Phillip, the two of them coming leisurely up behind him. Carl looked up at the sky, where the slanting October sun in his face burned like the sun of August. They walked past him talking, without a pause, talking about a girl. When Carl looked down they were getting into the car and sudden desperation seized him. A few steps brought him close enough. "Say, Woodrow," he said. "Phillip."

Even in the little MG only Phillip's head and shoulders were visible above the door. It was as though he sat swallowed up in the luxury of the car's plush red and gold, serene and almost listless, eyeing Carl with that same half-focused gaze. No reply, just waiting.

In a strained voice Carl said, "It's at a lot out on the highway, way on out." Then, "The MG I'm looking at. You ought to see it."

"That right?" His face was not unfriendly. But the other one was, the sharp face of Reed looking at Carl. Once more, struggling, Carl did not know what to say.

"See ya'."

There was only the hostile face of Reed looking at him. The car thundered, circled, and was gone.

Carl did not sleep much that night. He did not sleep much, if at all, the next night either, or for many nights. He lay stiff on his cot in the dark, fists knotted at his sides, feeling the rise and fall of blood in his face. Or he would steal naked out of the house and stand in the bare yard that he could not keep free of trash, until in the night's bitter air his shuddering flesh distracted him from his thoughts. In his few daylight hours at home he did not much notice his mother's questions or her looks of puzzled and ever-increasing vexation. "What's eating you? You up to something?" regarding him over the bridge of her reddened snout. He went outside. He cleaned up the yard again, down to the tiniest fragments of paper and the weeds he had missed before. Crawling he searched out litter under the house and he tightened and tightened again the sagging rusty strands of the barbed-wire fence. Then night came on and the agony of suppertime and after.

It was as if in some measure he had lost control not only of his thoughts but also of things he said and did. Not all at once. At first there had been only his timid and distant pursuit of Phillip, hanging back, resisting. It had been his eyes mainly that went where Phillip went, everywhere he went at school. That was it for a while, for some days after that day of casual rebuffs. Because this was what they were: he had accepted this later. Even so he had held on to the thought that it was a matter only of some key he had not found, that there were right words or a right gesture waiting to be discovered. So he waited and watched, watching Phillip.

Then he was discovered watching. One afternoon in the study hall Phillip surprised him by quickly turning his head and answering Carl's gaze eye for eye. Phillip's, though, was not a stare: it was merely a look, neutral and speculative. The stare came later, after some repetitions of that look, and with it a clenching of Phillip's brow that could not be read except as anger or worse. Carl felt it like a wound. For the rest of that school day he dared not lift his eyes from his desk. But the wound was festering. Overnight it produced the desperation that made Carl say and do the things he did.

His pursuit of Phillip was not distant anymore. Though always keeping a few steps back he went where Phillip went, hanging just outside the clusters that gathered where Phillip was. He saw the other hostile eyes and did not care except for Phillip's. If he could *speak* to him, *show* himself to him. One day, ignoring the resistance of bodies and the silence that fell, with his face on fire he shouldered his way in to Phillip. The MG, he told Phillip about the MG again, as if those words were all his tongue could master. And afterward the same stillness and his face flaming and Phillip looking at him.

"Why don't you shove off?"

It was Phillip saying this, in a tone that Carl, for all the drumming of blood in his ears, could not mistake. He hated Phillip. Just for a moment he did, with his hands clenched, wanting to strike the contemptuous mouth or to seize him by the neck. Nothing happened. Then he was standing alone in the hall and there was the sound of voices and some laughter diminishing in his ears.

He walked straight out the nearest door and across town to his home, thinking as he went that he would never again go back to the school. He would leave town, in fact—now, forever. He did not. The thought of that day's humiliation like a goad at his heart drove him, all right, but not to leave. It drove him out of his bed that night and, dressed as if for school, clear across town to the residential area and then to the house where Phillip lived. He knew the house well already, though by night, through the shedding maples and with only one high-up window lighted, it looked different, princely looking. He stopped under one of the maples. He was still in the grip of a fuzzy notion that having come this close he would find some way to talk to Phillip alone. It was not Phillip who appeared. All of a sudden he stood in a blaze of light and seconds later his arms were roughly pinned behind his back.

They kept him much of the night at the police station accusing and bullying him. Yet he went to school the next morning. He went in fact with an eagerness, as if he had a new start, a new self to present. He even made himself late, so that when he entered the room Phillip's and everybody else's eyes followed him each step of the way to his desk. The Strangler. As if this was his new identity, enveloping him like a visible and potent aura. The police had let him go, of course, only "under surveillance." Just now at least, when he was still shaken from last night's ordeal, this was enough for him. He sat in his desk taking their stares, hiding his tooth, trying to find what pose and expression befitted this new self of his.

This odd state of mind did not last very long. He was on the way to his first class, still feeling as if he walked on strange new legs, when he heard someone behind him laugh. When he realized that the laugh was at him he first thought of turning around, revealing his Strangler's face. But there was somebody in front of him near the classroom door, Reed with his hands lifted before his face in mock terror. And then a shriek. "It's the *Strangler!*" In the doorway beyond stood Phillip, looking at Carl. The expression on his face was something just poised between amusement and contempt.

For most of the day Carl endured the laughter and the mocking questions. For a little while, until the illusion was burned clean out of his mind, he tried to keep up his dangerous look, his Strangler's face. After that, pretending he too saw the humor, he tried to laugh or smile with his tormentors. Always his mouth went awry. He ended by fleeing again, not home but to a place in a thicket near his house where he stayed, trembling because the weather had turned cold, waiting for dark and suppertime. Then, through the window, he would steal into his room and take the few things he needed.

He got in without being heard, all right, and got the door to the rickety cabinet open. He never took anything out, though. The wall next to where he stood was thin and sounds from the kitchen and the dinner table there reached his ear almost unmuffled. He could hear them eating, chewing, like hogs at a trough. The few words that escaped him were those his father spoke with his mouth full. He heard his mother chuckle. "Strangler," she said. Then she laughed. She had a mean derisive laugh, like a winner's. "I reckon that's how come he ain't here. Out strangling somebody. Junior." She added, "Wouldn't he make some Strangler?"

He stumbled against a chair on the way to the window. His mother heard him and came into the room. Seeing the window open she leaned out and called to him but he was already gone in the dark. This was the last contact of any kind his family ever had with him. It was also the last that anybody at all in Okaloosa ever had with him, except Phillip.

He was already there in the garage when Phillip drove in in the MG about nine o'clock. There was an electric lamp on a wrought-iron post across the apron from the garage and it threw enough light inside to make Carl visible. Phillip did not see him at first, though, even in his headlights. He had switched off his lights and motor and already had his feet out on the garage floor when he first saw Carl standing there as if he had been nailed to the brick wall. The shock of surprise stopped Phillip cold for a moment. In that moment Carl never moved. He looked like a person waiting paralyzed for the spring of a fierce something or somebody that he could not hope to resist. When Phillip said to him, "What do you want? What are you doing here?" then he moved. He raised his hands, held them up palms-out with the fingers open and spread. It was a ridiculous gesture, like the threat of a child playing at ghosts. Even the look on his pale face was suited to such a game.

"Get your grubby ass out of here." Phillip was standing up by now. "Before I—" The car was right behind him and, besides, he was in no way prepared for Carl really to come at him. But Carl did, with a violence that in itself unmanned Phillip's resistance. Then he was on his back on the floor, with Carl's hands already around his neck. His outcries were almost stifled. They were not nearly so loud as Carl's own broken and animal ones.

Phillip's father heard the racket. When he got there he not only saw Carl coming out of the garage. The boy, seeing him, even stopped and with one finger pointed into the garage where Phillip lay motionless on the floor. Then he ran away.

Phillip was a long way from dead and he was already beginning to stir when his father reached him. The blows of his head against the concrete floor had done as much to put him out as had the choking he had got. Except for a headache and a very sore throat he was all right the next day. His father of course called the police at once. They made a big thing of it, combed the neighborhood and set up a net around town. It was no use. Somehow Carl got clean away. The police sent out a statewide bulletin and for a day or two continued their search throughout Okaloosa and in the countryside around. Then they began to reflect. They talked to Phillip more at length, to other boys at school and to Carl's family again. And they recalled again the details of their questioning of Carl only the night before the attack had happened. Nothing, neither the suspect nor the victim, fitted the Strangler's history. Within a few days, though they left the bulletin in effect, the police were practically sure that Carl could not be their man.

CHAPTER SEVEN

Bulwark

Throughout the summer and fall and afterward too there continued to be an inexhaustible stock of rumors. They were based mostly on nothing: somebody's speculations or a sign misread or a flimsy piece of evidence blown up and distorted. By late summer there had been already at least half a dozen people named and for a time suspected of being the Strangler. In August, after the murder of Ernestine Bell, still another one was added to the list. Then people, some people anyway, wondered how he could have been overlooked for such a long time.

As usual there was no real evidence. The rumor seemed to stem from a report that the young man, named Bucky Daniels, had been seen late that August night in the immediate neighborhood of the house where the murder happened. This evidently was the nucleus to which other things quickly attached themselves. The first of these things was the fact that Bucky was apparently not quite all there in the head. He was not any lunatic, certainly, or even really a moron, because in most ways he was plenty clever enough. It was said that he could have finished high school if he had wanted to and that there was no outward reason why he could not have got, in the four or five years since, a job much better than mowing just enough lawns to earn him the pocket money that his widowed and despairing mother continued not to give him. So it was not lack of good sense or even of any trace of normal ambition that produced the general impression of Bucky. There were plenty of other things about him, especially when people started thinking back.

They did not have to think back very far to get to the biggest thing about Bucky. Just three years ago gossip to the effect that he had sexually molested an eight-year-old girl was circulating all around the neighborhood. The matter never did get cleared up publicly and it finally went away, leaving nothing except a cloud over Bucky's apparently unconscious head. But it made people scrutinize him as they never had before and all the things they noticed or raked up out of their memories came back to them now, in support of their new suspicions. They recalled that even in childhood he had had no friends, as much because of his own indifference apparently as because the other children did not like him. They recalled in the child the same indolence and the same vacant expression they saw now when they looked into the yard where he lay, with one big bare foot hanging down, in the hammock between the hedge and his mother's little frame house. The foot reminded them how big he was, and fat, with a pasty face: big and strong enough. It was as though the pieces of a puzzle had come together.

When Angela Byrne, who lived in the yellow brick house at the dead-end of the same street that Bucky lived on, first heard the rumor it already was nearly full-blown. She did not talk to her neighbors much. Even her house, facing directly down the street and backed up to a swampy patch of thicket, was set apart at a little distance from theirs. She heard it at the high school, where she was teaching a summer class in history, and came home mute with indignation. That was the way indignation affected her, with muteness, and more and more as the years, forty-three of them now, passed by. Later she might try to tell her ancient great-aunt about it, but not now. She was thinking, turning it in her mind. Hers was one of the lawns that Bucky mowed. More than that, she had had him as a student in her history class not five years ago. And still more, when Bucky came to cut her grass she often sat on her porch and chatted with him for a little while, feeling friendly toward him, thinking he was a young man with gifts not yet discovered. It was like them, she thought, looking down the street at the rows of houses.

Angela thought a great deal about the town. There were nights when she would lie thinking for an hour of nothing else, envisioning ugly streets and suburbs and faces, half of them strange, glazed with that inward look of self-concern. And her students, with bright evasive pagan eyes and appetites where brains should be. No memories, no yesterday. She had tried showing them old photographs of the town, of Cot-

ton Street that had been little more than a beaten track to her
grandfather's cotton gin and of the old chaste and classic
courthouse across the street from where the present one stood.
A flicker of interest, casual. Eyes viewing an old slow world as
alien as China. It was no use for her to tell them about it,
about a world where people could be human, where these
rude children of today would have been only miserable without their motorcars. Yet the streets were lovely then. Even in
her own childhood there had been horses, there had been
wagons and mules and black people who tipped their hats
when she walked down Cotton Street with her mother or her
grandfather in his shiny black coat. They were dead, though,
and it had come to this. It had come to women strangled in
the night.

That Strangler. Angela had often thought about him slink-
ing through the dark, crouched and formless among bushes or
peering under a window curtain not drawn far enough. Like
a vengeance, waiting and inscrutable. That, she vaguely
thought sometimes, was why they had not and never would
catch him: because somehow he had no human form. So they
blundered here and there, chasing shadows, excited and for a
time convinced by every false report. Like frightened children.
Except they had a power to harm that children never had.

"They're like cruel children," she said to her aunt.
"They've got to fasten it on somebody, no matter." But it was
not certain whether Aunt Kate understood what she was talking about or even heard her speaking. The old lady's consciousness of things came and went and even at the best of
times was liable suddenly to slip away. It did not matter.
"That poor young man," Angela said. "It's not as if they
hadn't persecuted him enough already."

Aunt Kate sat in the shape of a question mark over the
kitchen table, the red oilcloth that she had already befouled.

Her tremulous spoon dipped at mush in a bowl and mush dribbled from the corners of her mouth. She looked as if the sunset breeze through the open window, blowing a welcome freshness in from the swampy thicket, might with a little increase lift her out of her chair. Angela stepped across the kitchen and with a damp cloth wiped the old lady's mouth and then the oilcloth around her bowl. "They'll think up some more bad things to pin on him now," she said, not even noticing when no answer came. She was looking out through the back door toward the thicket, standing straight, as rigid and slim almost as a standard-bearer. Except for some white streaks in her black hair there might have been a hundred years between her and the old woman bent and puttering over the bowl of mush. Unless somebody were to look carefully for a while at the two of them together. Then he might notice certain lines like prophecies around Angela's mouth and also about her eyes a hint of something remote, a sort of glaze beginning to form. The breeze stirred the window curtain, gave it a muted flap. Aunt Kate removed her hand from the spoon standing in the bowl. She suddenly said, "No . . ."

"No what, Aunt Kate?" Angela was still looking out through the door.

There was silence. Then, "I remember . . ."

"What do you remember?"

But Aunt Kate had forgotten. Angela looked at her tenderly, wondering what it was that had got away. A long-ago bright moment under an arbor, in a swing, with pleasant young men's voices? Her golden hair, her beauty shining. Angela had a photograph of Aunt Kate then, her beauty captured, set on the mantel in the living room where, at her work of sweeping and dusting, Angela would often stop to gaze at it. Now she gently wiped her aunt's mouth again and taking the limp hand placed it back on the spoon. "You need to eat. To keep your strength up."

There was a little back porch off the kitchen and almost every summer night after she put Aunt Kate to bed Angela sat out there for a while. Lights from the houses beyond did not penetrate the thicket in summer and the small backyard was dark and, except for an occasional voice straying in from a distance, quiet. She was not afraid, not anymore, not for this past month at least. Somehow it had come upon her, almost like a gift to her while she slept, that that danger, in spite of its reality for others, could not be her own. She still locked her windows at night, but now instead of fear it was prudence speaking. Here on her back porch in the dark she felt no uneasiness, felt only her indignation kindling all over again. And then at last pity for the boy, for Bucky, the goat for the rest of them. She made a resolution.

Milly Sparks, who lived in the house closest to Angela's, noticed when Bucky appeared the next afternoon. Given the sinister rumors about Bucky she would have noticed in any case, but when, without his lawnmower, he entered Angela's yard and went straight up and knocked at the door she was surprised. She was more surprised when she saw Angela at the door letting him in. And it was a full hour at least before he came out and went off, head bent, at his shambling walk down the street past Milly's house.

That was only the beginning. It happened again two days later and after that pretty regularly two or three times a week. Of course people had to accept that it could not mean anything ugly, not with Angela Byrne anyway and certainly not openly in broad daylight with an old aunt in the house. It was strange, though. Of course Angela was strange herself—a withdrawn defiant haughty kind of woman for no good reason unless it was that her name had once meant something in the town. That was it, they decided, watching this weird friendship demonstrated, without any explanation, two or three times each week in front of their eyes. It was an act of pride, an arrogant show of noblesse intended for a slap in the face to her neighbors. So with eyes that grew increasingly hostile they watched her, predicting secretly, half-hoping in the back of their minds, that one morning she would be found assaulted and strangled in her bed.

Angela felt it. When she went out into the yard or got out of her car—which she parked now in the driveway so that she could be seen—she was conscious of eyes watching from windows of the houses down the street. Her posture was naturally erect, high-headed, and now as she moved through the yard or stopped to examine a rosebush or a shrub she made of it a reflection of her disdain. When Bucky came, shambling onto the porch, she made a display of that too, showing herself as she held the screen door open.

They sat in the kitchen, at the table with the red oilcloth. At first Angela had served him cookies or pie she made. Soon she stopped that. He was too heavy, she told him, he needed to lose, and after that she served him yogurt flavored with fruit and coffee with honey in it. This was the first step of a campaign Angela had decided on. It included advice, reflections, lectures really on Bucky personally and on the town, the world he lived in. Bucky seemed always interested and never resentful, even when Angela's remarks touched him in the most personal way. "You shamble," she said. "Hold yourself up, hold your head up. People see what you think of yourself. Show them. Make them swallow their venom." Bucky, quiet most of the time, nodded his understanding. He was a listener, a learner. His glass-blue eyes could kindle at things she said to him and his mouth, normally a little slack and droopy

at the corners, could often express with eloquence an un-
spoken thought or passion. In no small part it was his big and
rather pasty face that hid his real nature from their eyes, eyes
that did not want to see. To Angela there was another face
beneath this pasty one, like the face the sculptor sees in the
lump of clay.

The kitchen, with its breezes and ticking clock, opening on
the small backyard and the bounding wall of thicket beyond,
was a good place for their talks and for sharing the way they
felt—like a secret place. Or secret except for Aunt Kate,
though her interruptions need not have amounted to anything. When she did appear she usually stopped at the dining
room door and stood gaping as if both of them, even Angela,
were people unknown to her and a little alarming. Until
Angela would say, "It's all right, Aunt Kate," and usually the
old lady would creep away. Once in a while, though, she
would come in and with Angela's help sit down in her place
at the table. It should not have mattered. She rarely said anything and her intervals, really her flickers of consciousness
could not have gathered the sense of what they were talking about. But Bucky did not like it. He sat there sullen, fingering or staring into his cup of honeyed coffee, maybe and
maybe not listening to Angela. The light that so often came
and went in his eyes never appeared in the times when Aunt
Kate was present.

That was how August went out, with the small difference
that now because school had started back Bucky's visits came
usually after supper. This little change, however, was like the
start of a new phase and Angela, thinking over the past few
weeks with Bucky, felt that she had reason to congratulate
herself. Already this soon, she thought, he was not the same
young man who had come to her as ignorant as a child, ignorant even that he was the one now chosen goat for all their vi-

cious tongues. She had seen the light come into his eyes—
come and go, but it was there. She had seen him lift his head
and seen his lips stir, flex themselves, trying hard to shape the
thoughts she had brought to birth in his mind. And then he
had begun to talk a little. If it was not yet very much it was
more than the tongue-tied answers that at first had been his
only contributions. "I been thinking and thinking," he said
one day and looking out the window paused as if this was to
be his conclusion.

"Thinking what?" Angela said, watching his lips that were
stirring, flexing, no longer droopy at the corners. It was one of
those moments when she fancied that a different face was
about to show itself.

"They been mean to me all my life. I never done anything
to them. Just mean. I hate them. I wouldn't care if he strangled everybody in this whole town." Then, "Except you," he
said, with a sudden timid glance her way.

"You mustn't feel that way, Bucky. You mustn't hate, even
when you're hated. That's what Jesus tells us."

Bucky lowered his big disheveled head, brooding over his
cup. "I do, though. Laying it on me . . . I wish I had been
born back there when you talk about. When everybody wasn't
. . ." He was searching for the words.

"Oh, it wasn't perfect then," Angela said. "There were bad
people then too . . . lots of them. But there wasn't all this
hate and suspicion. There was so much more kindness, broth-
erly feeling. So much more love," she concluded.

Bucky gave her another timid glance and looked out the
window, gazing as if determined to see the vision pictured
there against the wall of thicket. Angela across the table
watched him. Compassion had softened her mouth at the
corners and deepened the look of remoteness about her eyes.
She was thinking that almost she could see, under Bucky's

too-much flesh, the good clean lines of the face that would emerge.

Then, early in September, old Mrs. Gladys Stallworth was murdered. Because it had happened on the next street but one there was, if anything, more consternation this time than ever before in Angela's neighborhood. As usual there were no real clues, nothing solid to go on, and every baseless suspicion got itself redoubled overnight. In spite of, or maybe partly because of Angela, Bucky was once again a victim. Again there were whispers around the neighborhood that he had been seen abroad that night and this time somebody took it to the police. Bucky was picked up and hauled off to the station for questioning. Of course he was released but not as quickly as he should have been: the police, frustrated and desperate and thinking maybe they smelled something pressed him hard for a couple of hours. When they brought him home he got out of the patrol car shaking, sweat still running down his big face and neck into his wet collar. The first thing he did was head for Angela's house. She was not at home yet, though. In fact she was unusually late that day and it was almost Bucky's accustomed visiting hour, nearly dusk in September, before he got to see her.

Angela, standing at first, silent with indignation even when he paused in his account, finally went and sat down at the table with him to listen. It was no longer the voice of panic that she would have heard three or four hours earlier. For all the tremors in it and the breakings-off and confusions in Bucky's story, there was something reflective about his manner, as if he was trying to find the meaning of what had happened to him. Sometimes he would stop and look hard at the window where night was gathering. Again, lifting his big hands out of his lap, he would clasp and knead them together against his chest—at moments seeming to strain as if to press

the truth out of them. "They kept yelling at me, telling me I
. . . It wasn't me, though. Just 'cause I know that old
woman, cut her grass once. Even if I didn't like her. It wasn't
me, though." He stopped again, his hands kneading, straining
against each other. Angela watched them.

"I go walking a lot, at night. I can't sleep. So I go walking.
But that doesn't mean . . . They kept saying it and saying it,
yelling it at me. I felt . . ." He stopped again and for the first
time looked directly at Angela, appealing to her. "It wasn't
me, was it? You know it wasn't me, don't you?"

"Of course it wasn't," Angela said. "That's the way they
do." Then a pause and she saw the big hands slowly relax
and slowly part themselves and sink down into his lap again.
He was looking at her with worshiping eyes.

"Just you," Bucky said. "You're the only one. 'Cause
you're good. All the rest of them . . . Mean ugly faces
watching me, yelling at me." His hands in his lap had
clenched each other again. "I hate them all," he said with a
sudden vehemence that twisted his mouth. Then, his face
changing back, "I wish . . . me and you . . . we could . . ."

This time it was a movement of Angela's that had made
him break off. Her head had moved, a small startled movement, and when her eyes wandering for a moment came to
rest they were fastened on the dining room door. Aunt Kate
was there, gaping at them with that look of puzzled alarm. A
space of silence went by before Angela said, tenderly, "It's all
right, Aunt Kate." The old lady must have heard her, because she began the slow maneuver of turning to go away.
Still they watched her, both of them watching. When Angela
looked at Bucky again there was something in his face she
could not read.

But whatever Angela saw, it was as if a dim alarm had
sounded in her head, sounded and left in its aftermath a dis-

tress whose cause kept evading her. It hung there in her mind, clouding her thoughts, smothering the indignation that Bucky's words had fed. There were words again, Bucky talking to her again, but she did not hear the words, heard only his voice going, breaking and rising and falling. She saw his lips in motion and saw, once, the lips curl and twist his mouth and she saw when he looked at her with the light that came and went in his eyes. It was all like a sort of dumb show only, with only a wordless voice to give it sense. There was one moment though, an interruption, that cut like a shaft of light into her mind. Bucky, with just the slightest turn of his head, paused for another glance at the dining room door. Then the veil dropped back, the voice took up again.

Bucky was gone, the door shut behind him, and still her distress remained. It followed Angela to her room and was there still when she got up from her bed the next morning. It haunted her day at school, making her stumble among her facts, putting grins or looks of discomfort on the faces watching her. After school she dawdled and went home late on purpose. It was not until after supper, just as twilight started coming on, that she realized what the matter was. She was afraid of Bucky. All of a sudden, her dripping hands arrested over the sink, she was listening for the sound of his step on the porch.

Foolish, Angela told herself, and baseless. One moment, only one, when she had not been able to read his face. Ridiculous. Plunging her hands into the dishwater she took a plate and dried it. Yet she was listening. And she heard his step on the porch, his timid knock at the door. She hesitated. But she went and let him in.

That night was the start of it. Instead of two or three times a week, now it was every night, signaled by his footstep and his soft knock on the door. She tried to tell him. "You mustn't come every night, Bucky. I have things to do, you know, papers to grade." He, his head bent, his eyes looking obliquely at her with that light in them, would say, "I don't have to stay long. Just a *few* minutes." And Angela, uneasy, would always let him in.

But it was different in other ways too. No matter how Angela tried there were times when the old words, advice, reflections would not come to her lips; or, coming, sounded hollow and not to be believed. "There was so much . . . so much more feeling then. So much more . . ." Again she would notice her own intentness, the stiffness of her body, and try muscle by muscle to purge it away. No use. It was as if there might be danger in letting her gaze stray far from his face or from the hands that had grown nervous in these last days. Of course Bucky felt it. This was why his eyes increasingly had a haunted or maybe a helpless look when he lifted up his face to Angela, and it was why the hands wandered so, clenching each other, fingering the coffee cup. Big, powerful hands. Once in a while, in moments that always seemed vaguely frightening to her, Angela would see his mouth open and his lips moving in what was like a struggle for words stuck too tight in his throat. These moments were like small gaps in time and Angela, breaking the rigor of her posture, would say something or move in some way to put a stop to them. And night by night it grew worse.

But worst of all were the times when Aunt Kate appeared. Always there was that moment of suspension, almost perfect, when they turned, both of them, and met the old lady's gaping stare. It had been no use for Angela to warn her away beforehand. "Don't come to the kitchen when he's here, please, Aunt Kate. Stay in your room. Please." And Aunt Kate, nodding, seeming to understand, would say, "Yes, dear. I will." And yet she would come. Would forget? Or do it out of old-woman's perversity to vex Angela? Or was it something better, design in it, a will however muddled to defend this house from evil? In any case she came and stood gaping at them from the door, stopping everything, stopping even Bucky's nervous hands. Angela would glance at the hands. And then came the night when Bucky, in the middle of one of those still moments, said something. It was said in a voice almost too quiet to hear and yet in Angela's head it was like a shout. "Tell her to go 'way. I hate her."

Angela, drawing a breath, it seemed long afterward, said, "It's all right, Aunt Kate. It's all right."

Angela had already taken to locking her doors and windows with scrupulous care at night. But on this night, going the rounds at bedtime, she kept being afraid that somehow she had missed one and she went the rounds a second time and finally, in her nightgown, once again. She left lights burning in the living room and kitchen. Pausing at Aunt Kate's open door she saw a window shade not drawn, not all the way, and once again on quiet slippered feet she entered the room. The shade drawn she continued to stand there. Through the narrow space at the edge she could see out into the yard and see, fifty feet away, the shadow wall of thicket, solid shadow. And nothing but a window glass between herself and it. One sharp rap of a man's big knuckles . . . that fragile. As fragile, she thought, standing there, as the sound of Aunt Kate's breath in the room behind her. Or could she really hear it? With a start of panic Angela turned around. The bed was barely visible and the old lady among the pale sheets was not visible at all, not until Angela bent down. Even then for full assurance Angela had to touch her. Yes, she could hear the breathing now, however faint, like ghostly breath. Her hand rested on Aunt Kate's arm. Softly her fingers encircled it, feeling how small and dry it was, feeling after a little while the thread of pulse against her fingertips. Or was that only her own pulse she was feeling? Her fingers must have tightened on Aunt Kate's arm. The old lady stirred, waking up, and muttered something unclear. "It's all right, Aunt Kate," Angela said. "It's me. Go back to sleep."

But Angela spent the rest of the night in the chair by Aunt Kate's bed.

In the night, though, she had made another of her resolutions. She had told herself that she would execute it on the dot of seven-thirty, just before she set out to school, and she had her jacket on already and her briefcase sitting on the chair when she reached for the telephone. Her hand closed on the receiver but that was all. There was such a tightness in her throat. A little later. She would have to be late to school. She went into the bathroom and in front of the mirror, observing the pallor of her face, the deepened creases around her mouth and eyes, adjusted her hair. In the next room Aunt Kate was stirring. Angela went back to the telephone but once again she did not pick it up, not for a minute or two. Then she did something she had never done before. She telephoned the school and lied, saying that her aunt was indisposed. It was necessary.

Angela puttered about the house, tending to Aunt Kate, dusting things and forgetting and dusting them over again. It was noon before she could master herself, picking up the phone, speaking out of a tight dry throat in a voice that might have belonged to somebody else. Afterward she could not remember her words exactly. She remembered Bucky's better, such as they were, that were mainly stutterings and small protesting explosions of breath. And the one clear word, "Please . . ." like a whine. But she had been firm, very firm. Hadn't she even, in the face of his persistence, mentioned the police? It would be all right now.

She puttered the afternoon away. She baked some cookies, sweet and light without eggs in them, that would do for Aunt Kate. She manicured the old lady's nails and gently with mineral oil on the cotton cleaned her ears. Then she combed Aunt Kate's hair. Standing behind her at the kitchen table Angela combed and combed the white hair, combed until it flowed like silk and whispered between the teeth. Aunt Kate fretted. And she was puzzled. "Who . . . who's coming? Is he coming now?"

"No. He's not coming anymore. Not ever," Angela said. But she looked out the window. Then she bent and kissed the cheek that was fine and cool as wax.

Once in the afternoon she saw Bucky. On one of her trips to the dining room window in front she saw him down the street. He was a good distance away and he was just standing there looking toward her house. This redoubled Angela's nervousness, but it was not until dusk when she saw him a second time, standing a little nearer this time, that she did something about it.

After dark the neighbors across the street saw a police car stop in front of Bucky's house. The policemen called him out and the two of them stood talking to him under the streetlight beside the car. The neighbors could see Bucky shaking his head. Once, just for an instant, they heard his voice. It came almost like a sob out of the general quiet. Then the policemen drove away and left Bucky standing there under the streetlight with his head bent down.

Nobody saw him again that night or the next day either. He was seen on the following day, for a while, sitting on the steps to his front porch bent over with his head on his arms. And he was seen again that night.

Milly Sparks' husband Cal got home about eight o'clock and getting out of his car he saw Bucky on Angela's front porch. Bucky was in plain view because, as had been the case every night lately, the porch light was burning. He obviously saw Cal also because, after knocking at the door again, Bucky would turn and look in his direction—defiantly, Cal said later. And the knocking got louder. Cal thought about doing something, calling out or phoning the police. But before he could do anything Bucky stopped knocking and after a pause left the porch and went shambling slowly away down the street out of sight.

Cal was still wondering half an hour later if maybe he shouldn't do something and he went to his front door and opened it. That was when he heard a scream, followed quickly by another one. Cal ran, across his front yard and in through Angela's gate and, because the front door was shut, around to the back of the house. He met Bucky coming out, not exactly running even, just sort of jogging and stumbling as he went. He was crying, sobbing as he passed around the corner of the house. Cal did not try to pursue him, he ran right in.

Both women were on the kitchen floor. But only Aunt Kate was stretched out, lying with her head on Angela's lap, her head that was entirely hidden in Angela's embrace. There were no screams now. There were only Angela's moans and broken phrases, in the voice of a desolate child pleading and pleading. Every little while she would loosen her embrace and bending farther kiss the old woman's forehead and eyes and cheeks. Her kisses left marks, as could then be seen, because her mouth was bleeding. Also her blouse was torn from one of her shoulders.

The story of what had happened came out later, piece by piece, through Angela first and then through Bucky, who had been found within the hour lying in the hammock beside his house. Bucky had come to the kitchen door. He had knocked and kept on knocking, harder all the time, calling to Angela through the glass. The two women, or at least Angela, had been too terrified to move from the table—at first anyway. And besides, what was Angela to do: run away, leave Aunt Kate? It was only when Bucky began to bump against the door with his shoulder that Angela stood up and drew Aunt Kate also to her feet. Then the door flew open and Bucky was in the kitchen, raving. Aunt Kate was the one he came to first. He seized her—by the neck, Angela said—and threw her like you would a chicken against the wall, where she fell. Then he went for Angela. It must have been her screams that saved her, right in his face that way. Anyhow he suddenly looked frightened, let go of her and stepped back. Then she was down on the floor with Aunt Kate. When, some moments or minutes later, she saw him moving toward her again, raving again, that was when she started screaming the second time. Those were the screams Cal heard.

Bucky was never very clear. He always cried when they pressed him for details and answered only in fragments. "I just wanted . . . I wanted to tell her . . . She kept hiding, running behind her. I just pushed that old woman . . . out of the way. I wouldn't hurt her. Not Miss Angela. Not never! I *love* her." That was as much as they ever got out of him. They kept him in jail for a few weeks and then sent him off to a mental institution. If Bucky was the Strangler—and most people doubted it—there was never any evidence to convict him.

Curiously Aunt Kate did not die, not then, not for a couple of years. But she never was in her right mind again or even able to walk around. After a month they brought her home from the hospital and Angela gave up her teaching job and just about everything else to take care of her. Her situation would probably have won her some friends among the neighbors if she had not remained so haughty, refusing every offer of help. Her grass grew up and even after Aunt Kate died she had it cut, by professionals, not more than once or twice a season. She never taught school again. By the time Aunt Kate had been dead a year Milly Sparks was saying that given another year or two Angela would be the spitting image of the old woman.

CHAPTER EIGHT

Rage

The rumor circulating among the white people of Okaloosa that the Strangler was known to be a Negro found its way to black ears too. When Herman Coker, Sim Denny's son-in-law, heard it he said, among other things, "Yeah. *Knowed* to be. Got to be a nigger. It's me, maybe. I hate them white som'bitches bad enough to done it."

Herman's response was predictable—and understandable too, up to a point. He had grown up in a black slum in Birmingham, in a two-room tenement apartment that, as he said

later, a farmer wouldn't keep his hogs in. There were six children and the mother but no father that Herman could
remember. Until she died when Herman was seventeen his
mother worked as cook and maid for a white woman, a job
that made her have to travel twenty miles by bus back and
forth every day except Sunday. Herman saw the white
woman two or three times and later, after he learned to hate,
remembered her with hatred both for his mother's toil and for
the ugliness of that wrinkled old white face.

The mother, who was both pious and ambitious for her
children, managed to make them all go to school for a while,
and Herman, the brightest one, longer than any of them. By
the time he got to high school the first whispers of racial troubles to come were already in the air. By the time he got out,
quit in the middle of his next-to-last year, he had a seething
bitterness toward all white people and a cynicism that made
him mock his mother's piety and her stupid ambition for him.
She died not long after that and Herman had to go to work.

There were several years of jobs like loading trucks and
stacking lumber and putting down pavement. The jobs mostly
ended in about the same way, with Herman quitting in a rage
or getting fired because he made his hatred of whites too
plain. He drank too much and got in fights, though always it
was black people he fought with. By the time he was nineteen he
had a big pale ridge of scar tissue on his neck and also a reputation. Most people steered clear of him. When the real racial
protests got started in the early sixties Herman was right in
the middle of them. He was put in jail twice. Even after the
blacks won some victories and things generally had cooled off
a good deal he was not much less bitter than he used to be.
But then he met Maybelle, up from Okaloosa.

Herman was ripe for the meeting. By that time he had practically lost touch with his brothers and sisters, and lonesomeness

had taken him to, and brought him back from, two or three other cities where he did not find anything. Then he met that glad timid grin of Maybelle's that fled away and suddenly came back and astonished him. It was as if she had come, bringing some of it with her, from a place that was brand-new and fresh like a garden on the old soiled map. That was how it was for a while. It was long enough for Herman to marry her. It was even long enough for him to go with her, a few months later, back to her home in Okaloosa.

It seemed to Herman that he had stepped back in time a few years. What had already happened in Birmingham appeared to be just getting under way in Okaloosa. But Herman was more prudent now, if not less bitter, and he managed to get and keep a job at the Rayburn Textile Mill. He was a doffer, supplying loaded spools to long rows of rumbling clicking machines that passed the yarn from spindle to spindle like running webs. It was easy work, forgetful work. Except for the white people he had to work for, and sometimes with, he liked it fine. And he would have liked living in Maybelle's house in Creektown if the house had not really belonged to his father-in-law Sim Denny, who was nothing better than an Uncle Tom. After the first few months, even after Sim started trying to act as if he was part of the Movement too, Herman had got so he couldn't speak a word to the old man without there being a sneer in it.

"Leave him be," Maybelle said. "He old."

"Yeah," Herman said. "Leave him be. If niggers like him hadn't been sucking up to honkies all their life we wouldn't be where we at. He ain't earn *nothing* from me."

"This his house," Maybelle said, but mildly, not looking at Herman any longer. Her sullen expression, the outthrust purple underlip, did not quite hide the fact that she was afraid of him.

"*His* house, yeah. Till a white man decide he want it for something. Ain't nothing *his*."

More and more nowadays that tone of his voice was like a signal to Maybelle. She hushed, and if Sim was present she always cast a warning glance his way. There was no need for it. Sim was afraid of him too and at supper, almost the only time he had to be in Herman's presence, he sat in silence with his gray bullet head bent over his plate eating. Those meals were mostly silent. If there was other talk than a necessary word from Maybelle now and then it would nearly always come from Herman. The chances were it would be some angry or mocking thing ending, as likely as not, with a cut at Sim or the question: "Ain't that right, Uncle?" A grunt from Sim, an agreement and a protest both, would be the only answer. And Herman would grin, maybe, a hard little flash of a grin, and go at his food again as if he had forgotten until now what he was at the table for. He wolfed the food, quick with his hands, forking up beans or cornbread or a piece of pork at random. His mind was busy and under the hanging light bulb, weakened by the paper shade, the white in his eyes suggested eyeballs reversed and gazing backward into his head. For Sim it was a little like sitting at the dinner table with something that just might all of a sudden spring at him.

After Herman's first few months in town the feeling that he was somebody to be avoided was pretty general among people who knew him even fairly well. And this was true in spite of his deliberate efforts to be friendly. He tried to enter into things and he kept his rage in check. A week after he came to town he joined the Improvement Association. He made contributions and went to all the meetings and when he talked, seeing how things were in Okaloosa, he always throttled the violent words that had used to come boiling up like acid in his gullet. Sometimes he had even gone to church and sat nodding agreement with Brother Dick's pale diatribes. Finally, though, it was all no good to him. There was not any curtain he could draw against their glimpses into his soul.

Herman had not quite stopped hoping, though, and several times in the course of that spring and summer there were occasions when he thought his hour was at hand. A row between blacks and whites at the high school was one of these. There was anger in Creektown and words spoken with feeling that might have come straight up out of Herman's own heart. The aftermath of that second old white woman strangled made another occasion. A Negro, the white people said, and said it this time in the newspaper, as though it was a fact already proved. Hershel Rawls answered. He answered from the steps of the First African Baptist Church and made a speech out of it that blasted Whitey the way he ought to have been blasted and lifted Hershel's voice quite out of its old suave accents. For Herman it was like a friend's voice speaking to him. And the crowd around him, touching him, the black heads nodding and murmuring and shouting Amen where Hershel left a pause: suddenly they too, all of them, were his friends. At least for a while they were.

But the big moment, the one that seemed to be *it,* came at the end of summer when the white police killed poor old deaf and dumb Earl Banks. It was not just a moment, either, it was two or three whole days of moments running successively. Herman had friends everywhere. He met them on Creektown street corners talking in noisy threatening voices under the streetlights and saw them pass by in speeding cars and heard, against the wail of police sirens, their shouts in the distance. On into the night and all the next day and into that night too, Hattie's Cafe was crowded. Bottles of whiskey, pillaged from the white-owned store at the west end of Creektown, stood openly on tables or passed from hand to hand through the drifts of smoke. One of the hands was Herman's. His voice, running unbridled now, sounded no different from other ones made audible in the break when his own voice stopped. "Yeah," he said, lifting the empty paper cup almost to his lips. *"Had* to be a nigger. So they got them one. *Any* one, it don't matter, niggers is all the same. Little bad luck and it'd been me," he said, addressing the big black man with the missing tooth.

"That's right. Sho it would," the man said. He pushed the bottle of whiskey across the table to Herman. Pouring, Herman said,

"Yeah. And you know what they going say when that Strangler kill him another old white woman? This here was just a little *mi*stake. A little *mi*stake," he repeated slowly. "And what *we* going do?" He lifted the cup and tossed the raw whiskey into his mouth. It burned, seared its way down his gullet. Through watery eyes he saw the faces watching him now, waiting, making around him a pool of quiet among the strident voices in the room. "Yeah," he breathed, with a breath that felt like flame. "I hate them som'bitches. I hate them goddamn white faces." The bottle was empty. He held it by the neck, gripping until the knucklebones whitely defined themselves through the skin. When he suddenly threw his head back they could all see the pale ridge of scar above his collar line and they were still looking at this when, too quick for thought, he raised and hurled the whiskey bottle with all his strength against the wall. The explosion made a hush in the room that he remembered afterward.

They put him out of the cafe, though not roughly, and somebody with a hand on his arm walked the three blocks home with him. Drunk, in the dim streetlight, Herman did not know who it was or what raging words he had said to the man. He seemed to recall this much only. The hand on his arm and the low voice had answered in spirit to the violence pouring out of his mouth. On the front porch alone, standing propped against the door, Herman could feel yet the pressure from that hand holding his arm, holding him upright.

But that interlude was illusion like the others—just bigger this time and longer-lived. About three days, little more, and again the streets were quiet at night. There were bursts of laughter once more and mellow voices and clusters of boys instead of men standing under the streetlights on the corners. As if it had not happened, Herman thought, seated at Hattie's counter with his glass. There was no crowd at nine o'clock, and eyes that stopped for a moment on his face seemed barely to remember. A few did. He got a greeting or two. Wait a day, a week, he thought, and knowing how anger would pitch his voice too high he did not answer the greetings. A few days more and not one pair of eyes but would look at him in the old way, uneasy or afraid of him, lingering a moment on his scar. Slowly he lifted his chin and made the scar like a badge plain to see. And he remembered, when he had hurled that bottle against the wall, the stillness of all those faces looking at him.

Herman remembered something else that night. He remembered it at Hattie's and he remembered it again afterward as he passed along the deserted street, walking a little unsteady because of the whiskey. It was the man who a few nights ago had walked him home from Hattie's. Herman had no memory of anything except a dark figure, maybe tall, and a hand on his arm and answers that appeared to second his own raging words. What words, though? It seemed to matter and he tried to recall. No use, the words were gone: no memory but the sound of his own voice pouring out his soul. It did not matter.

This was what Herman told himself then and also later

when the thought recurred. Somehow it did matter. It mattered enough to keep on calling that question back, as if in his drunkenness he had laid bare a dark and ugly secret about himself. What secret, though? He had no secret. Even so this answer was never good enough to finally silence the question. It came back in his sleep that night and still the next day, through the forgetful clicking hum of the doffing machines he tended, went on repeatedly asking itself like a voice from over his shoulder.

He was at Hattie's again by eight o'clock. In fact now he was at Hattie's every night, seated where the counter met the wall, an elbow propped beside a glass of beer or moonshine whiskey. Somehow he thought he would know the man who had walked him home that night. The one still figure in that room full of voices and movement and dinning jukebox music, Herman sat and watched. His eyes were secretly busy, passing from face to face, lingering when a new one entered the room. After the first few nights of course not many new ones entered. It made no difference. By eight o'clock he was there on his stool and busy with his eyes.

That was the week Sim Denny died. Of course it was expected, it was only decent that Herman go to the funeral of his wife's father. He did not go. From the first, feeling the way he did about Sim, even Sim dead, he did not want to. And he wanted to less and less when he thought about how it would be watching Brother Dick, the preacher, by the coffin with his black face turned up to where he could see, he would say, old Sim's soul already washed clean as a lamb and on its last bright journey. And Jesus waiting, holding his hand out. A white man's hand. Like all those notions were white man's notions cooked up to keep the niggers quiet. Precious Jesus. Those black voices wailing it out in that old nigger graveyard where you had to pick the cockleburrs off your ass before you

could sit down on your chair. While Jesus looked down. Just
like He had looked down when Herman was one of six little
pickaninnies in two hog-wallow rooms in a stinking tenement
house.

The clincher came when, the evening before the funeral,
an old white woman showed up at the front door. It was *Mrs.
Mister Will*, old Sim's white man's lady. With some flowers
she had pulled somewhere in that big green yard of hers and
looking tearful, sad about the good old days when niggers
were niggers and Sim was Mister Will's own personal nigger.
Except the ones in that living room were still acting like such
niggers, jumping up all around like giving that old white
woman a chair was the biggest thing that could have happened to them. Herman left the house.

He left the house but he did not leave that white face
behind him. Even his vigil at Hattie's and all the whiskey he
drank that night did not dislodge it from his memory. As
usual his eyes were busy, though half the time they were looking inward instead of out, seeing the folds and creases in those
pink-white cheeks and the melted look in the eyes and the
tight mouth that had no flesh or color either one. He remembered that woman his mother had worked for. He remembered a hundred, a thousand old white women's ugly faces,
that looked at him like they were blind when they passed him
by. Finally, late that night, he kept seeing the face like an
image printed on his eyeballs, as if his eyes had been mirrors
holding it. The whiskey was the reason. He left Hattie's and
made his way home in the swimming half light from the
streetlamps.

The walk did not clear Herman's head. When he saw the
lights on and then, as he stumbled up onto the porch, people
in the living room he stopped and stood there confused for a
moment. Through the door the people were all looking at

him, all silent, and the shiny head of the coffin reflected the
floorlamp by the wall. Swaying a little he pulled the screen
door open. A voice and then another one spoke. Herman only
stood there against the doorjamb making the round of faces
with his gaze. The white one was gone. They were all black
faces, all turned on him like masks with living eyes, evasive
eyes. "Yeah," Herman said in their stillness. "Yeah," and settled his gaze on the motionless head in the coffin in the
lamplight. A mummy's head. "Old Sim, there," Herman said.
"Gone to white folks' heab'm." Around the room the eyes fled
from him. "Yeah," he said and after one uncertain step,
watched by the eyes, passed among them through to the
kitchen and entered the bedroom door. He slammed it shut
behind him.

Maybelle's startled face from the pillow met him in the first
stroke of light. Herman looked back at her, waiting, waiting
for her parted lips to move. Then he said, "Act like you ain't
never seen me before. This here your husband done come
home." Swaying above her on the balls of his feet he felt like
something fiercely perched and waiting. The parted lips went
shut, said nothing, and the eyes escaped behind her fallen lids.
"Better look see is it Herman," Herman said. "Might be some
bad guy come in on you."

"I knows it's you," Maybelle murmured and did not open
her eyes.

"Like that Strangler dude. White folks say he black just
like me. You better look see."

A long breath lifted Maybelle's bare shoulders but her eyes
stayed shut. "Wish you'd get to bed, Herman. I tired."

"Yeah," Herman said. To steady himself he put a hand on
the iron frame at the foot of the bed. A low voice from the living room was audible but he was still looking hard at
Maybelle's face. "He don't go for black, though. It's white he

after. Like that ugly old white woman come in this evening. Crying for good old Nigger Sim." Herman drew a breath. "I knows just how that Strangler guy feel."

He saw how Maybelle's body had got stiller on the bed— except her underlip, poked out a little. He said, "I reckon she be at the funer'l. With some more tears in her eyes . . . I ain't going to no funer'l." Herman's hand had tightened on the bedframe.

"She ain't hurting nothing." Maybelle's voice was so low he could barely hear it. "Her old man, he dead too."

"*Mister* Will," Herman said in a voice much louder than hers. The knuckles of his hand were almost white. "You think you going get me at that funer'l? I might do like that Strangler, I might wring that old white woman's neck."

"Hush up, Herman, they hear you in there." Maybelle's eyes were open, her head lifted.

"Like a chicken," Herman said louder than ever. "I hope he do it to her. I be glad if he do."

"Hush up, Herman."

"Yeah," he said, very loud. "I might just do it for him." He suddenly gave the frame a yank that pulled the bed out from the wall. Then he found that he had to hold on with both hands, because now the walls were slowly wheeling around him. Maybelle's face was in it, with eyes showing white, passing and not passing across the track of his vision. The walls were spinning, getting closer. He opened his mouth but nothing came out. He handed himself along the bedframe and plunged face-down into the mattress, feeling the walls come down dark upon him.

Herman waked up almost blind, with something like a wedge embedded in the middle of his brain. Once he could remember things, the pain made fragments of them. Maybelle was gone, there was stirring in the house. He lifted himself slowly and felt between the flashes inside his skull last night's rage coming back. No need to dress. Walking with caution, balancing his head, he went into the kitchen and, watched by eyes from the living room, out into the backyard. Midmorning sun glazed his vision. After a minute he saw the big black hearse and people dressed like Sunday standing out front. The flicker across his brain was pain and rage at once and, watched by the eyes, he went through the hedge into the yard next door and away down the street.

As late as it was, Herman went to the mill, walking the whole two miles in the sun, with lights that would not stop flashing inside his head. A brief hassle with pop-eyed Pinky Danford in the office and Herman was back among his machines again and it was better. Down the long deserted aisles neon light from the ceiling bulbs fell bland and dreamy clear. An empty spool. He replaced it and farther on replaced another one and turned at the end from this aisle to the next. The hum and click and web after web of yarn running from spool to spool became after a little while like something that went on inside his own skull, crowding thought, purging his mind. At least it was this way for a time, an hour. Then something happened. He did not know what had happened but suddenly he was nervous and his hands, when he changed a spool, trembled a little bit. He could not think of any reason except the white woman who tended the section next to his and whose boiled wary face, frightened of him, had peeped at him through the webs a while ago. No matter. All afternoon he could not shake the nervousness that followed him like a presence from aisle to aisle.

Herman did not go home that evening. He ate a sandwich at a place on Bean Street and sat until nearly eight o'clock. At Hattie's the whiskey burned his throat but it cleared his head. It seemed that his ears never had been sharper or his eyes more able to read the meaning in faces that answered his gaze. All hostile. Even Hattie's when she served him, always in silence, her stove-black face drawn up in wrinkles around her bulb of a nose. Herman was used to this. The new thing, getting slowly worse, was his nervousness. He began to feel trapped in his corner where the counter met the wall and his hand on the glass began to tremble slightly. He was sure that something was about to happen.

It was a while later when it happened. It came in a lull when the jukebox had stopped, when even the voices had seemed to fade and then to hush for a moment. The clap of the screen door was unmistakable. Blurred in the corner of Herman's eye a figure stood hesitating, then moved out of his sight. The jukebox came back, thumping, screaming in the room. When finally Herman turned his head it was only a little, a fractional movement, but it was enough. The man, seated not far away at a table with two other men, was facing Herman and the smallest elevation of his gaze would bring it squarely up to Herman's face.

A whole half hour must have gone by. There had been lulls when Herman could hear the man's voice though he could never hear the words. It was a low voice and once for several minutes running it hovered just at the margin where hearing stopped. Those two heads at the table with it heard, were bent to hear. And that was when, the voice pausing, those two heads turned to look at Herman. He thought they had: his glance came an instant too late to catch the certainty of it. He had caught one certainty, though. *That* man was looking at him, looking straight, from under a knitted bone-ridged brow.

This had been a while ago and now a wild voice out of the jukebox made a featureless babel of voices talking in the room. Herman was waiting for it to stop. Then it did. A glance showed him an empty chair where the man had been sitting. Suddenly Herman was on his feet. Hattie's cry pursued him but it did not make him pause.

The street was empty. At the intersection below Hattie's he looked down each dim street, then turned and hurried back up the block to the intersection there. He was too late, there was nobody. He set out at a venture down Jacob Street, at a walk that kept breaking into a jog, slowing only for a look when other streets crossed Jacob. At last for no good reason he turned onto one of these. Two blocks on and he turned again and did not even know where he was anymore. There was a police car. He saw it under a streetlight prowling toward him and he stopped. There was a tree in the yard beside him. He lunged for it and stood behind the tree trunk while the car went past. He stayed there catching his breath, beginning to think again.

He was outside Hattie's when it closed for the night. He had been waiting where he could see through the door the two men still at the table and when he saw them stand up he took a few steps backward into the dark. He was lucky. They were the last two customers and when they came out, the door shut behind them. Finding Herman in their path they stopped, peering at him in the gloom. He had a speech but it failed him. What came out was, "Who that guy was setting with you all? While ago. Hour ago."

It was wrong. The men just looked at him and finally one of them, the big one, said, "What you want know for?"

Herman's mouth opened and shut and opened again. "Wants to talk to him." It came out too sharp, staccato. "Wants to tell him something."

The men peered at him. "What?" the big one said.

Herman's throat had shut down on him.

"I tell him you looking for him," the big man said. He

meant for Herman to get out of his way but Herman did not move. Instead, in a voice still pitched all wrong, he blurted,

"What he tell you? I seen him telling you something. 'Bout me."

The men just looked at him. He tried to see their faces. "I never meant nothing, telling him that. Just drunk talk, I was drunk. He telling it on me, ain't he?"

"Telling what?" the big man said.

Herman tried to read his face and then the other face beside him. It was too dark. They were waiting. It was a trick.

"Get out the way," the man said, advancing, brushing Herman's shoulder as he passed. The striding figures drew away, receding in the dark, with muttered inaudible words passing between them.

There was no light burning in the house. Tonight Herman was glad for this and even when he entered the deeper dark of the bedroom he did not reach for the light switch. He did not mean, at first, to speak to Maybelle at all and he moved quietly, hoping she was asleep. But her breath that came heavy always when she slept made no sound in the room and this told him she was awake—awake and lying with her eyes open. Unfriendly eyes. He unbuttoned his shirt with nervous fingers and laid it over the shadowy chair. Some words, almost spoken, died on his tongue. Seated on the chair he bent and took off his shoes and afterward stayed that way, bent over, lest even in the dark a glance might show him what her expression was like. It was a long while and the second or third try at it before he said, "It go all right today?" It was just a murmur, so quiet it might have escaped her. He said it again, and he was almost ready to add something else when her silence struck him. His anger flickered palely and went away.

Later, still sitting bent over on the chair, Herman said, "You got to listen to me, Maybelle. They b'lieve any kind of lies on me. They lay it on me if they can. Police will too. You the one got to tell them. It's some man, I don't even know him. I never meant nothing, just talking . . . You listening to me, ain't you, Maybelle?"

There was no reply, nothing.

"Ain't you even going answer me?"

Again no answer and after a moment Herman lifted his head. There was such a stillness where she lay, no breath, not even the faintest stirring, that he stood up and leaned over the bed. Where Maybelle ought to have been there was a wadded garment lying. He switched the light on. He called her name, but not loud. He did not find her in the little back bedroom or anywhere else in the house. Nothing, gone, no message. Where? He looked again for a sign, looked harder. He turned the lights off and stood in the dark with his heart beating.

In the night Herman kept thinking that soon he would leave here and he thought about how he would go and what he would take with him. He did not think about where he would go. On this his mind shut down, too tired, as though whichever direction he looked would show him still another Birmingham. A little rest and then he would leave, and in the dark, stretched out shoes and all on the bed, he kept thinking that each next minute would be the one. A police siren he heard, or thought he heard, kept making him lift his head. He always settled back again, too tired, still waiting for the minute to come.

What Herman was really waiting for came to him late in one of his fits of sleep. Maybelle entered the room. Even in the dark he could see her plainly and see the glad timid grin that pouched her cheeks. Her eyes, as used to be, kept fleeing and coming back to him—the look that once in Birmingham had astonished the evil mood clear out of his heart. He reached out his hands to take her. This ruined everything. First her underlip pouting, swelling, and then unmistakable fear blooming in her face. Her cry was real terror, a bolt of sound that left the room empty in its wake. Herman woke up with his hands extended.

Even just to run away again Maybelle did not come. The dream was what made Herman think she would and kept him suspended there in the house all morning pacing the rooms and thinking of words that never in his life had passed his lips. It was noon when he gave up and went next door. But Lena Brooks said no, she couldn't help him, and so did Mary Gaines across the street. Or wouldn't help him. His last try, at Mildred Echols' front door, was a little different. She didn't know, she told him through the screen she kept latched shut, then added something else. "I wouldn't tell you if I did. She want you to know, *she*'d told you."

It was the same tone, the same face as the others, clamped shut. Herman said, "I ain't never lain a hand on Maybelle."

"Well, now you ain't got no chance to."

At dark he would leave. Back in the house he stuffed some clothes into a laundry bag and money from deep in a dresser drawer into his pocket. His switchblade knife was there. He put that too in his pocket and stood with his hands empty looking around the room. Maybelle's things, everywhere. She would have to come back. Later when he heard a woman's voice from someplace he lifted his head and focused his ears to listen.

They were nervous hours. Voices from the neighborhood sounded much closer than they were, like muffled voices just outside in the yard. There were passing cars that seemed to slow down in front of the house, and once he thought he recognized a car that had passed by two or three times already.

About four o'clock, for a space of fifteen or twenty minutes, a man Herman did not know stood on the other side of the street talking to Leon Echols. Except a snatch now and then he could not even hear their voices and he saw that they kept looking toward the house.

But Herman did not leave that night, or any night, as he had planned. Suddenly, late in the afternoon, he had heard Maybelle's voice. That was what he thought when, thinking it had come from out on the porch, he got up off the bed. There was nobody on the porch, though, or anywhere else in the house or the yard, but these moments nevertheless had made a difference. It was as if something, a passion, had got hold of him. Minutes later in the full light of sunset he went out the door and up the street toward Hattie's.

It was around ten o'clock when Hattie finally telephoned the police. Ordinarily, being afraid of the police herself, she never did this even when things got right up nearly to the cutting stage. She had never had to because, just as was the case tonight, there had always been enough other people around who were willing and able to put a stop to it before the blood got flowing. Tonight she did, though, and did it even before Herman came out with the knife she had already known he would have. She had thought for a week and more that, besides his being just plain a mean nigger, there was something wrong about Herman. In fact she had heard some funny talk about him only this afternoon. And then he had come in, two hours before he usually did, and said some things to her that fitted right into what she had heard.

Herman had not said anything at first, not for most of an hour, but Hattie noticed the difference in him. Before, he had always sat there at the counter very still, just drinking and watching, sneaking long hard looks at first one person and then another. This evening it was Hattie he kept sneaking looks at. But at that early hour there was nobody else in the place and his looks were not what she noticed especially. What she noticed was how nervous he was, with his hands and his mouth and the way his Adam's apple kept jumping. He had Hattie nervous too before he ever even said anything to her. She had her back turned and she kept it that way, only moving her head sometimes so she could watch him out of the corner of her eye.

"They telling lies on me," Herman said.

"Who is?" Hattie mumbled. She was drying glasses. She wished somebody else would come in.

"Ev'ybody, now. It's a man. I just seen him in the dark, and me drunk. He mistook me . . . what I told him." Herman pressed his lips together and then, still watching her, took a drink from his glass. Finally Hattie said,

"What you tell him?"

"It's what he say I told him. I never meant that. He telling it on me . . . All of them is, now. Ain't they?"

Hattie did not like the quiet in the room. "How I know?" she said, carefully wiping the glass in her hand.

"Don't tell me you ain't heard them talking." It was practically a threat.

"I ain't heard nothing," Hattie said quickly. She heard him move and this made her hands stop. When he spoke again his voice was pitched higher, excited, as if it might break into a yell.

"They wants to lay it on me. All them old white women. 'Cause I won't be no nigger uncle like they is. Ask Maybelle, she know it ain't me. She be back, she . . ."

What stopped him there and what stopped Hattie from making the retreat out the back way she had already planned was a man, two men, coming in the door. She thought at first, right after the interruption, that he was about to start up

again, but he did not. He only stared, with eyes that in just
the last minute or two had got almost crimson, at the two
men who came up to the counter and ordered beers. He had
forgot about Hattie. For a long time after that, while the
place filled up with customers, except to order a drink once in
a while he did not speak again.

By nine there was a good crowd for a week night. Hattie,
serving up beers, was too busy now to think much about Herman. Or was except when he signaled for a drink and she saw
again how red those eyes were, as if they had a glaze of blood
across them. In fact she was back in the little pantry reluctantly getting Herman still another drink when she first noticed that something had happened. It was a matter of
sound: not the music but the voices had suddenly gone quiet.

When Hattie got back in there the first thing she noticed
was heads turned and the next thing was Herman seated at a
table with three men. Their faces were anything except
friendly, watching and not watching him, while Herman,
leaning over the table, turned from one face to another with
his red eyes. The jukebox was blaring but Hattie could hear
his voice and sometimes snatches of the words, words she recognized. She heard Maybelle's name. The men kept swapping
glances, while Herman's voice rising broke in a sort of plea
and sank again. One of the men got up and left the table.
This left two: the voice went on. Until, in the quiet when the
jukebox hushed, these men also got up from the table.

This had seemed to be the end of it. After a little while
seated at the table he had emptied, glaring around at faces in
the room, Herman got up and left the cafe. He was gone for
maybe half an hour. Hattie was taking beers out of the cooler
and when she turned around he was standing over a table
where there were four men. Just the look of him, the way his
head jumped and his voice rose and broke in the hush, set off

something like an alarm in Hattie's brain. It was not just that she knew he was dangerous drunk and would have a knife somewhere in reach of his quick hands. It was something worse. She went to the telephone by the pantry and called the police. Even from back there she heard Herman's voice before she put the phone down.

Everybody was standing up and it took Hattie a moment to move where she could get glimpses of Herman backed up there in the corner of the room with his knife out. She could hear him plain enough, though, his voice broken, as if he had something in his throat, crazy. "Yeah, me, lay it on me. Couldn't been no *Tom* nigger . . ." He seemed to swallow something. His red eyes burned and that shining knife blade, held at ready, quivered under the light. "Not none of you . . . white folks' niggers. Yeah, I the one. That's right, that's right. Call the *po*lice . . ."

"You crazy, man," somebody said. "Put that thing down."

But he lifted it higher. A swipe of his hand made the blade flash. "I the one. Choked them. All them wrinkled old white necks. Go 'head. Call the *po*lice."

"Man . . ."

There was the wail of a siren, startling, pitched like a scream that gathered force as it approached the cafe. Then heads that had turned away turned back and saw, just for a second, Herman with his red eyes and knife-hand frozen standing like a man impaled in the corner. Blue light flashed in the room. Herman's eyes moved suddenly, sweeping the rank of bodies in his path. Just to his right there was a half-shut window. He made a leap and then another and took both glass and window frame out with him. He hit the ground on his face but there was not even a pause before he was on his feet running, straight through a hedge, disappearing into the yard next door.

What Hattie told the police right after that was enough to get them heated up and within a few minutes there were three or four cars prowling the area. But if it had been only escape Herman was thinking about, probably he could have got away in those few minutes. At least he could have got out of the neighborhood. Instead, after that initial burst of panic fear that carried him through Hattie's window and the next-door hedge and straight on through many other hedges and yards, he changed his mind. Or, better, his mind changed itself, because he was still not very clear about what he meant to do instead of keep running. He was clear enough to move with caution, though, and nobody saw him again until about half an hour later when he turned up at Mildred Echols' house where he had gone that day at noon. He came to the back door and he had knocked softly at first. The yelling and banging started only when Mildred, from inside the locked door, told him for the third or fourth time that she did not know where Maybelle was. Then he was yelling that May-belle, she knew, and would tell them it wasn't him. Herman tried next to break the door open with his shoulder and Mildred's husband Leon had to stand there holding it while she called the police. Herman was gone when the police got there a couple of minutes later.

They found him at home. The house was all dark but they thought he might possibly be in there and they went in to look. He was in the bedroom standing on the other side of the bed when they switched on the light, and he had his knife out. There was a window he could have gone through, as he had done at Hattie's. He never even glanced at it. He stood there warning them. He had cut white throats before, he said. And then, like an afterthought, he said, "Choked some, too. Ugly old white-woman th'oats." With the blood and gashes all over his face and the wild red eyes and that knife in his hand he looked, the policemen said, like the devil himself.

They brought Herman in alive. After the Earl Banks uproar they were afraid to use their guns and so they went for him, three of them, with billy clubs. It was costly, though. One of the policemen got the knife in him, or rather across the side of his neck, and was taken out of there squirting blood. That was what Herman got sent to prison for, because they finally came to the conclusion that his claim to be the Strangler was probably all lies. For one thing the details he brought in support of his claim were garbled and never were the same the next time he was questioned. He could not identify a single one of the houses where the women had been murdered or cite one piece of solid evidence. These things along with others mounted up. So, after a week, they dropped the charge, even while Herman went on claiming that he was the Strangler. It seemed he really did want what such a conviction would have got for him. As it was, however, he had to settle for five years, and the permanent loss of Maybelle who never came to see him even while he was still in jail in Okaloosa.

CHAPTER NINE

Break

When old Claude Manning got hit by a car that broke his hip he collected enough money so that he could finally quit his job at the shoe store. Once the money was sure almost the first thing he did was write a letter of resignation to his employer, Cecil Peck. It was much more than a letter of resignation, though. Counting the interludes while he raked through his memories, and the time spent choosing his words and getting them spelled right it took Claude a whole day, and the result was a bitter detailed account of all the reasons he had for hating Cecil. He spared nothing: the letter was meant to give as much pain as it could. Claude only wished, when he read the letter over, that he could be there to watch Cecil's face.

He would have been more than satisfied. Most people receiving such a letter would have thrown it away before they got through the first page. Cecil did not. He almost did but something stopped him. With his face burning he read it all the way through. Afterward he did throw it away, in the trash can in the little office at the back of the store, but that was not the end of it. Later, with his hands trembling, he took the letter out and read it again. And after he closed the store at five o'clock he did the same thing still another time. It was as though the letter reflected, clearer with each reading, an image that both appalled and fascinated him.

Cecil left the store by the back way and went down the alley to Cotton Street and walked home. He did not remember that walk. He was surprised to observe his feet on the yellow stones that led, for a dozen steps, up to his own small boxed-in front porch. He forgot to pick up the newspaper lying there and he even forgot, when he entered the house, to go straight back to the kitchen and kiss his wife Edna on the cheek and offer to help with supper. Instead he just sat down in the living room, in the chair where he always sat, and stared into space that customarily at this hour was blocked out by the newspaper in his hands.

Edna found him there and it put her off. For once, though, Cecil barely noticed. It was only at the supper table when Edna's voice got sharp and bit into the silence that she managed to compel Cecil's attention. But even then his account of his day at the store was not satisfactory. "You look like you've been taking dope or something," she said. Her eyes were indignant. It was a spare face but even so the dewlaps had made headway lately—as had the wrinkles like stitches around her mouth, making her lips seem tight and hard at the corners. Not a pleasant face, Cecil thought. The observation surprised, even alarmed him, as if it might have been overheard. And there was laughter, or chuckling. This came across the table from his son Hal, fifteen, who thought that that about his father and dope was the joke of the week. Derisive. So was the gaze from the close-set brown eyes fastened on Cecil—always derisive. A small tide of unaccustomed anger welled up into Cecil's throat and just for a second threatened to spill itself in some answer. Then it was gone, swallowed. It was as if Cecil did not know, not in this house, any words to express so lawless a feeling.

Later he thought of this moment with shame, as if it had been one of the instances cited in that letter. Under his lamp with a book, pretending off and on to read, he watched himself, watching his feeble and timid responses to Edna's growing vexation, watching out of his mind's eye his furtive hands caressing the feet of lady customers at the store. At bedtime sleep was far away. He lay stiffly on top of the covers staring into the dark at the thin figure that was himself, a self with sparse receding hair, with black horn-rim glasses and hands that moved with a nervous quickness as though the things he touched were too hot for his fingers. Only once in a while, and that still indirectly, did he think about his treatment of old Claude Manning. For that was where the real pain lay. The clock chiming eleven was a distraction.

"Cecil, shut the windows now."

He heard her but, as it seemed, only after some time had passed, as if her voice had reached him from down a crooked corridor. She repeated the words, with impatience.

"It's too hot," Cecil said. The thought that this was a reck-

less thing to say came only afterward, like an indifferent strag-
gler, surprising him.

"I'll do it myself."

A sudden shaking of the bed and one of those accustomed
starts of alarm brought him upright and sent him to the window across the room. He shut this one and then the back window.

"The others too." But this was later. Her tone made Cecil
realize that he had been just standing there looking out into
the small sideyard where the wooden chairs and Hal's now-
broken swing appeared in a flash of heat lightning. He turned
and left the room and went about the house closing windows.
At the foot of the stairs, though, he forgot. After a minute he
turned back to the bedroom and already had his hand on the
bedpost when Edna's voice came harshly out of the dark: "I
didn't hear you go up to Hal's room."

"Nobody could get in those windows."

"There's such a thing as ladders."

He went. But after all he did not shut the windows. Half-
way across the room, in the sound of Hal's breath fluttering
out of the dark, Cecil stopped. It was the pain again, almost
like a seizure, like some of those moments this afternoon while
he read and reread that letter. The truth, wasn't it?—his own
true image on those ink-scrawled pages. A mind after all in
Claude's submissive head, and a secret rage lying in wait this
whole eight years for its chance. Cecil drew a breath, sucking
air from the airless room. Those open windows. He looked at
them. Suddenly in place of the pain, like an answer to those
windows, a rage of his own came on him. He turned and went
downstairs.

It was not rage enough to make him tell Edna the truth:
he said he had shut the windows. Such as it was, though, it

persisted, and on into the night he lay there thinking, thinking, on top of the covers because of the heat. Sometimes his
rage would fasten his thoughts on Edna and in and out
among these thoughts he would listen to her sleep, to her
catches of breath and the snufflings as though she was clearing
her throat for an order. Something blunt, irresistible, a voice
that brooked no trifling. Except (the shame made Cecil writhe
in the dark) that was his own voice too, his store voice, the
one in which he ordered old Claude around and abused him
in front of the women customers. Shriller, though, not so sure
—more like a feist dog's voice. "Not *those* shoes, Claude.
Don't you know pumps from sandals? After all these years?
Please hurry, Claude." Shaking his head for the benefit of the
lady. And old Claude, his head down, in a hasty shuffle back
to the shelves again . . . Feist voice, bullyboy, playing with ladies' feet.

That, on until nearly dawn, was how the night went for
Cecil. The hour's sleep he finally got did not help much and
at the breakfast table in the white spotless kitchen he kept forgetting to eat. "There's *something* the matter with you,"
Edna said. "What is it?" Sleep had deepened the wrinkles,
made her mouth still harder at the corners. An accidental
curl, escaped in the night, dangled in a sort of stiff and mocking coquetry over her forehead. An ugly word that Cecil
pushed back in his mind still threatened to speak itself. Hal
said, "Dope. Dope's the matter," and the wide smile split his
face in two.

"Nothing's the matter," Cecil said. "I just didn't sleep very
well."

Edna's eyes did not relent. "It's probably your blood. You
need to take something." This seemed to satisfy her and she
raised the cup of unsweetened tea to her lips.

Cecil thought about it being his blood, not having enough

red or white corpuscles. He thought of his strong father who, when Cecil was twelve, had died of a stroke while trying to pull a drowning man out of flooded Okaloosa Creek. His mother, a timid woman, was the one who had given Cecil his blood, and there was not anything he could take for it. Dope, he thought; but this was a laughing matter. Rage, he thought, if it could be taken in capsules in daily doses, that was said to change the chemistry of blood. He thought of himself striking the table with his fist and his voice in a roar, transformed from a feist dog's voice. And Edna's face with the mouth open, hanging loose, for once. Except that her face was looking at him now and the mouth was not open. "You're going to be late," she said. "Stop mooning and eat your breakfast." He watched the fork in his hand spill the thickened yolk from the egg on his plate.

Cecil waited on two women that morning. One of them, Mrs. Myra Nettles, was an old customer with familiar feet. Kneeling before her with the shoes, his head bowed, he tried not to touch, not even to let a finger graze the stockinged foot she extended, half-listening while she talked with one breath about the fit or the style of the shoes and with the next one about the fright she had suffered, because she thought that somebody had tried her window last night. That horrible Strangler. Why couldn't they catch him? Cecil shook his head and trying not to touch forced the too-narrow shoe onto her foot. He did not know the second woman.

The woman did not buy any of the shoes she tried on or even let Cecil know what her name was. As she left the store his eyes followed her as they might have followed an apparition. When she was out of sight he took off his glasses and stood squinting out through the plate glass window beyond which she had vanished. No matter that, if, the young clerk Joe Robbins was looking at him: it was as though this nameless woman had bestowed on Cecil a radiant new vision. And it was a sort of vision, starting with her foot. The foot was bare when she extended it but this was only the first thing. It was also sleek and small, with skin like a flower petal and with tiny oblong polished nails. Then he noticed, could not help noticing, how it seemed to join without any joint an ankle that rose as fine as a stalk to where the gently swelling calf began. And then the white knee hooded in shadow under the hem of her dress. It was not a decision, he simply lifted his head and found her looking straight into his eyes. The moment was a terrible one. It was like the aftermath of a seismic shock in which for sheer desperate need he could not draw his eyes away from hers. It was she who looked aside and also she who disengaged her foot from his hands. For he had been holding it! And would hold it again, as it seemed to him, unless that foot was removed beyond his reach. Some words she said gave point to Cecil's confusion and springing to his feet he headed for the shelves of women's shoes. When he turned back she was already leaving.

That confusion followed Cecil all day and into another though differently sleepless night. He thought and thought about the woman, wondering who and where she was. That little foot, that ankle, that white knee hooded in shadow. And himself. Or was that him, in those moments, holding her naked foot, looking straight up into her eyes without thought of himself or thought of anything? Not Cecil. He might, if she had not spoken he *would,* have seized that foot again—and seized it with a mindless violence impossible for him. And then what? For seconds at a time, for a whole minute now and then, the blood pumping from his heart seemed thrust along in gouts too big for his arteries. It was pain, and once he had to get out of bed and stand breathing, burning in the dark. Edna was lying there. Her shape was a shadow and on his knees on the bed Cecil reached and put a hand on her hip. He heard the catch of breath in her throat and then her brusque half whisper, "What's the matter?"

Cecil had no answer.

"Did you hear something?"

Cecil took his hand away. "No," he said.

"Are you sick?"

"No."

Edna stirred and turned over. After a moment she said, "Did you lock all the windows? You didn't last night, in Hal's room. You'd better go check."

Even in the dark he could see the thickness of her bare legs on top of the cover and it might have been this that started his rage. Holding it behind his teeth he got up from the bed in silence.

With that rage in his throat Cecil passed through the hall, switching on the light, and into the living room. Her will driving him, always hers. He would not check the windows, that much he would not do. For show he made a little stop in the living room and without even a glance at the windows went on into the dining room. Another little stop and then he was in the sun parlor at the far side of the house with windows all around. A longer stop was needed here. But as he stood glaring blindly out into the dark yard there came a flash of heat lightning and in that shuddering moment of illumination something struck his eye. It was a figure among the shrubs out there. He jumped, hit something and an object fell clattering to the floor. Then silence. Lightning again and he could not see the figure now. He heard his name called, Edna calling him. There was no figure, nobody among the shrubs: it never had been more than the shape of his own fear. Always his fear. Feist voice, bullyboy, playing with ladies' feet. Shame assailed him, turning back to rage. Then Edna's voice once more, with a note of alarm that by and by registered on Cecil. He just stood there.

It must have been two or three minutes before Edna called to him again. Her voice was not so loud this time, he could barely hear it. But he heard plainly enough that quavering note and he did not move. He could feel the silence swelling, himself the core of it, as if his heartbeats fed it stroke by stroke. He did not need eyes to see her there in the bed sitting stiffly upright, holding the covers to her breast. Reflected light from the hall made her face look stark in the room, and her mouth was hanging loose. For a moment he almost laughed. But even this was not enough, not yet.

Finally he moved, passing slowly into the dining room toward the light from the hallway door beyond. He would tell her . . . The floor creaked under his foot and he stopped. There was silence. Then Edna's voice again. "Cecil?" It was low, with a plaintive fluttering in it that was terror. Terror in her face too, if he could see it. He thought of answering and did not answer, not yet. He let it grow, feeling the resonance of his heart and the thrust of blood through all his body. Like a different body. Powerful.

Maybe a minute but maybe a much longer time passed before he thought to end it. Two steps brought him into the light and another into the hall, strong purposeful steps that carried his weightless body. He knew what to tell her. He said it as he entered the bedroom and saw her in the light from the hall sitting exactly as he had imagined, with her mouth hanging loose and her face as white as the sheet she hugged to her breast. "There was somebody out there."

No answer came. He looked at her without any pity and sat down on the bed. There was still that strong and pleasant surging of his blood.

"The police," she whispered. "Call the police."

"No use now, he's gone. Whoever it was." Then, on inspiration, "I went outside to look."

"Call them anyway."

"The police get a hundred calls like that. They'd think I was just imagining. Anyway whoever it was is gone."

There was a silence, with her eyes fastened on him. He straightened his pillow, prepared to lie down. Suddenly, in all but the old commanding voice, she said, "I want you to call them."

It seemed to be the stroking of Cecil's heart that held him rigid, withstanding the moment, gazing not quite at her in the half light. She had dropped the bedsheet, exposing the bare flesh and throat above her gown. This was where his attention fixed itself. Then Edna moved, brusque movements that carried her past him to the bedside and up and into the hall. He heard her dial the telephone and her voice loud, raised in command, abruptly stopped two times by silences. Her voice, then stillness, as if hands had shut on her throat.

That was what Cecil dreamed about that night, after the police came and walked around in the yard with lights and reassured Edna and left. Only once, to tell him in a vindictive voice that he had imagined it all, did she speak to Cecil again and she went to sleep with a hostile back turned on him. It was much later when Cecil slept, though the sleep was half like a torpid reverie. He was conscious of Edna's snufflings and of the silences, sometimes long ones, that fell between them. He dreamed of that dark powerful figure in the room, near the bed, just waiting. He finally dreamed that the figure moved to the other side of the bed and with extended hands, in a shuddering light, took Edna by the throat. The snufflings stopped, everything stopped, even the beating of Cecil's heart. He never moved or tried to move. He only lay there marveling at the power in those hands.

That was a strange night for Cecil. He waked up next morning thinking of it half in alarm, recollecting all this as if it might in fact have happened. And there, right off, to affirm it all, was Edna's manner toward him. No call to the breakfast table, not even a nod when he appeared. He tried humility, sitting at the table like a man not fully licensed to be there, a humble guest. A cold hasty hand set his eggs in front of him and not a word was said directly to him. "They didn't find one sign of *any*body," Edna said, speaking to Hal. "There never was anybody, it was just *his* imagination. Just dreaming." But Cecil, eating his eggs, suddenly was not so sure of this.

That grin, ear to ear, was on Hal's face again. "Dope," he said, "Daddy's on dope," and went on grinning. Cecil, eating his eggs, was not so sure any longer. There was something different.

He noticed the difference all day. It was as if he knew something important that, when he tried to put his hands on it, eluded him every time. It was vaguely like a presence behind him: he would feel it and turn around, only to find it gone. The feeling, though, like company, stayed on with him hour after hour and not only stayed but became finally, despite its teasingness, welcome. It supported him. It overheard with approval when he gave a subdued order to young Joe Robbins and seemed to be the reason that his hands when he fitted a shoe on a lady's foot were firmer than they used to be. He found that he could look up almost without blinking into a woman's eyes and could speak with a sureness he had not felt before.

Cecil had thought that it would be gone by the time he got home that evening. He was wrong. It was there between his wife and him like a sort of transparent curtain that in some curious way filtered the voice and the image he received. It was the same Edna, face and voice, nothing obscured: so what was the difference? A sense of remoteness, he decided, as if this one day at the store had somehow lasted not for mere hours but for weeks or months. He watched her obliquely and listened, submissive, when she spoke. Seated in his chair under the lamp he felt like a man imitating himself and efforts he made to shut out of his mind unseemly or brutal thoughts were not real efforts. Ugly. That was the word that stuck in his mind whenever his eyes happened upon her face. The mouth, the chin, the neck that had begun to wither. Her voice. It was the voice of a crow . . . or a hawker of fish. "Stop reading," she said from her place beyond the lamp, from over the needlework in her hands. "You need to go to bed and get some sleep. Or something." A glance at her mouth was all he allowed himself.

Cecil kept thinking that it would go away. But it was with him when he waked up the next morning and all that day and right on into his sleep that night. A whole week made no difference. At home and at the store he went through all his usual paces, fitting the shoes, shutting the windows at night, keeping his head down—like an actor who has his part too well to forget a single gesture. Even so, there were moments: Edna's eyes were too sharp. But there was not anything she could get her teeth into and she had to settle for a mood of almost constant vexation. Almost, because a couple of times there had been small interruptions. These had been as uneasy, as uncertain for Cecil as for her. They had been moments when, caught with his gaze on her, he saw what looked like second sight darkening her eyes.

Nobody else could have noticed any change in Cecil, though. Old Claude Manning, if he had been still working at the store, would have noticed, and maybe a lady customer who came there often enough. Neither one of them could have noticed any difference in him at home. Unless they could have observed one trivial new habit. When Cecil got up to shut the windows at eleven o'clock he had invariably started with the windows in the living room and proceeded to the dining room and the sun parlor and then to the other rooms. Now he had changed this order. He came last to the sun parlor and when he had shut and locked the windows there he always stood for a while looking out into the yard. He was convinced now that he had in fact seen a figure among the shrubs and he kept thinking that he would see it again. There were moments when he was sure it was out there, among those same shrubs, crouched down. A chill would start in his spine and run like a cold tide up into the scalp at the back of his head. He would imagine the figure rising up, full height now above the shrubs, the black torso just visible against the blackness of the hedge. Then Cecil would turn and hurry, because he hated her voice calling him, back to bed.

This was what happened every night. There was a difference, though, night by night, that nobody could have observed. It was a difference of intensity, of Cecil's gathering expectation every time he stood there. Then one night, in a certainty that the figure would appear, he felt himself shivering as he never had done before. It was like an attack, the violence of a fever seizing him, and for a moment or some interval of time his mind went perfectly blank. That was when Edna called, called twice, called still another time. He seemed to hear her finally from out of that void in his head.

Then there was light, a blinding stroke of it in his eyes, and next he saw Edna as if she had been a hateful specter taking shape in the glare. Her voice came at him, something harsh and accusatory that twisted her lips. ". . . to frighten me." Cecil understood this much. He did not know whether it was

this that plucked some nerve in his chest and made him lunge
and reach out for her.

It was her neck he was after. For a few seconds, while
Edna's astonishment was still so great that she could not lift
even an arm in her defense, he did have hold of her neck—
with both hands and with all the strength of that rage that
had clutched his heart. Of the details he remembered afterward this was the one most vivid to him—this and the way it
made him feel to see her mouth gaped open without sound.
Except for her strength he did not think that he would ever
have let go. And the proof was that when they fell to the floor
and he was there on top of her—between her big naked legs,
actually—he had been trying for that same grip again.

So it was only Hal who had saved her life. Wasn't it?
Cecil's own amazement, coming within seconds after Hal had
pulled him off her struggling body, out of the confusion of
her screams and of objects falling around them, was another
witness. For that, his real intention, was what amazed him so.
Looking down at Edna on the floor holding her throat and
sobbing and not even thinking to cover her big white thighs,
he was for just a moment all but persuaded that it was the
Strangler who had attacked her. Not Cecil. He almost said it
out loud. It was Hal who spoke. Crouched at Edna's side and
looking up at his father as if he did not recognize him, he
moved his mouth and faintly said, "You gone crazy . . . ?"

Crazy, he was crazy. This thought, planted so suddenly in
Cecil's mind, had seemed at the time to explain everything.
Mad, a lunatic . . . and dangerous. There on the floor, with
Hal crouching beside her and also sobbing, was proof of it.
He took a step backward and then another. Dangerous. There
was need to remove himself, he thought, and bumping first
against the dining room table he turned and went into the liv-
ing room and down the lighted hall toward the back door.

Clothes, he would need clothes. He snatched them from his room and out in the backyard behind the garage dressed himself.

Three hours later, after walking all this time, Cecil checked in at the Cotton Street Hotel. He was not crazy, he was sure of this by now. Nor, he was nearly sure, was there anybody pursuing him. What he felt as he entered his hotel room, almost everything he felt, was that first amazement over again. Not Cecil. He shook his head but nothing changed. The room itself as he looked around him, with its faded curtains and chandeliers and ghosts of whores and seedy drummers, ministered to this feeling of amazement. Presently he took off his clothes and having no pajamas stood there naked in the middle of the floor. With the lights still burning he lay down on the sagging bed, and stared. At the foot of the bed the bureau glass reflected his naked image. It was Cecil's body, and thin and white. And yet it was dangerous.

Cecil did not go home the next day or any other day. He did everything through a lawyer, refusing even to talk to his wife, who tried two or three times to call him. He did not so much as send home for his clothes. Instead he bought new clothes, of a kind with a sort of subdued flashiness about them that made him look a little seedy, or maybe sinister, as if he might have had underworld connections. They were certainly not the right kind of clothes for the proprietor of a quality shoe store and no doubt they were a part of the reason that his business declined. But also there were the complaints some women made about his freshness, that he seemed to be making awkward passes at them when he tried on their shoes.

The decline of Cecil's business did not affect his new ways, though. The sight of him walking around town late at night, in those clothes, got to be a common one, and so did his presence at all the honky-tonks and dance halls in and around town. Most of the time he would sit at a bar or a table in silence drinking beer. But now and then he would make a sally. He would make, rather awkwardly and crudely, a try for a girl or else he would initiate a conversation with some lone drinker close by. These conversations usually led nowhere, because he did not have anything to talk about except one subject. The subject was the Strangler. Cecil had a lot to say about this, and people reported that he never failed at some point in the conversation to hint, with his head lowered and his gaze deep in his beer glass, that he had more than just a notion who the Strangler was.

CHAPTER TEN

Self-portrait

Okaloosa was never notable for its hospitality to the arts, but the town always had a few people who at least called themselves artists. In fact they were nearly all just dabblers, eccentrics, or ladies who in the old style did such as china painting. There had been one honorable exception, a gifted young painter named Crayton who moved on years ago to greener pastures. And there was the much less honorable exception of Joel Trotwood who, during the summer of the Strangler, moved on to a different kind of green pastures. It was right to

call Joel serious about his art, though in his case the word art
needed a good deal of qualification.

The Trotwoods were an old family and Clinton, Joel's father, was third in a line of Trotwoods who had been circuit
judges in the district. He died when Joel was only twelve, in
an auto crash with a Negro boy, but he left his wife Elaine in
comfortable circumstances, with plenty to educate two sons
through college and generally to keep up the family name.
Among the things he left was his old house on Grove Street
near the Calvary Presbyterian Church. It was a one-story
house and not large and sat even then on a lot greatly re-
duced from the original acreage. Still it remained, with its
shade trees and sheltering shrubbery and wide white-
columned porch in the classic style, the nicest home on that
residential street. That was where the boys grew up and
where, later, in the attic under the dormer window, Joel had
his studio.

Joel's yen to be a painter did not come from his father and
certainly not from his mother. If it had any family origin at
all it must have come from his father's sister, his Aunt Lett, a
withdrawn delicate maiden lady who was an indefatigable
painter of china. As a child Joel spent a lot of time at her
house watching her paint, watching the hand that trembled
slightly, that had to be held steady by the other hand on her
wrist, draw the tiny brush through intricate patterns over the
surface of a plate or a teacup. She liked to have him come
and watch and she always had some cookies baked for him.
Joel went half in secret, though, because his mother, who
thought Aunt Lett vain and foolish, unserious, did not ap-
prove. After Judge Trotwood's death, she put a practical stop
to the visits. His mother wanted to raise *two* judges.

From the looks of her first son, Clinton, Jr., six years older
than Joel, she might have raised one judge anyway. But

World War Two was on and young Clinton died in it, her second great blow in two years. There was Joel left, a Joel also shaken. His mother turned her energies on him.

Not that Joel seemed at this time an unlikely prospect for the bench. He had shed his babyhood quite cleanly and he had a solemn look in his eyes. His performance at school, if not quite up to that of Clinton, Jr., was good, as was his general conduct. He had friends of the better sort, perfectly normal boys, and though he was a little small he was wiry and played at sports. His mother saw nothing then to disapprove of, no signs of an artist. And she was gratified by his attentiveness to her. It was not just a matter of small attentions, acts and gestures that were a help and a comfort. It was more that he listened to her, really listened. Then she was reminded of his father, the responsible look in the brown deep eyes, the way a troubled light would come when she expressed complaints or indignation. And starting in those years after the war, when the town began to go the way of all modern flesh, such expressions were more and more on her tongue. Half the time now when Joel looked at her, listening, that troubled light was visible in his eyes.

Joel's interest in painting started when he was away at the University. He had gone there to study law but he decided pretty early that law was not for him. Without telling his mother he changed his major to art. His mother was a watchful woman and as soon as she caught on, which wasn't very long, she put a stop to that. So what Joel did, finally, was flunk out of the University.

That was only the first of many things he flunked out of. He went to Atlanta for a few months and flunked out there and came home again. In the course of the next few years he flunked out of the Cannon Insurance Company and Farnsworth Chevrolet and his own real estate agency. Then there was the furniture business, the grocery business and so on, a considerable list, with each new venture seeming shorter-lived than the one before. He even flunked out of his one engagement to be married. Finally there was not anything, no longer even a pretense of a job. Unless his painting could be called a job. Of course he had been at that all along, in his hot attic under the dormer window, at least from the time when he had worked for Cannon Insurance and had come in every morning with paint on his hands. In the end he simply pronounced himself a painter and let it go at that. Even his mother, in despair, had to accept it at last.

She did not accept it with grace. It was not only that Joel had betrayed her dream of another judge in the family—and betrayed it finally in never taking a wife. There was also the cliché, the comic side of it all. She knew that people made jokes about him, about the ne'er-do-well dreaming over his "art" in his mama's attic. She even knew the nickname they called him by: Raphael. The very thought made her bitter and made the muscles show along her jaw and the small jawbone tighten like a horseshoe. She was not a large woman but she had authority and an eye cold enough to freeze the loosest mouth. She got into the habit of freezing mouths. Often, just back from an outing where she had indulged her habit, she would turn that cold eye on Joel. There was nothing for him then but to escape as best he could, into the backyard or the street or up into his attic.

Probably what made life tolerable in that house through all those years was the fact that Joel, even after he became a painter only, was never much in evidence. Most of nearly every day he spent in the attic and not long after supper at night he either retired to his room or else went out for one of his "walks." As a regular thing he was with his mother only at suppertime. Seated at opposite ends of the big mahogany

table, under the cut-glass chandelier with three of the five
bulbs gone, they talked in sallies and afterward fell silent over
their food. There was less talk than silence but now and then,
above the clicking of china and silverware, one voice or the
other would launch a reflection or a topic of the day. More
often it was his mother's voice, louder than Joel's, from a
mouth that until she spoke looked as if it had been bound
shut by an invisible stitch at the corners. What she said was
likely to be something that Joel would answer only with nods
or grunts or else with a topic of his own intended to counter
hers. "They will take over this town," she said, meaning the
Negroes. "Once they start pushing they never stop. I saw it
coming years ago."

Joel grunted, bending to receive the stick of cornbread his
hand lifted to his mouth. Hunched over the massive table he
looked no bigger than the woman stiffly seated at the other
end. Her lips came unstitched at the corners again. "It's just
another part of this whole thing, this whole decline. And
nobody left who can, or *will*, do anything about it. Please sit
up straight."

Joel sat up: It was raining. Big drops blown against the
window coursed in faintly silver patterns down the clear glass
pane. Hard to catch in paint.

"I told you, I told them all . . . years ago," his mother
said. "Even before they started inviting these 'factories' in
here. It's a moral breakdown."

"I'll bet you didn't shut your car windows, Mama."

She looked at him icily. "I *did* shut them." Brusquely she
took the clay pot beside her hand and poured tea in her cup.
Joel's gaze went back to the windowpane. A tint of blue in
the silver would be needed.

His painting was a thing that Joel never mentioned in his
mother's presence. At first he had, long ago, and sometimes,

on fire with pride, he had come down from the attic bringing a picture just now completed, a landscape usually. A moment's attention, a toss of her head. "Very nice," she might say as her gaze moved on. The paintings might have been crude toys a child had knocked together. There was a last time, a time Joel remembered clearly. The landscape was a deep vista with a hill and a winding column of trees that mounted up to a sky streaked with rose and violet. His mother had looked at it with more attention than she was accustomed to do. What she said was, "Aunt Lett would probably like that."

Despite the sting in his mother's words they had given Joel an idea. For a while after that, the only such interlude in his life, he had an audience. In secret, two or three at a time, he would take his canvases to Aunt Lett's house and bask in the praise she never failed to give. It was more than praise out of Aunt Lett's mouth. She, with Joel beside her, would sit for many minutes at a stretch gazing and wordless in front of a picture, as though her eye had lost itself in the depths his brush had rendered. He would watch her face, remote and delicate. Blushing with pride he would turn back to his picture, living it again, wandering in its distances. But Aunt Lett went away. She went to live with an ailing cousin far off in Mississippi.

There was a period when Joel tried sending his pictures away to exhibits. They were never accepted and he soon gave that up. Once he put on an exhibit of his own, at the town library, but almost nobody came and nobody bought a picture. That was his last attempt at a public. Someday, he told himself, somewhere in the future this would come of itself, and he went on painting. Already the attic was crowded with his old paintings and the day came when something had to be done. Weeding among them he took almost half and in the alley

behind the house burned them one night, watching the blue
and yellow flames, watching the plume of tinted smoke drift
away in the dark. He painted that picture from memory,
painted it several times and called each version "Youth."

Joel was thirty-one then and not quite yet a full-time
painter. Within a year, though, he lost the job that was to be
his last. He never tried for another. Painting was his job, these
landscapes and still lifes done in oils. The still lifes were
mostly recent work, scrupulous studies of flowers in a vase or
leaves of the cottonwood tree by the dormer window or the
birdbath under the tree. But the landscapes, in pastels or water-
colors, remained his specialty. He did them all from imagination and a person familiar with three or four of his landscapes
would be likely to recognize his hand in practically any one he
had ever painted. There were always the soft lines and colors
approaching the exotic and always a perspective that drew
the eye into deep distance. He would, if need be, spend days
getting this effect, painting over, starting again, stopping to
shut his eyes until the vision had set itself against the dark of
his lids. There were nights when he could not sleep for thinking about an effect, trying to see it right. Sometimes, as
stealthy as a thief in the night, he would get up from his bed.
He would make his way back through the kitchen to the stairs
and, mounting into the attic, work, until dawn at the window
behind him changed the light on his picture.

This was Joel's life, it seemed, established and final by the
time he was thirty-two. In fact it was only most of his life.
There was a small part that he kept hidden, especially from
his mother, with all the discretion of a master spy. Those
night walks were his occasions. He had known since his teenage years where whores could be found and at some point
along in his twenties he began to use them. He kept it at a
minimum and chose his women with care, older ones if he

could find them. And since most of his walks were innocent and took him only to innocent places, nobody seemed to notice anything. At least his mother, the important one, did not. Even on the occasions when he came in with that sensation of filth all over his body and found her still awake, still up, her manner never hinted at suspicion. Or so he would realize later, in his bed. Because there were times when, meeting her this way, he was sure that the whole ugly story was spelled out in his face.

As for the rest of Joel's life, at least to all appearances there was nothing to hide. His days were the same, his hours in the attic and the times of his going up and coming down. Eyes at the dormer window would have seen him, draped in a too-large paint-smeared workman's shirt, brush in hand, before his easel painting or through long intervals without movement staring at his work. Of course he would sit down sometimes, on a stool or the end of the bench where his paints were laid out, but his look of entrancement was not broken. Through half an hour, maybe longer, he would just sit there holding his brush, looking no different than he looked when his eyes were fast on a painting. Except once in a while. This was something an observer would have noticed and wondered about, seeing him suddenly come alert, tighten his posture, glance toward the bolted attic door. Yet the only sound would be that of his mother's footsteps in the kitchen below. There was always an interval, a matter of minutes, before his look of entrancement would come back, erasing completely his troubled expression. Eventually, though, as his life approached the crisis that was preparing for him, such interruptions began to be serious matters. At last instead of minutes it was likely to be whole hours before he could recover his serenity.

When the first of the stranglings happened, in early May of that spring, Joel was nearing forty. By the time there was such a perfection in the routine of his days, so much like clockwork, that, left to itself, his mind would have done little more than record the event. Except for his mother the event might even have passed him by entirely, because he rarely looked at a newspaper or talked much to people. But there was his mother. There had not ever been a time when Joel could make complete silence of her indignant voice in his ears or screen from his consciousness the hardest of those looks she sent him down the supper table. In this instance, though, his strategies counted for nothing at all. His mother had known the victim, and all she expressed of horror and outrage was, it seemed, directed at Joel's head.

"Rosa Callahan. She was not much older than me, you know." His mother paused, her mouth stitched tight at the corners again. Sitting erect, so that she seemed the taller of the two, she looked at him over the teacup suspended and forgotten in her hand. Or glared at him: that was how it appeared. "In her own home. Assaulted . . . You see what kind of monsters they're raising up. Where is it all going to stop?" It seemed, when she set the teacup down, that she was waiting fiercely for Joel to answer. But she said, "Aren't they even going to defend us? It could just as well have been me, you know."

Joel opened his mouth. He said, "You don't live in a house by yourself like she did." Instantly he was sorry he had said this.

"You would be up in the attic. Painting. Or out on a walk."

Joel shook his head. Waiting for more, bearing her eyes, it was all he could think to do.

That was how it went for a week and more. From her massive high-back chair by the front window, in her own pool of lamplight, she would straighten herself and looking directly at him over the newspaper in her hands say, "Not a clue, nothing at all. He's walking around like anybody else." In answer Joel might say, "They'll catch him, Mama, don't worry." Or else, finally, pinned down by her gaze, "Mama . . ." he would begin and not remember what he had started to say. There was no escape for him—as if even his thoughts that used to fly away so quickly up those attic stairs were trapped here in the room with her.

"You see what they've made of this town . . . this whole country," she said, holding him to it, making him look. Until she grew tired and released him.

That week was ruined. The same picture sat there unfinished on Joel's easel, impossible to finish. There was a setting sun in the picture and however many times he altered or erased and painted that sun again it always emerged like an eye looking back at him. He tried removing it from the picture. This was wrong. There over the landscape were the slanted lights and the pools of shadow and not any sun to cast them. A strange picture. He paced about the attic. He reviewed old pictures or stood with his eyes shut trying to call his vision back. Or he listened. He found he was listening much of the time for the sound of his mother's footsteps in the house. There was one time when he thought he heard her approach the attic stairs and pause at the bottom. Would she put a foot on the steps? When he heard her again she was somewhere else but the blood in his neck went on pounding.

It was temporary, or seemed to be. In another week, when his mother's intensity_had faded, Joel was almost himself again, painting again, finished with that picture now. *Almost* himself, because the interval had left a recurrent dream that kept troubling him some. It was a vague dream in which whatever happened happened behind a sort of curtain, waking him in the night. It was a small distress, though. In a few weeks it was gone. But then it was June and June was the month when two of the stranglings occurred.

Then indeed there was no escape for Joel. No matter his efforts, the paint from his brush lay flat and dead on the canvas. Now the attic echoed with footsteps from the house below and his bolted door, it seemed to him, would not have withstood a determined push of her hand. Even his walks were ruined. The innocent ones, that had been most of his walks, that had led him in the pleasant anonymity of night here and there through the half-lit streets of town, were charged now with an anxiety whose cause evaded him. It was fear all right but not of any man. It was as if the quiet in these nighttime streets, the stillness of the houses, was all somehow unreal, a concealment or a preface maybe to a gathering though undefined disaster. He had given up the whores. The last of those furtive and guilty walks that took him to a house behind a cafe at the foot of the Smiths Road bridge ended one hot June night in the littered yard by the door. He had reached out for the doorknob. Imagined or not, what stopped him was an odor. It was the smell of her body, he thought, a reeking musk enough to stifle breath inside that room. His arm sank down to his side and he went away.

Such walks as Joel still took at night got fewer. Part of the reason was his mother. "Why do you have to go out? I'm here in the house alone, you know." And usually he would go to his attic instead. But the day came, after that second murder in June, when he had to do even this over her protests. As likely as not, if he went to the attic anyway, she would come after a while to the foot of the stairs and call to him. Once she climbed the stairs and knocked at his door and kept knocking, while Joel stood there with the brush in his rigid hand, feeling the hot blood pound in his neck. She liked best to have him in the parlor with her, in clear sight where, knitting under her lamp, she could speak to him when she chose and unburden herself. He would try not to listen, knowing it all by heart, answering by rote and nods of his head. "I know, Mama." Nodding. Her eyes observed him from out of her pool of light.

There was a night of rain. It ticked at the windowpanes and whispered in the shrubbery outside. "It doesn't have to be a Negro, like they say," his mother said. "It could be anybody, nowadays. Anybody."

Joel was thinking of the picture on his easel. No life. Dead. Ruin, it seemed, was waiting for him.

"It could be somebody on this very street, that we see every day. Walking around like everybody else. It's that kind of a world."

Walking in the night, Joel thought. What face? Rain whispered in the camellias outside the window. Hidden among the camellias, looking in at her, the strong hands tense and the blood racing. He killed old women. Her knitting needles ticked in the room. Her mouth, compressed like a seam too tightly drawn, would open wide in her agony. Joel said out loud, "He's crazy, though."

"It needn't show," she said. "I've read about it, what doctors say. He may seem just a little peculiar. Withdrawn. In other ways like anybody else. Nobody could guess."

Her needles ticked. Joel had been looking directly at her and still was when she suddenly lifted her face. It was an odd moment. It was as if the thought he saw pass like a wing across her eyes had come that instant to light in his own mind. For her it was gone, she was at her knitting again. For Joel it was a thing settled and already growing inside his head.

The thought was still there, still bigger when Joel went to his room a little later. Lying stretched out in the dark, in the whispering of rain, he could not sleep. Back in his mind her needles ticked. At last he got up and stealthily, in the dark, dressed himself again and made his way to the attic. For a long time he sat on the bench under the bright bulb, just sitting, gazing into nowhere. Finally he stood up and removed that dead picture from the easel. Working quietly he put another canvas on. He got his oils out, arranged them on the bench and, brush in hand, stood before his easel. He dipped his brush and made a stroke. A little while and he made another stroke, and later on another. He had made the outline of a human head. This was as far as he got: he was gazing into nowhere again. Soon he turned from the easel and carefully cleaned his brush and put it back in its box. Switching off the bulb he made his way in silence down the stairs and out the back door of the house. It was only for a walk, but this walk, with all the stops and pauses, lasted until almost day.

Nearly two weeks later, up in July, Joel was summoned to the police station. The police were fairly discreet about it because of his family name and also because they did not really have anything. What they did have were two reports that Joel had been seen, on foot, at hours of the night when nobody went out. More than that, one of the reports placed him in the yard of the house where the Strangler's last victim, Marilyn Barfield, had lived, and died. Acting strange, the report said, and used words like "furtive." Joel already had the reputation of being peculiar, and in those days of pressure the police were not overlooking any kind of a possible lead. So, in spite of their near assurance that they would be questioning a harmless crank, they called him in.

When Joel left there, however, they were not so sure any longer. His explanation for his night walks was simply that he could not sleep and, so, walked until he was tired. He did not remember being in Marilyn Barfield's yard, though it was possible, barely, that he might have paused there a moment in passing by. This statement contradicted the report, which was fairly specific, but probably the police would have been satisfied anyway if it had not been for certain other things. Of course Joel's inability to sleep would have explained his look of haggardness and also the nervous motion of his hands, smeared with paint, that were constantly embracing and kneading each other. They did not think it explained the slow uncertain way he answered, as if he was sorting things in his mind. Except for one moment he kept throughout the interview an air of distance, of forgetfulness even, that was hard to fathom. But there was that moment. One of the two questioners, a detective named Farrell, asked him suddenly what he thought about women, old women. This struck Joel. It stilled his hands, which settled onto his knees, and made him look down at the floor. He said he liked them as well as he did anybody else. His voice, however, as the two policemen thought, was charged with something.

They let Joel go of course, only cautioning him with some sternness not to take late-night walks anymore. They had it in mind already to watch him, and their minds were not changed by his mother's expressions of outrage when, later that day, they called her also to the station. This, the outrage, was to be expected. But it was possible too that they got a glimpse of what this pitch of her indignation was meant to hide—even from herself. It was the thought that had so lightly crossed her mind that night two weeks ago. Here, reflected in sober official eyes, it had a sudden and terrible weight that would not let it pass on out of her head. Now she was even made to recall that this thought had come more than once in recent days.

She had seen Joel's haggardness, watched it grow. She had also observed that now, at least at the dinner table, he ate almost nothing. "You don't look well," she had said at first, like a challenge. "What's the matter with you?"

"Can't sleep," he mumbled, not raising his head.

"Don't mumble." A few days before she had had heavy wire grilles put over the windows and she said, "I don't think we have to worry now, with these grilles in the windows. If that's what's the matter."

Joel did not answer but he lifted his head. He did not look at his mother, he looked past her, at the dining room window. This was something else she had come to notice lately: that as a regular thing he had stopped looking directly at her even when she spoke suddenly to him. It had angered her before. It angered her now. "I think you owe me at least the courtesy of an answer. I don't expect much else from you." When Joel still did not look at her she said, with real ice in her voice, "How could I expect anything?" And then, "I wonder what you *would* do without me to breathe for you." Then Joel looked at her.

It was the first time his mother had seen that look and it stopped her, hard. It was not the last time, either. On each occasion, after the initial jolt, after that brief look had passed and she had got her thoughts adjusted, she ended by reading it as mere insolence and withdrew into icy rage. Not anymore, not after that day and that hour at the police station. Official eyes were watching. Recollections came to her. A little peculiar always, just a little. Withdrawn. And all his walks at night, even those nights when the stranglings had happened. Though of course it could not be true. Of course not!

His mother's manner toward him changed. Her voice, her tone was softened when she spoke to him and it was a rare thing, a moment of lapse, when one of her old barbs was cast his way. At the dinner table and at other times she studied him with secret glances, and she also studied what to say to

him. They were kindly things when she could think of them.
And Joel, up in his attic, never heard her voice calling him
anymore. Several times she even inquired about his paintings,
as though she cared. He never answered, just looked at her
that way.

It was a change nobody could have missed. Out of his haggard face Joel observed this change, watched its progress. It
was like homage, growing with his power. That was how he
felt, seeing his mother's anxiety, seeing that now they had a
spy who watched from across the street at night. And
watched without the breath of a notion how easily he made
fools of them all. From the back door, ever so quietly, passing
like a shadow from bush to bush, laughing shadow laughter at
them. Then it was lawn to lawn under the trees, through
hedgerows and alleyways, ducking once in a while the beam
from a prowl car out in the street. And the people, the houses
asleep. He was like somebody moving through their sleep, a
dream they were having. It would be a recurrent dream, with
his figure coming always nearer, passing always closer to their
windows. Night after night.

In the day, in the attic on the floor, was when Joel did his
sleeping. It was almost never good sleep, the forgetful kind.
Mainly it came in fits, full of dreams that made it more like
his nights abroad than like sleep. In his dreams it was
different, though. Among other things the perspective was
different. Instead of in he was outside the figure of himself,
watching it from a distance a little too great for the fullest
clarity. It was a black and white figure and some of the time
independent of him, vanishing and appearing again from
behind a hedgerow or a tree trunk. Now and then it approached and stopped, just stood there under the dark window of a house that was familiar to him. He waited, his
breath stifled, to see what it would do. One night it climbed

up and vanished into the window. He heard a woman scream. It was Marilyn Barfield's voice. And finally one night, just before Joel waked up, the figure was standing under the window of a house that he knew to be his own.

It was no wonder that the face his mother met at the supper table grew more haggard day by day and that his hands seemed never to get quite still. Joel knew how he looked. He saw it daily in his mirror and saw it again reflected in his mother's secret glances. He would not have hid it if he could. It was part of his power, part of the mystery of himself, and he held up his haggard face like a banner for her to tremble at. He saw through her pretenses, always, to the fear they were meant to mask. He *had* to see a doctor, she kept saying: he was so pale and didn't eat. Joel would just look at her, knowing what, in her fearful heart, she took to be the meaning of his pallor.

There was pleasure in it, a growing pleasure. Weeks had passed in which his mother had not once mentioned the Strangler. When there was mention of him now Joel was the one. He did so rarely, discreetly, by indirection if he could, watching for that small flicker in her eyes. There was just a single time when his prudence all but failed him. Some gesture of hers or one of those displays of pretense meant to hide her secret fear must have spurred the surge of violence in him. Breaking the silence he said, "All these weeks and still not a clue," and saw her eyelids blink over her teacup. "It's got to be somebody you'd never guess. He could live on this street, maybe." He stopped his tongue. Too much? He saw her eyes trying not to not look at him and her mouth loose at the corners where the stitch used to be. Then Joel thought that someday soon he would show his mother the picture on his easel.

That, the early days of August, was Joel's heyday in the

house. From the power, the freedom he felt in it now this might have been his own house to do with as he pleased. He took no care anymore. A chair pushed out of place or an afghan wrinkled or tumbled onto the floor or a spill on the kitchen table did not, if he even noticed, concern him in the least. At the dinner table, that old arena of his mother's tyranny, judging from the look of them it was no longer she but Joel who presided. Even behind an unlocked door he was safe in his attic now.

He saw less of his mother and heard much less of her footsteps in the house. She went out often now and when she came back walked softly and stayed sometimes for hours in her room. She lay on her bed or sat by the window with a book, listening for him. They had called her another time to the police station. They had wanted a psychiatrist to talk to Joel. She had refused, flatly, once more making a show of her indignation. Her lips had trembled, though. Over her book they often trembled again. But release for her was not far off. It was to be a strange kind of release.

On the night of the seventh Ernestine Bell was murdered. Joel's mother got the news only late the next morning when she went out onto the porch to get the paper. The news made her head swim. She stood there until she got straight in her mind what it all meant and then a great tide like a blessing swept over her. About ten last night and Joel in the house. Hadn't she heard his steps in the attic and seen him face to face in the kitchen not long after ten? Proof, she had proof. Standing there on the front porch in the quiet August afternoon she almost laughed out loud.

Then, quite suddenly, her mood went sour. Anger compressed her lips and made her small breast heave and she turned and entered the house. Her footsteps now were the old unguarded steps, making straight for the attic stairs. She

climbed them noisily and knocked three times and then tried
the doorknob. The door was not locked. Joel's haggard face,
in anger or alarm or both of these at once, looked down at
her. She handed him the paper. With her head high and stiff
she turned her back on him and descended the stairs.

It was *her* house again. All afternoon she went about stepping as she chose, cleaning and straightening, restoring things
to order. She thought of calling the police, and did, her indignation over the phone ringing out as clear as a bell. She
wanted him removed, that sneaky man who watched her
house at night. Her son Joel, the very idea! And all the while
she was watching the attic stairs, sure that at the top, through
the cracked door, Joel was listening to her. Crestfallen: that
was how he looked. Caught in his childish act, his little game
all over with, restored to his shamefaced self again. And her
image of how he must look was soon confirmed. Right after
she put the phone down she heard the attic door go softly
shut. She wished she could *see* his face, though.

At five she started preparing a gracious supper. At six she
called from the foot of the stairs and went back to her oven.
She had the roast on the table before it occurred to her that
she had not heard Joel come down. She understood, she
would be gracious—coolly gracious. When she called again
there was barely an edge of impatience in her voice.

The impatience was clearly there the third time, though,
and still there was no answer. There was no sound at all. She
called again, then climbed the stairs, angrily, and called and
knocked and then tried the doorknob. This time it was locked.
In there sulking, she thought: a child pouting behind his door.
She thumped back down the stairs and into the dining room
and ate her angry supper by herself. When, an hour later, she
climbed the stairs again, the attic door stood open and Joel
was gone.

Her lips clamped tight, her face a mask, she removed the cold supper from the table. Joel would get no supper. He would get . . . She put away the dishes and the silver and with her knitting sat down in her chair in the living room. The knitting lay neglected in her lap. Defiant child! Spasms of anger made her small head shake sometimes. She turned her chair to face the front door.

Night came on and the hours ticked away. She was pacing now, peering out from doors and windows. At intervals she went onto the front porch and stood scanning the lighted street, the yards around. She was there when the distant courthouse clock stroked midnight. And she was there when it came to her that Joel, in one of the intervals while she was out here, might have sneaked in through the back door. She hurried, glanced into his room and then went to the attic stairs. It was dark up there but she could see that the door stood open still. "Joel," she called. No answer came. She climbed the stairs anyway and felt for the light switch on the wall inside.

No Joel in the attic before her eyes. Unless he was hidden, buried among the chaos of his "art"—pictures stacked and heaped and hanging crazily, litter of rags and paper and paint spills on the floor. And his easel under the light bulb. There was a picture on it. Her eyes passed over the picture but they came back. It was a face, an ugly, a brutal face, all cruel bone stretching the skin and glaring merciless eyes. Hideous. She switched off the light and descended the stairs. She had got to the bottom before she saw that the hideous face still hanging there in her mind was somehow Joel's face. Though she shook her head the recognition stuck.

This was what made her break down finally and call the police. Yes they would look for him, the voice said lightly, bored. But nothing happened. A little after three she called again and afterward, exhausted, went into her room and lay down on the bed.

Then it was dark, though she had not put out the light when she lay down. This was her first thought. Her second one was that this was not the reason she had waked up. The reason was a sound somewhere. It was not "somewhere," it was in the room, and it was not a sound but a presence. Looking up she saw it, a figure standing over her bed like a giant. And up there in the dark that hideous, that Strangler's face. She screamed. She put her arms up over her head and screamed and screamed again.

Something happened. It was as if her screams had displaced the figure, had distanced and diminished it to where it stood at a sort of crooked angle against the wall. Then, even though she was still screaming she heard a small outcry like a sob, and another one just after. The figure was gone, its steps retreating through the house. She heard his running feet on the stairs and the attic door slam shut.

In the steely light of dawn from her windows she sat still trembling on the bed, hugging herself, her cold hands melded together and pressed against her throat. No sound. The sun rose and occasional humdrum traffic passed by out on the street. She heard nothing. Later on somebody knocked at the front door and then went away. Still later she heard the telephone ringing. It kept ringing and finally she crept into the hall and answered it. It was the police. Had Joel come home? "Yes," she said, "Yes," and stood there holding a dead receiver. No sound from the attic.

Until almost noon, with the door cracked just a little, she sat in her bedroom listening, waiting. At last, though, she grew desperate and crept out of the house and crossed the street and begged Mr. Kelly to come. Seeing her he hurried. He pounded on the attic door for a time, calling to Joel. In the end, while at the foot of the stairs Joel's mother stood with her pale face turned up, he had to break the door open with his shoulder. Mr. Kelly never crossed the threshold, though. He stayed there, before he turned and came back down the stairs, just long enough to see that Joel had used a piece of the wire he kept to hang his pictures.

CHAPTER ELEVEN

Ashes

Late that September Mrs. Stella Echols, the owner and proprietor, died in the fire at the old Cotton Street Hotel. It was
not the flames that killed her, it was smoke inhalation. By a
near miracle the fire was put out before it could destroy the
whole building or even the whole second floor that by then
constituted most of what was left of the original hotel. The
flames themselves got nowhere near Stella's own private room
at the front corner but of course the whole place was thick
with smoke. They found her in her room lying with her head

against the door where she had been trying to get out. She was dressed, though haphazardly, with her skirt on backward and without any brassiere. From appearances there had not been anybody else in the hotel that night.

So they naturally thought at first that it was just one of those sad accidents. But this was before they found the signs of abuse on Stella's body and also before they noticed that the fire had either proceeded very peculiarly or had been deliberately started at several different places in the hotel. Then of course they checked the guest registry. Of the few recent guests only one, who had registered three days before, had not checked out. The name on the registry was William Johnson and the address listed was a Birmingham one that on inquiry turned out not to exist. Nobody, neither the part-time desk clerk nor the one maid presently employed, remembered anything significant about the man. Just a middle-aged man, black hair with a little gray, average-looking. There was no evidence in his room, 210, because there was not any room there, that being one of the places where the fire seemed to have started. So there was reason to suspect foul play all right, but what were they to do? From among Stella's personal possessions they got a couple of leads that led nowhere. They checked and found out a good deal about her personal history. However, these things did not bring them anywhere near a solution of the crime, assuming there was a crime. The matter was left standing on the police books with a permanent question mark after it.

Stella was originally from out in the country, where her father was a rural mail carrier, and when after graduating from high school she came to town nobody knew her. Nobody much knew her when a couple of years later she married young Mason Echols and became proprietress of the Cotton Street Hotel. The hotel, through the death of his father, had just recently come into Mason's hands and he had this as a second reason for suddenly wanting a wife. He was crazy about her, though, for a while. The coolness that presently grew between them was, people thought, at least partly attributable to the hopelessly declining situation of the hotel itself.

It had not been much of a legacy. Because of the motels that had sprung up around town the hotel, a big block-shaped old-brick building on the corner of Cotton Street and Fourth Avenue, was already well on the downgrade when Mason received it. This continued and then, in the mid-fifties, the crowning blow fell. Cotton Street, or those couple of blocks where there was a loop in it, was relocated and one morning the hotel found itself overlooking a street called Old Cotton that for traffic could not begin to compete with the new one. Now something had to be done. Mason decided that by pulling in his horns he might be able still to make a living. What he did was sell off for office space most of the hotel's ground floor—there were only two floors—leaving himself just the lobby and the coffee shop at the front. Then, with his debts nearly paid off and only the twelve rooms upstairs to keep rented, he was able at least to drag along. He did this for about a year. Then he decided that something else had to be done. What he did this time was much simpler and more complete than what he had done before. One summer night he packed his suitcase and left hotel, wife, town and all and never came back again.

Stella was in her mid-thirties then and already tired-looking and getting too thin. The sunken places under her cheekbones that later came to resemble marks of starvation had already appeared and so had that burnt-out look that people most commonly met in her gray eyes. It was no wonder. For all but the first two of the nearly fifteen years she was married to Mason she had been the one who really ran the hotel. She not only ran it. Often, because help now was hard to keep at the wages they could afford, Stella had to clean up the rooms herself, occasionally as many as twelve or fifteen of them in a day. There was the fact too, as people thought, that she was childless and after the first years of marriage never had had a proper home. The hotel was her home, two connecting rooms on the first floor. Until the first floor, or most of it, was sold off. Then her home was the single room at the top of the wide staircase. And that room continued to be her home after Mason ran out on her.

When the hotel became Stella's alone people thought she would sell it, even at the low price she would no doubt have to take. She did make a few inquiries but these did not add up to a serious effort. It looked almost as if she was too tired for that kind of an effort. Either that or else she was for some reason content to stay on running the place by herself, doing most of the drudgery with her own hands. Why she would be content, though, was hard to see. It was true that the hotel, what was left of it, had a certain antique charm. There was the old-time spaciousness of the rooms and hallway, with wide heart-pine floorboards, scatter rugs, glass chandeliers, and window drapes. There were even the old brass spittoons stationed along the hallway. But the charm could not have been anything like enough to compensate her for the drudgery and also for other things. One of these was the kind of clientele she mostly got. Often she had to shut her eyes to what went on in the rooms. Another thing was the loneliness. Much of the time the hotel was empty or nearly so and the big gloomy hallway closed in everywhere between shut doors magnified the silence like the inside of a drum. The door to her room overlooking the street corner was not enough to keep that silence out.

Of course Stella was not always alone, or alone with only

guests, in the hotel. Until she closed the coffee shop for good
there was a cook and a waitress or two and after that there
were still, usually, a part-time desk clerk and maids that came
and went. She did not have much life beyond the hotel but
she went out some, occasionally to the Methodist Church on
Sunday and fairly often, until he died in the early sixties, to
visit her father in the country. There was nobody who could
have been called a friend, though, only acquaintances in
nearby shops whom she stopped to chat with sometimes. With
the hotel guests she almost never chatted, even when, judging
from her expression, one of them interested her. For there was
one now and then. Most of the guests encountered, across the
lobby desk, an almost silent face with starved cheeks and eyes
close to the color of a cigar ash, that registered nothing while
it took them in. But a few of them saw, when she looked at
them, a change come in her eyes, the ash kindle suddenly.
Then she might look them straight in the face for a longer
time than was comfortable, searching them, seeming to be
about to put a question. She never did and the light died out
and all was hotel business once again.

This was about as much as was generally known about
Stella Echols when she died in the hotel room at the age of
forty-seven. It was at the end of that long summer of fear,
when people locked and barred their doors and windows and
looked suspiciously about them at every cranky neighbor.
A lone woman in a near-empty hotel on an empty street could
not have helped but be afraid sometimes and those last
months leading up, like an unidentifiable preface, to her
death were anything but comfortable ones for her. Now instead of on the lobby desk she had the buzzer that buzzed in
her room upstairs installed outside the hotel entrance door.
The nights when she kept the desk herself she locked the door
about eight o'clock, opening it for each guest, and when it

was the young clerk who was on duty she was always there at eleven to let him out. The sound of that buzzer in her room at night, even early in the night, frightened her. She would always lift the window shade and stand there as if the glimpse she could get of the person waiting on the sidewalk below was going to tell her something. At the door, pretending to fumble with the latch, she was actually scanning the face on the other side of the doorglass. Then there were those moments just after she let him in, watching across the desk the head bent over the registry, wondering what in this better light the face would look like when the head was raised. The pen, scratching on the page, filled the silence. Often now, and more and more often as that summer dragged by, she refused to answer the buzzer at all after dark.

In fact toward the very end this was the pattern that increasingly prevailed in her life. The young part-time clerk Paul Betts was called on now, even for daytime duty, much more often than ever used to be the case, while Stella remained in her room upstairs. He could see that she was afraid and he thought her fear was affecting her health as well. She looked more tired than before, the starved cheekbones sharper than before and the eyes now almost exactly the color of ashes. This, he thought, was why she grew negligent about keeping the rooms cleaned up, not caring when the maid left early, leaving this room and that for days at a time in states of disorder. At the end it could be seen that more than one room in the hotel had not been cleaned or even touched for at least some weeks.

She stayed in her room, behind the shut door on which she had had a second lock installed—a big brass one, the kind that operates with a turning wheel. Of course she came down to the lobby sometimes, as carefully dressed and unrumpled as ever, to give some piece of instruction to Paul or to go out for purchases. Or else to examine the registry. She had grown very interested in this. If there was a new name on the page Stella would stand looking intently at it, as if to study it letter by letter. One day, in her most veiled and flat tone of voice, she said, "What does he look like . . . Thomas?" She had her thin finger on the name, pressed hard enough to hold the finger in a slight inverted arch.

"Big fat guy," Paul said. "Got a mustache."

"How tall?" Stella was not looking at him.

"Oh, tall. Over six feet." ·

Stella did not look at him, might not have heard him. Her finger relaxed on the page and then withdrew and she left the lobby without saying anything.

This was only the first of several occasions when, her eyes fastened on the registry page, she asked these same questions of Paul. And then came a time, just days before her death, when she pressed him hard, wringing out of him every last detail he could recall about the man—named Foley, this one. What color were his eyes, his hair? What kind of a voice and what kind of manners? This time Stella watched Paul's face while he answered, and not only watched but watched intently, as if to discern the truth behind his answers. He was surprised at her intensity. He was more surprised at the difference he saw in her eyes. He thought they changed color. Instead of gray like a cigar ash they were, for a few moments anyhow, a luminous bluish-gray that he thought very beautiful.

Paul was a good deal puzzled. She could only have been expecting somebody, somebody she knew quite well indeed. And more than that, he thought, somebody she loved. Then he thought about her fear and how she kept the entrance door so carefully locked and stayed so much of the time behind her own locked and double-locked door upstairs. It had to be the

Strangler she was afraid of and kept herself locked away from. How could she know what he looked like, though, much less feel love for him? Paul could make no sense of it. The man, Foley, as harmless as a dove, checked out the next day. Stella, having shown no further interest in him, was in her room at the time. She, not Paul, was on duty the day when that last man, the one supposed to be still there on the night of the fire, registered at the hotel.

The police could not find any evidence that might lead them to that man, but somebody with imagination finally put his finger on who Stella thought the man was. Not his real name. That was never known, or was not remembered except by Stella herself. She, at least, thought that the man was the same one she had had the brief affair with a couple of years before she married Mason Echols. This, about the affair, was a fact the police inquiry pretty soon turned up.

It had happened during World War Two. To the extent that the man, a young man then, was remembered personally it was for the fancy Marine Corps togs he wore throughout the whole of his short stay in town. Or for how they made him look, rather, because he was to start with remarkably handsome, in a Spanish way, as erect and slim and fine-boned as a Castilian is supposed to be. To the young waitresses at the cafe where he ate, a block up from the Cotton Street Hotel, he was like something freshly stepped down from the screen at the movie house. To Stella, who was one of the waitresses, he was more than this. He was a vision, the very incarnation of all the romantic dreams she had ever had.

It was not only that Stella was vulnerable in the way that small-town girls confronted with such a dream man are expected to be. She had just recently come out of the country, real country, and even by Okaloosa standards, even the standards of that day, she was still a good deal of a bumpkin. That early in her career, anyway, Okaloosa itself seemed like a step in the direction of romance. But the real depths of her vulnerability came at least in part from a special kind of preparation.

Stella's father, the rural mail carrier, was named Henry Dupree. Once upon a time the Duprees had been a family to be reckoned with in the county, a great plantation family. That had been before the Civil War and by Henry's generation there was nothing left of it except the name and some cloudy memories. Henry had some of these memories. Along with his natural good intelligence and sickly constitution they seem to have been the reason for his perpetual discontent. He hated carrying the mail, the meanness of his circumstances, and did not know what to do about it. So he complained and had visions of a better estate and, half on purpose, passed on to his only child a version of what he felt about life.

Having lost his wife when Stella was eight, Henry Dupree and Stella were very close. In summer she used to ride with him on his mail route, up and down the gravel roads trailed by a wake of yellow dust, stopping in front of sun-bleached shacks and houses while she put the letters into the mailboxes for him. She always noted carefully where the letters came from. Mostly they came from Okaloosa or some other close place of little interest, but once in a while there would be a letter with the postmark of a city so far away it was like a dream. She would shut her eyes and think about that city, seeing it with towers maybe and with people in the streets who did not look like the people she saw in overalls and straw or dusty felt hats and shirts with a dark half moon of sweat under the armpits. Clear eyes and faces. And smooth hands with fingernails as bright as if they had been honed.

One summer, just that one, there was a place on the mail

route that Stella always waited for with growing excitement.
It was a large artificial lake surrounded by pinewoods and, at
spacious intervals, elegant cabins made out of brown stone
and cypress logs that looked exactly like each other. There
were shiny motorboats tied to floating docks or else out on the
water flashing in the sun and towing behind them figures
standing magically erect on skis. Now and then she would see
somebody in one of the yards or on a dock but always it was
by glimpses, through the trees. She knew what they looked
like, though. They were the ones who peopled her visions,
who came from far away and passed with never a stop
through the land of dusty cotton fields between their places
and here. She put their mail in the boxes with special care.
One day there was a letter from Italy! She stole that letter,
sneaking it under the car seat. It was written in Italian and,
as the police found, was still in Stella's possession when she
died.

This was the girl who, soon after her graduation from that
country high school, came to Okaloosa and in a matter of just
a few weeks met the Spanish-looking young man in the Marine Corps uniform. He was staying at the Cotton Street
Hotel and that was where he took her, by way of the fire escape door in back, to his room. The hotel then had not much
declined from its original proud estate and all the splendor, as
she saw it, inevitably wove itself into the fabric of those
nights. The young man's looks did not belie him. He was as
gallant and tender and worldly wise as Stella had dreamed he
would be and words he spoke survived in her mind long after
her memories of his inflaming hands had faded. There were
the usual promises, which Stella believed, which maybe he did
too for a while. A short time after leaving Okaloosa he sent
her a postcard from South Carolina with a romantic picture

of a cypress garden on it. The card said, "Dearest—Am remembering. And waiting for the day when . . ." It was signed simply G. She still had the postcard too when she died.

But Stella was no fool and she caught on by and by. She tried to put him out of her mind and finally did, in a way. It was only in a way, though. It was as if G had left in Stella's memory a sort of model or paradigm that she was always searching for in the faces and manners of the young men she met. She was a pretty girl, with distant blue-gray eyes and auburn hair, and she had some young men after her in those days. At least one or two of them seriously wanted to marry her. But the man who fitted never appeared. She kept thinking he was somewhere in one of those great cities and she kept making plans, making even a few brief forays to cities like Birmingham and Atlanta. She always came back looking tired, dull around the eyes. Two years later she was still in Okaloosa, working now as a clerk in Holman's Jewelry Store. Then, after only a brief courtship, she married Mason Echols.

It looked as though it ought to be a good marriage, despite that Stella was nobody in the town and that there were some whispers about her. Nothing of this bothered Mason. He clearly showed his pride and pleasure in her and went at the hotel as if determined to put into it the new life he felt. And Stella, except she was too withdrawn socially, seemed quite suitable. After the first few months, when it became obvious that the hotel's decline was not to be so easily arrested, she began to take a part. In fact she fell into the routine as if she had been born to it, working in the coffee shop kitchen, cleaning rooms, sometimes, even as young as she was, standing in as desk clerk in the lobby. It looked now as if Mason had found the perfect wife for him.

This did not last long, though—not the part that kept the look of contentment on Mason's face even while he spent himself daily in his efforts to renovate the hotel with his own hands, to bring it back in spite of the odds to its old prosperity. One day Stella looked at him with different eyes. It might have been a day when she was keeping the desk and he came down into the lobby with paint on his rather bulbous nose and on his hands and wearing a discolored and sweaty workman's shirt. Maybe, with a humorous groan and one of those small oaths characteristic of him, he sat down on the bottom stairstep and drew a dirty sleeve across his face. "Hell's bells, it's hot. How goes it down here, baby? Any new victims?" He regularly joked about the guests, calling them victims, or prey, or "scalps." "Got any new scalps?" And he called her "baby" instead of her name no matter where they were. On such an occasion as this one she must have looked at him and for the first time seen him in the light of all the things he was not, and wondered at herself.

How could she have married him? Stella thought and thought about this now, always first reciting the reasons that ought to have been enough, the practical reasons. But these were never enough anymore. They were not enough because, in a way that practical reasons never could have inspired, that she would not have allowed in any case, she had been in love with Mason. She had thought she was, really thought it. There was real fire when he embraced her and a sense that beyond, on the other side of his embrace, lay a mystery, a life that was entirely new waiting there in the gloam. As if his embracing arms would take her there. And yet it had not been real. From the other side she saw a man she could never love, a vulgar man who would be content forever with his "baby" and "scalps" enough. Here on the other side, in the lonesome twilight of the hotel's rooms and corridors, Stella was still waiting for that new life.

So it was with her marriage. Mason, feeling it by and by

and not understanding, struggled against it. Too much work, he thought, was the reason for her growing coolness, her seeming indifference toward him, and he tried to lighten her load. He hired a maid they could not afford and insisted that Stella spend only her mornings working at the hotel. It did not change anything. In a few days' time, over Mason's protests, Stella was back in the afternoons again, pursuing the new maid, correcting her sloppiness, at last in an ugly scene driving the woman to quit. Then there was the period when Mason tried with gifts, some of them expensive ones, a gold bracelet once. He would wait to catch her alone, cleaning a room maybe, and to surprise her suddenly produce the gift from behind his back. Always there would be an anxious little tuck in his brow, his eyes waiting for her response. It was never what he had hoped for, tried to see. In the end there was no misreading thanks wrung only from the will. It was not to be expected that Mason would not at last stop trying.

Of course Stella saw when he stopped trying. She saw too when his eye first began to rove and when, later, he had in fact become unfaithful to her. Except for one short hour, though, when her pangs were like those of old losses remembered, she was indifferent to this too. She did think, then and many other times afterward, that now in good conscience she could leave Mason and go wherever she wished or the wind listed. But thinking more about it she did not know where she could or even wanted to go. Not now at least, though the time might come . . . *would* come. Meanwhile, since Mason had turned his gaze elsewhere, the hotel was practically in her hands and this, for now, was what she gave her life to. There was only one more time, and that after nearly ten years, when Mason really asserted his authority. It was when he sold off most of the first floor for offices. Stella suffered that like an amputation. Certainly it was no such blow as that when, a

year or so later, Mason walked out on her. It was not a blow
at all. Now there was not even his physical presence to sometimes draw her attention from her work.

For a while after Mason left her there was naturally talk
and gossip about them and some sympathy for Stella. She received a good deal of free advice. But by and by the subject
palled and Stella, even less in evidence than before, increasingly ceased to be on anybody's mind. The same thing went
for the Cotton Street Hotel, which by now was fast becoming
the kind of hotel people forgot to mention when they named
off places to stay in Okaloosa. The clientele continued to decline, in quality as well as numbers. In a few more years there
were not many who looked even fully respectable and there
were some who looked enough like vagabonds as to make no
material difference. Yet the place was kept up. Nobody ever
came away complaining about dirty linen or mildew in the
bathrooms or any disorder anywhere. The most elegant of
guests, if Stella could have called them back from the past,
would have been able to find no fault that her tireless hands
could remove. At least it was this way until that summer at
the end of her life, the summer of the Strangler.

Paul Betts, the part-time clerk, described Stella in her last
weeks but he never understood much. He was not even there
when the man, the one that Stella took to be her old lover,
registered at the hotel two days before the fire and her death.
It was Stella at the lobby desk watching the man's head, dark
hair going gray, bent over the registry, while the pen
scratched in the silence and she waited for the face to appear
in the good light over the desk. Then the scratching stopped
and the man looked up at her. There may have been a moment before she could drop her gaze from his face, feeling the
blood surge hot into her neck, confusion in her throat. Until
she could turn to the board behind her where the room keys

hung and with a slow trembling hand select one from a hook.
She laid it, a click of sound, on the desk in front of him. Side-
long she saw his retreating face, dark face, black brow, jowls
obscuring the chin line. The back of him climbing the stairs,
the cant of his head as he turned and vanished at the landing.
It was terror. It was as if the void in his wake swallowed even
the air she was fighting to breathe. Not then but minutes later
she remembered what key she had given him.

A little later that evening another man registered at the
hotel and broke the spell on Stella. The plain face asking
across the desk for a room was the face of everyday fact
breaking into her dream. She watched him write with effort
on the registry page, gave him a key, watched him with his
frayed handbag go heavily up the stairs. Mistaken again. Illusion. Her blood paced slow, thick and tired in her veins. Too
tired to move, to lift her hands from the lobby desk.

And yet . . . The words, as she climbed the stairs an hour
later, were the first stutterings of illusion fighting back. Standing at the top she gazed down the wide hallway where three
yellow night-lights barely held the dark suspended, barely
limned the brassy shapes of spittoons along the walls. All doors
shut. Silence. No echoes from her million million footsteps
along this hall, door to door, rag and broom in her callused
hands. She stared at the door where her footsteps first had
started, that one at the hall's end where she had put this man
with the dark black-browed face. Her mind's eye held the
face before her. Her heart began to beat again.

That night behind her locked door Stella spent the hours
until almost day listening for his footsteps. There were spells
when terror shutting like hands around her heart made her
gape and strain her lungs to draw the sullen air. Imagining
the footsteps she would try in vain to cry out. There were moments of another kind, a sort of stirring and tingling like seeds

about to open in her blood and her heart swelling and the air more and richer than she could breathe. At these times she would get up from her bed or chair and stand with her head resting against the door. Then doubt would come again. Mistaken again, illusion. The morning's clear light would show across the lobby desk a face she never had known.

The man did not leave the next day, or the day after that either. He came and went a few times, watched by Stella from the desk or through her own cracked door, but mostly he stayed in his room. What for? As if he was waiting? Once when he passed through the lobby that name, *his* name, sprang into Stella's throat. It got no farther. It lodged there like a stone to choke her, bringing the terror back. Then on the third day the last guest but him checked out at noon.

That or the night of that day was when it happened, after her long afternoon in the hotel alone with him, her hours behind the lobby desk that now she dare not leave, while from up the stairwell the silence hummed in her ears. At supper-time she heard his steps, his feet on the stairs, and watched him pass through the lobby to the door. Gone. Then he was back and it was dark. This time he looked at her, saw her. The look was brief but hard, with an aftermath of shock, as if in passing by he had shouted something terrific into her face.

That had been maybe an hour ago and in all that time, except for the slow heave of her breast, Stella had not moved. Then she did, like waking up. She went and locked the lobby door. She climbed the stairs and after a long pause staring down the silent hallway she went into her room. She never sat down. There was too much blood raging through her fragile veins, making terror that now somehow was one thing with her yearning. Yet her hand was steady. It did not tremble when she took up the comb and before the mirror combed her dark and not yet graying hair. No need of rouge for those starved checks: they were not pale any longer. She laid the comb down carefully and drew one long full breath.

It was like a journey walking down that soundless hallway over the million invisible prints of her feet to his door at the end. As she lifted her hand she had one pang of regret. There were rooms that lately she had neglected, like flaws in a perfect life. Never this room, though. Her hand, still not trembling, touched the door.

From the moment when Stella first stood facing that man through the open door there must have been doubts already trying to start. Or maybe it was just a little later, when she could no longer meet the dark eyes where a light was growing and let her gaze fall away to the undershirt he wore and then to the room behind him. All disorder there, things strewn about, crumpled bedsheet on the floor. She must have gone into that room with her eyes shut and kept them shut when his hands took her, taking her clothes away, touching her body. She would have shut her ears too for as long as she could, listening back into her memory, making the old gentle voice prevail against the obscene one pressing in. She could not have kept it so for very long and the pain would have made her open her eyes. By then it was much too late. There was nobody in the hotel to hear her cries, and her struggles were nothing against him. In the end she found herself lying dazed on the bare mattress, naked, alone in the room.

To find the will and then the strength to lift herself up must have taken Stella a long time. At last she found her scattered clothes, all but the brassiere, and painfully dressed herself. Then what? Silence. She had to sit down again, in this room with the bedclothes on the floor and the lamp broken and the night table overturned. And cigarette butts, ashes scattered around her feet. She stared at these, heard nothing. She did not notice, or hardly noticed, the pain in her body.

On the dresser lay a package of book matches. When Stella finally did get to her feet she picked it up and looked under the cover. There were matches there. She tore one out and struck it, holding it until the flame burned her finger. Then she turned around and struck another match and held the flame to one of the window drapes.

She set fire to drapes on a window at the end of the hall and also to those in a second room. Then, no doubt to get some things she wanted to take with her out of the hotel, she went back to her own room. It may have been that, once there, she passed out for a little while. Or else she found herself suddenly just too tired and sat down to collect her strength for a minute that turned out longer than a minute. Then it was too late. She made it to the door and, staggering, knocked it shut instead of open. She fell against it. She must have made another try or two. Probably she did not try very hard.

CHAPTER TWELVE

Familiar Spirit

When, in the winter before the stranglings started, Douglas Bragg came home to Okaloosa he found that his ancient grandfather was living in his mother's house. In fact the old man, Todd Quick, because his other daughter had died, had been living there for most of the whole year while Douglas was off wandering. The old man's room was upstairs too and especially because of this Douglas thought that his presence would be nothing but a nuisance and a bore. After about a week, though, Douglas changed his mind. He was amused.

He was amused at the old man himself but he was still more amused at the old man's relationship with his daughter, Gloria, Douglas' mother. On almost every question they were the most perfect of opposites and anything from a skirmish to a downright pitched battle was likely to break out at any time.

Besides amusement the old man's presence supplied Douglas with another benefit. Not even Gloria could keep up the moral indignation needed to do justice to both Douglas and his grandfather and therefore Douglas had a good many moments of peace in the house that he would not have had otherwise. Of course there were still enough of the moments Douglas had anticipated. The years of his absence, at college first and then out roaming, had not brought any decline in his mother's spirit of dedication and Douglas had not been back in the house a full twenty-four hours before she was giving him a good look at it once again. In fact on that occasion there had seemed to be even more of it than in the past. She had good reason, though. Douglas was a great disappointment, even to himself, and it had been a long time since his mother had had a chance to express herself on the matter.

"What *are* you going to do?" she said. "At *least* you could have gone on and *graduated*. Even if you were wasting your time taking courses that are no use to anybody."

"I told you. I found out I hate sociology."

"Then *psy*chology. Or *some*thing."

"I did take something. Those things all sound like bunk to me."

Gloria was an angular woman nearly as tall as Douglas and she had lean cheekbones that colored like little lamps when she was angry. She was angry then, so much so that it looked as if her lips might have got clenched shut this way for good. The room where they sat, a parlor when the house had been her husband's, had long since been her study, and books with forbidding titles and covers lined the greater part of one whole wall. They told her, she said, how to understand and help people. Quite beyond her job at the local Welfare Department, this, helping people, was her profession and there was hardly an improvement project anywhere in the county that she did not have a finger into. Not with any support from Douglas, though.

"You think everything's bunk," she finally managed to say. And then, with a change of tone, "What ever *happened* to you? You used to be such . . . such an idealist."

Douglas, sprawled in the one armchair with his feet out in the floor, sighed. "I ran out of steam," he said. This was about true. It had been like that, a little more steam escaping every day, the limpness coming on.

Gloria, just looking at him, sat there with her scuffed loafers side by side on the floor. "And now you really don't care, do you? About anything . . . or anybody. Whether they live or die. You are just plain callous, Douglas."

"Well, maybe you're right," he said. On inspiration—it was his familiar spirit speaking—he added, "In a world like this, though, a man's got to keep his calluses up, hasn't he?"

The look Gloria gave him as she got up from her chair told him how little this was funny. In fact Douglas did not think it was funny either, especially afterward. In fact this was one of those times when he saw his own flippancy as pretty deplorable and, with a few minutes' real despondency, his mother's description of him as just about right. He *didn't* care, it was true. And "callous" was probably not the wrong word, either. But how did you go about caring when you didn't, or get interested where there was not any interest for you? Maybe you pretended and that was the way it came—by acting a thing until at last it got real in your head. Maybe. Anyway it was mainly on the strength of this thought that he did what his mother had been bedeviling him for weeks to do. He got a job. The job was not much, he was a gas station attendant. It would have suited him all right, though, except for having to listen at home to his mother rant about the waste of his "fine mind."

By this time Douglas was already friends with his grandfather. The two of them shared the second floor where Gloria did not often come and when he was at home Douglas, like his grandfather, was always up there. Reaching the top of the stairs he had almost never failed to see through the door to his right the old man at his reading table. If Douglas did not go in he would get a summons. Usually, to start with, it would be a call to listen to some passage from one of his grandfather's Civil War history books, probably a passage he already had nearly got by heart. Then the lecture would come. "General Bragg th'owed it away. Th'owed Chattanooga plumb away. Forrest tried to tell him. Attack! Called him coward to his face. Wasn't a bit of use." The old man's blue eyes, enlarged through his gold-rimmed spectacles, blazed at Douglas across the reading table. "So Bragg just set there on top of Lookout Mountain studying . . . Th'owed the whole West away. Nothing left but running, after that . . . You ain't got much of a name, boy. I hope you ain't any kin to him."

Douglas did not know. His absconded father had not stayed around long enough to tell him.

Douglas had never known or cared much either about the "waugh," as his grandfather called it. Now he found himself interested. It was not so much interest in the war itself, though, as it was enjoyment of the old man's passion about it, the way excitement reddened his cheeks and blazed out of his eyes and, as it often did, lifted his voice to the pitch of old-time oratory. But this was only one of the things that amused

Douglas. Another was his grandfather's habit of dress, or un-
dress. Living alone upstairs the old man had grown forgetful
and was liable to appear with a garment on backward or
inside out or else missing completely. Pretty often Douglas
found him in nothing except his socks and ragged long-under-
wear, the seat flap hanging unbuttoned maybe, and the brown
felt hat that never seemed to be off his head. Half the time at
least he looked like somebody got up for Halloween. Not less
than once a week at suppertime the old man was driven by
Gloria's outraged cries out of the dining room and, in spite
of his high blood pressure, back upstairs to put on the pants
he had forgot about.

Most of all Douglas enjoyed the running battles between
his grandfather and his mother. At the supper table especially
it was easy to set them going. A calculated remark or two and
then he would sit back and watch like a man at a tennis
match. Any of half a dozen topics was almost sure to work.
The Civil War, which his mother considered a Southern folly
much better completely forgot, was the least of them. Child
rearing and sex education were more productive topics. The
latter one especially was, because it made his grandfather
blush first and after that sputter with rage. Most productive
of all, though, was Civil Rights and the Negroes. Douglas was
not on his grandfather's side in the matter but he did not care
much either and it delighted him to see how the old man's
antique rhetoric about niggers and everybody in their right
places made not only his mother's cheekbones but her whole
face go livid. On her best days she simply turned her head
away in disgust. There were her other, her irritable days,
however, when she fired her vilest epithets straight into her father's face. "That's plain reactionary bigotry. It's racism!"
she would say between white lips. It was part of the fun for
Douglas that, to his mother's repeated frustration, these

broadsides never had even the least effect on the old man. Those were nonsense words, spawned in the scrambled brains of a day when half the population ought to be locked up in an insane asylum. He would have included his daughter too, but he never did say quite this.

Except his grandfather, Douglas did not find much else that winter to keep him interested. There was nothing at the gas station, unless he counted Mr. Bush, the proprietor, whose talent for going to sleep the instant he sat down in his glass cubicle of an office—"bushed," a display in a store window— led Douglas to some fairly interesting speculations about time and whether life seemed long or short to somebody who slept through most of it. There was Lola Shanks, whose grasp he had slipped into. She came into the gas station one day, a woman in her thirties already getting dumpy, and she fell, as she told him, for his cold eyes and windswept hair. As it turned out, she was married. As it also turned out, Douglas was glad of it, because it kept her mouth shut and limited her capacity to become a nuisance. Her lecherousness put him off and after four or five desperate rounds in bed with her he tried to make an end of it. It kept on anyway, though, to his consternation, exactly like an obscene habit he never could quite break.

Then it was spring and things abroad in the town got suddenly more interesting. The less interesting matter was the growing racial trouble. Douglas kept up with events, but after all it was the same old story almost in detail that he had heard before in other places. Nothing short of a bang-up riot could have got him really interested. Of course it was not an old story to Gloria. The evening after the brawl at the high school she came to the supper table flushed and bristling, just as if she had entered the presence of the bad white people who were responsible for it. That was one time when her in-

dignation silenced even her father. Or so it appeared.
Throughout the whole meal in fact, sitting with his head bent
over the plate and his jaw slowly working, he had the look of
a man gone deaf on purpose to escape her.

The events that interested Douglas a great deal more were
the ones that began, the first week in May, with the strangling
of old Miss Rosa Callahan. He even walked to her house and
stood around listening among the crowd still gathered there
late in the afternoon on the quiet street. The white front of
the little house crowded among the pine and locust trees
looked back at him like a question. He did not have an
answer then and he did not have one in June when, each time
late in the afternoon, he stood in front of two other houses
where the Strangler had paid visits. Of course his mother had
an answer. "It's perfectly clear," she said to him one night, "if
you've read any psychology. Some poor victim of an ignorant
parent's repression. We live in the most repressive society in
the whole country."

"You mean a *mother's* repression," Douglas said. "They've
all three been women."

Gloria ignored this and went back to her writing. They
were in the study, where Douglas had spent some fruitless
hours among her books looking for something to read. He had
been unable to find even one that was not full of the kind of
jargon she was giving him now.

"I expect he's middle-aged," she said, "because they were
all old people."

"Then you haven't got anything to worry about." He had
noticed her attention to keeping the doors and windows
locked shut even on those hot July nights. Not that he
thought she was seriously afraid. As one of the town's most
active liberals, at a time when the local blacks were getting
unrepressed with a vengeance, she was too busy to be much

afflicted by trivial emotions. There were meetings to be arranged and letters, like the one she was writing now, to the newspaper. "Anyway," Douglas said, "maybe he goes for old women just because they're easy pickings."

"That doesn't make sense." Her pen went on scratching in the stillness.

Leaning back Douglas put his feet out in the floor. At last, his familiar spirit rising again, he said, "Maybe that's what's wrong with me—early parental repression."

This got Gloria's attention. To address him the better she put her pen down on the desk. "You know that's nonsense. Even your father, for all his faults, was never repressive."

"Too drunk, I guess," Douglas said.

Her lips met, then parted again. "You had every freedom. I saw to it. And you know that's true, too. You even had a chance to graduate from the best and most enlightened university in the South." She looked at him a moment longer, then took up her pen again. "I don't know what's wrong with you."

She was not the only one, Douglas thought, and went outside for a smoke.

That was a bad night for Douglas. The cigarette was no cure for his restlessness and he set out walking and ended up at a place named Dorsey's Grill. The beer he sat drinking for a good two hours did not help either. In fact it depressed him more, and so did the bad light and Mr. Dorsey and the boys at the pinball machine. Down the counter from him two old men talked and talked about the niggers and then about the Strangler and then about the niggers again. The flat daze he walked home in made the streetlight drift a little, as if he walked through a medium denser than air. He wanted to *do* something, throw, break something, and once he stopped and looked around him. He saw a police car coming down the

street. But there was one better moment, at the last. His
mother's house was on a street that dead-ended at a low railroad embankment. There was a moon and from the front
porch he could follow with his eyes the ribbons of silver track
on out to the edge of town and away south under the moon.
He stood for a while looking.

The porch light was on. His mother was that much frightened, anyway, and also frightened enough, when he let himself in with his key, to call to him from her bedroom. He answered and quietly climbed the stairs. His quiet was no use to
him, though. The door was open, the lamp burning, and the
old man at his table was looking out at Douglas from under
the hatbrim. "Come in here, boy, you got to hear this." So
Douglas went in and sat on the only other chair and tried to
listen.

It was General Sherman again, his march to the sea. Of all
the old man's readings this was the one that angered him the
most and Douglas, without his old anticipation, sat waiting
for the eruption to come. It took a while, the old voice growing thick at times, grinding on, his head bent low and thrust
out over the book. His books filled half the bookcase just
behind him and his other possessions hung on the wall above.
There was a Civil War saber and a discolored bugle he said
he could blow and a picture, a daguerreotype, of eleven now-
faceless men in uniform. One of the men was his father but it
was not possible to make out any features. Except for these
things and his clothes nothing belonged to him—in this room
or anywhere else that Douglas knew of. The chair he sat in
was not his, nor the table or lamp or bed, and certainly not
the television set, his daughter's doing, that he had turned
around to face the wall. Most likely he did not think about it,
though. His voice ground on in the room, and might have
been what made the skimpy window curtain stir. Out there

forty feet away at window level a streetlamp burned and Douglas watched the insects pointlessly circle and circle around the light.

"Damned rascal," his grandfather said. "Vandal. Not a bit of sense in it but just to destroy. Atlanta nothing but a heap of ashes when he got out of there. Burning every house he come to. Stuffing people's milk cows down in their wells. Damned vandal!" The hot flush from his cheeks had spread all over his face before he stopped, and the stop seemed only to let his pulse recede. Douglas finally looked away from him.

"Why didn't they just surrender, Granddaddy? They knew they were licked."

"Hunh?" his grandfather said. He pushed himself a little back from the table. "Why, no such a thing. We had a good army yet. And General Forrest besides. Fools wouldn't put him in. There was a fighting man, Forrest was. He was . . ."

"A slave trader, you told me," Douglas said, looking out the window. "Fighting for his niggers. Was it worth all that, just to keep some poor niggers slaves?"

He did not know why he had said this, there was no point in it. He could hear the old man drawing breath.

"Niggers, nothing! That wasn't even half of it. Boy, ain't I taught you a thing?"

"What *was* it for?" Douglas said, hearing his mouth run, regretting it. He shut his mouth tight and kept on looking out the window.

"Boy . . ." There was a pause, silence. "I can tell you one thing for sure. You come natural to knowing nothing."

"You're probably right, Granddaddy," Douglas said and after a while of being looked at in silence he told the old man good night and went to his room.

That was not the end of his night. An hour later, fully dressed again except for the shoes he carried in his hand, he descended the stairs and left the house by the back door. Twice on his way, with a curse in his mouth, he came to a dead stop and almost turned around and went back home. She stood there in his mind's eye leering at him, saying, purring to him, "It's a *wide*-open invitation, honey." Douglas, rebelling, clenched his teeth, but in the end he went on.

Those patrol cars seemed to be everywhere tonight, because, just as he came up to Lola Shanks' driveway, another one turning the corner ahead almost caught him in its headlights. He ducked behind a bush until it had passed. Lola's porch light was on but a few quick steps put him beyond its range and in the shadows under the tree at the back corner of her little house. A glance showed him only the one car: no Arthur Shanks. Another glance showed him, darkly, her "flag" hanging from the window. It was a pair of panties, her idea of humor, and seeing them he was to knock at the screen and then go to the back door where, as naked as a frog, she would let him in. And in fact he had taken a step or two before he stopped again. It was his rage come back. He stared at the panties, thinking how it had been ten days and here they were, bespeaking that smug knowledge of hers that he, if not tonight then the next, would be coming back for more. He clenched his teeth. He heard her voice. "Doug, honey? That you?"

He did not move. She could see out here where he stood only the shadow shape of a man, and her voice when she called his name again, not as softly this time, had an unmistakable tremor. He did not move—not unless his mouth did, in what felt at the corners like a grin that could not stretch his lips. He got a blast in his eyes. It was an outside light that glared for a second or two and then went off again. From the window he heard, "You trying to scare me, hon? Come on in here and let me see what kind of a strangler *you* are."

And Douglas went.

It could have been those moments of fright that gave her lust its special edge this time. It had always been too much. Tonight's engagement went beyond too much. Afterward in the dark, lying in his sweat beside the breathing woman on the bed, Douglas recalled the details as if each one had been part of an assault on his naked helpless body. His lips felt bruised and the flesh on his back where her nails had fastened stung like tips of flame. Claws, he thought, and he thought about her cries and the squalls of mating cats and neighbors roused from their pillows, watching. A gust of shame made him stiffen. A gust of rage was what brought him suddenly onto his feet by the bed.

His movement had not waked her and Douglas stood looking down at the pale shape of her too-much flesh on the bed. All that sated flesh, he thought, breathing from deep in its bliss. He could see that her mouth was open, a dark hole where the breath and also the cries and the obscene words came out and did not mean anything, meant nothing. This was the thought that all at once ran like a spark in his blood and made his clenched hands start up from his sides and locked his teeth together until there was pain. It lasted maybe a few seconds. Afterward, astonished, turning away to find his clothes in the dark, he thought about those seconds. He felt his teeth still throbbing. He wondered how fine the hair's breadth was that had stood between him and his violence.

But this was not the end of Douglas' night, either. On the way home, at a blind corner, he walked up on a patrol car parked against the curb. The trouble was that he recoiled and without thinking stepped back out of sight beyond the corner. Then he heard the shout, the car doors, the footsteps coming, and then, with his back to a five-foot wall, he was facing two big uniforms and a white and a black face glaring at him.

The simple truth was not enough for them. It was clear they thought he looked like somebody who would go around strangling people. "For God's sake!" Douglas said.

"Let's have the woman's name, boy," the white one said, breathing his foul onions into Douglas' face.

In the end they locked him up in the back of the car and drove him home and, each with a wrestler's grip on his upper arms, stood holding him in front of the door until his mother appeared.

That was almost the end of Douglas' night. He meant that it should be the end, and once liberated and safe across the threshold he made straight for the stairs. But the sound of the front door slamming behind him barely preceded his mother's voice. "You just wait one minute, please."

"All right." He had a foot on the stairs, but he turned half around.

"Do you mind telling me what you were doing out at four o'clock in the morning?"

"No. I was looking for somebody to strangle."

The way she looked at him, without so much as a blink, suggested that maybe his answer was one that ought to be considered. Finally she said, "Thank you," and went on standing there tall in her night-robe that made him think of a blanket cut to shape. Douglas put his foot back on the step.

"You have to do *something*," Gloria said.

"I am doing something. I'm going to bed."

She blinked. "Something worth doing."

"Like what?"

Gloria hesitated. "I could suggest something for a start." She hesitated a second time, her record perhaps for consecutive hesitations. "You could come to our dialogue group. We're meeting tomorrow . . . *this* afternoon." Her lean face visibly brightened. "It's our first interracial meeting. It's so important now . . . You could help, you know."

Her "love group," she meant. And mixed besides. He thought, "My God!" but he stopped himself. Why be cruel? "I'll see about it," he said and started up the stairs. From the turn at the landing, when he saw she was still watching him, he added, "Thanks," and went on to his room.

Douglas did not hear his alarm clock go off and he did not wake up until after noon. Mr. Bush, who already had a replacement, fired him. Douglas did not protest or even say what was in his mind to say, that a man with Mr. Bush's habits ought to be at least a little tolerant of oversleepers. There were other gas stations, other jobs. There were other towns, too. But this was something he had been thinking about anyway, ever since he had waked up and remembered last night and the police and a possibly vengeful Arthur Shanks. Not to mention Lola, whom he tried not to think about. What was one good reason he had for staying in this town? Or any town? Unless he counted the Strangler. Now that he thought about it, this, to see the answer to it, was maybe about the only reason he had not left before now.

Douglas went home and found, to his surprise, his mother in the kitchen. She was making sandwiches, tuna fish sandwiches one after another, and cutting them into quarters and piling them on a tray. The unaccustomed exertion had made her face red. "It's for our group meeting," she answered him and went on making sandwiches.

"You mean it's going to be *here?* With black folks?"

"It's time to stop worrying about what the neighbors will think. It will be a good object lesson for them. It will help them get used to it."

Not that Douglas minded. In a small way it was even interesting to think about how the neighbors would take it. And there was his grandfather too, if in his world up there the old man happened to notice. Douglas even thought that he might himself take a look in on the meeting. But he said nothing about it and Gloria was too proud to ask him again.

His grandfather was dozing over a book when Douglas passed his door upstairs and went into his own room. The bed invited him and he lay down and after worrying a little bit about Arthur Shanks and cursing himself a little bit he went to sleep. When he waked up, the light had changed. He wondered if he had missed the meeting and he went out into the hall to the top of the stairs. No, there were voices down there. His grandfather called to him but Douglas ignored the call and went down and in through the kitchen and into the dining room.

Through the wide door across the hall Douglas could see most of the circle of people seated around the living room. There were a dozen whites, as against four blacks. At the head of the circle under the mantel was a card table where Gloria and one of the black men were seated. They were the discussion leaders but the discussion seemed to be pretty well confined to the two of them. For once, though, Gloria had the minor role, deferring and nodding her perfect sympathy, content most of the time simply to elicit the black man's wisdom. "And don't you think, Dr. Smith, that if white people . . . ?"

Dr. Smith thought so, at length. "I think you are accurate, Gloria. If white people could be persuaded to understand . . ." He was as black as a black could get and dressed for Easter morning and his big solemn voice rolling out suggested lessons in elocution earnestly taken and flunked. "The evil," it said, "of prejudice is . . ." Douglas took a sandwich from the tray on the table and ate half of it, thinking how much it needed something. So did the discussion, he thought. When he heard the word brotherhood for what must have been the fifth or sixth time he put the half-eaten sandwich on the table and went through the kitchen and back upstairs.

"Come in here, boy, you got to hear this."

His grandfather was excited. He had got hold of a new book some way and there was stunning information in it. There had been just south of town a Civil War skirmish he had not even known about and, what was more, the Confederate major in command who had got killed was a local man named Ward. "Kin to them Wards in the grocery business, I don't doubt," he said. He pointed toward the window. "Wasn't a mile from here. Right where them train tracks cross Okaloosa Creek. Was a ford there. 'Tween a cane thicket."

Bending to his book the old man began to read, his voice husky. As for the looks of him he was at his worst, or his best, today. It was not only that he had forgot to shave and had white bristles all over his red cheeks and chin. He had also forgot to put on his shirt and his pants both and his long underwear had two or three sizable tears and a yellow stain on one thigh. That was not all. Douglas, sprawled back with his feet out in the floor, noticed after a couple of minutes that the underwear flap behind was not buttoned, so that when the old man stood up his naked butt would be exposed. It was then, while he sat envisioning this, that Douglas' familiar spirit came upon him. It came like a seizure and made him sit up in his chair and brought something like a bubble of hilarity into his throat. "Granddaddy," he said. The old man's voice stumbled and Douglas said, louder, "There's a nigger downstairs. He'd like to see you."

"Hah?" his grandfather said, looking up from under the hat at Douglas. "Is it Dick?" Dick was the old black man from out in the country who brought him a package of pig's feet or headcheese every couple of weeks.

"I don't know. He might be named Dick." Douglas preferred the truth.

His grandfather got up from the table and took his cane from against the wall and hobbled out to the stairs. He went slowly, taking each step with care, and Douglas, a little distance behind him, kept wishing he would hurry. That bubble in Douglas' throat felt as if it was already about to burst.

The old man reached the bottom and had already turned left toward the kitchen door when he suddenly stopped. It was the big solemn voice rolling out into the hall. The old man stood there for a minute like a question mark. Then, with his head still thrust out, he hobbled on to the living room door and stood there peering in.

The old man stood in touching distance of a white woman who had turned her head and was looking up at him as if he had been an apparition. So were all the faces in the half circle visible to Douglas, but his grandfather was not looking at them. He was staring straight ahead at his own private apparition: it might have been General Sherman there at the table with his daughter. Douglas heard his mother's voice, like a blade. "Go upstairs, *please,* Daddy!" The old man did not stir, not for a space. His mouth hung open. Even from his place on the stairs Douglas could see how red his face had got.

Then the moment came. It was when the old man turned around. That woman's face was not many inches away from the backside of him and her expression suggested that maybe she had something, a shriek maybe, stuck in her throat. There was not time for Douglas' laughter, though. His grandfather was coming toward him, faster than a hobble, thumping hard with his cane, and Douglas turned and hurrled back upstairs. It had not been as funny as he had hoped, but he pushed this thought from his mind.

In fact there was still some hope. His grandfather, coming on at laborious top speed, had almost reached the head of the steps, and his eyes were blazing. So was his language, even though his gasping breath made the words obscure. He came thumping into his room and, still heaving, stood there staring at Douglas. A moment passed this way. Then, "Nigger down there," he said as if it had been Douglas' fault. "Room full of them. The *living* room. By God!" He thumped the floor with his cane. "Big old black buck. Setting there . . . telling them. Like he was God A'mighty."

"That's the way it is nowadays, Granddaddy," Douglas said. He was maybe a little sorry.

"In my living room, by God!" He thumped the floor with his cane, then thumped again, harder.

"You'll have your daughter up here." Something clicked in Douglas' mind. Suddenly that spirit was up again and he could not resist adding, "You're right over the top of them, Granddaddy. They can hear that."

He looked at Douglas, his eyes almost as red as his face and magnified through the lenses. Douglas saw the idea take hold. "Let them, by God!" his grandfather said and thumped again hard and kept on thumping, using both hands now, striking heavy regular blows on the thinly carpeted floor. The cane had real weight and from downstairs it must have sounded a little like a well-digger overhead.

It had got hold of Douglas again, that hilarity, and he felt it spreading the grin across his face. Almost laughing out loud he said, "Go to it, Granddaddy. Thump them out of the house." But all at once he had a better idea. His eye had struck on the old dented and tarnished bugle on the wall and in a sort of transport he seized it and held it in front of the old man's eyes. "Here, Granddaddy, they can hear this."

The cane thumped one more time, but lightly. The old man stared at the bugle. His eyes when next he looked at Douglas were a really startling crimson, and for a second he peered into Douglas' face as though to discover whose face it was. Then, with a jerky motion, he took the bugle.

Somehow Douglas was not prepared. It was not only that the blast deafened him, or that the old man's billowing cheeks, in which the crimson mounted, had drawn the familiar creases out of his face. The real crux of it all seemed to be a sensation under the base of Douglas' spine, a shrinking in his groin. Even when he saw the cheeks collapse and knew that the blast had died away, this echo went on pealing inside his head. It was as if there had been an answer somewhere in the distance.

But something was wrong. It was the shape of his mother, bolting in between the old man and him, exactly as if she had breached a dream he was having. She had shattered it, in fact, and she snatched the bugle out of his grandfather's hand. "Have you gone out of your mind? What's the matter with you?"

The old man's lips were still pursed a little. When they moved, no words came out. But his eyes, redder than all his face, did not evade her.

"Have you gone crazy?" Her color was nearly a match for his.

"I saw that nigger."

Instantly Douglas noticed the curious constriction of his voice. His mother did not.

"Can't you even be decent? Does that give you a right to . . ."

"Setting right in my living room," he said in a kind of hoarse burst.

For just the shade of a second this made her mouth shut tight. "*Your* living room? It's *my* house! You only live . . ." Her voice died off. Even in her rage she had noticed the vivid color draining fast out of his face. The old man's lips twitched a little, then pursed as though he was trying again to fit them to the mouthpiece of the bugle. Douglas saw him begin to sway, his hand grope for a chair. The cane fell with a thud and awakened Douglas just in time to catch the old man as he started down to the floor.

Douglas of course never told his mother what had really happened. In fact except once, briefly, they never talked about it at all, even after the old man was in the ground. That once came a few minutes after they had lifted him onto the bed, where he lay barely breathing and not looking like himself without the hat and glasses. Gloria, whose face had not even yet quite lost its expression of supreme astonishment, said half under her breath to Douglas, "Why didn't you stop him?"

Douglas did not look at her, he had no answer. He had already put the bugle back on the wall and when his eye lit on it now he said, after a pause, in an undertone like his mother's, "It was his bugle." That was all he ever said. But why had he done it?

It was not much of a funeral, a skimpy ritual conducted all at the graveside under two big cedar trees. Nearly all of the old man's generation were dead and, including Douglas and his mother and Mr. Knowles the preacher, there were only eight people. Dick, the black man who had used to bring him the headcheese and pig's feet, was one. He stood throughout by the trunk of the closest tree, with his head bowed and both

hands holding his hat against his stomach. Another mourner
was entirely a surprise. He said his name was Tom Ketchel
and he came from the county where Douglas' grandfather
had grown up. He looked too old to have even his senses
about him, but he had come by himself and all the while he
sat there tears, the only tears at the funeral, kept streaming
and streaming down his lank gray cheeks. Douglas gave him
at most a few more months, reflecting that this was surely just
as well.

The day after the funeral Douglas took a walk. He went up
onto the railroad tracks and followed them a mile or so to
where the bridge crossed Okaloosa Creek. Below him on a
road that dead-ended at the high embankment there was,
backed up to the creek, a cinder-block building with a sign
that said: HONEYS CAFE. He tried to shut this out of his mind
and he walked out to the middle of the bridge over the creek
and sat down on a rail. There were trees along the creek bank
but no cane thicket, and no ford. He could see these in his
mind's eye, though, and holding them there as background he
tried to picture Major Ward and exactly how he had died.
Douglas was not very successful. The best he could do was a
tall Confederate soldier on a horse, his heart's blood streaming
between his fingers and his twisted face lifted up to the sky.
Even this much of a picture would not stay clear. There was
something missing, something needed to focus things the way
a memory did. He could not find that something. It was as
though his grandfather had omitted, or Douglas had failed to
hear, a crucial detail right at the heart of the scene his voice
described.

A week afterward, just one day before Ernestine Bell was
murdered, Douglas left town for good. Except his curiosity
about the Strangler there was nothing much to hold him, and
by now, after six weeks with no new attack and still no serious

suspect, he thought it pretty useless to stay around. He did not forget about the Strangler, though. In fact he began to dream about him, and always the same dream. From his window at home he would see a figure out in the night half-hidden by a bush. Douglas would go down and approach the bush and, with fear at his heart, begin to circle it. Suddenly he would confront the figure. He could never see clearly at first but always, after he stared for a minute, the darkness over the face would seem to thin. Then what he saw, with an increment of his fear, was a face that lacking a twist or two could well have been his own.

Epilogue

The stranglings stopped in September and since then nothing like them has happened in Okaloosa. Neither has any evidence ever appeared that might have led to the Strangler's identity—unless you could count that strand of human hair. That, because you cannot count the rumors and suspicions that survived for months and years, was the one thing the police were left with. In a fanciful way it was comforting that they had the strand of hair, tangibly real. At least this was something to prove that what they had been pursuing was a man and not some kind of a phantom. Because it was like pursuing a phantom. And from the perspective of time, long after the murders had stopped and still nobody to blame, it seemed even more like that. It was almost as if a spirit, having finished its evil season in the town, had gone back in just the same way it had come to whatever place it belonged.

Bestselling Books

- ☐ 16663-3 **DRAGON STAR** Olivia O'Neill $2.95
- ☐ 46895-0 **LADY JADE** Leslie O'Grady $3.25
- ☐ 55258-7 **THE MYRMIDON PROJECT** Chuck Scarborough & William Murray $3.25
- ☐ 65366-9 **THE PATRIARCH** Chaim Bermant $3.25
- ☐ 70885-4 **REBEL IN HIS ARMS** Francine Rivers $3.50
- ☐ 78374-0 **STAR STRUCK** Linda Palmer $3.25
- ☐ 02572-2 **APOCALYPSE BRIGADE** Alfred Coppel $3.50
- ☐ 65219-0 **PASSAGE TO GLORY** Robin Leigh Smith $3.50
- ☐ 75887-8 **SENSEI** David Charney $3.50
- ☐ 05285-1 **BED REST** Rita Kashner $3.25
- ☐ 62674-2 **ON ANY GIVEN SUNDAY** Ben Elisco $3.25
- ☐ 09233-0 **CASHING IN** Antonia Gowar $3.50
- ☐ 75700-6 **SEASON OF THE STRANGLER** Madison Jones $2.95

Bestselling Books

☐ 80701-1	**TICKETS** Richard Brickner $3.25	
☐ 21888-1	**EXPANDED UNIVERSE** Robert A. Heinlein $3.50	
☐ 38288-6	**JANISSARIES** J.E. Pournelle $2.75	
☐ 23189-6	**FEDERATION** H. Beam Piper $2.95	
☐ 47807-7	**THE LEFT HAND OF DARKNESS** Ursula K. LeGuin $2.50	
☐ 48518-9	**LIVE LONGER NOW** Jon N. Leonard, J.L. Hofer & N. Pritikin $2.95	
☐ 48522-7	**LIVE LONGER NOW COOKBOOK** Jon N. Leonard & Elaine A. Taylor $2.95	
☐ 21772-9	**CASCA: THE ETERNAL MERCENARY** Barry Sadler $2.50	
☐ 80581-7	**THIEVES' WORLD** Robert Lynn Asprin, Ed. $2.95	
☐ 34232-9	**THE HOLLOW MEN** Sean Flannery $3.50	
☐ 83288-1	**TWILIGHT'S BURNING** Diane Guest $3.25	

Available at your local bookstore or return this form to:

CHARTER BOOKS
Book Mailing Service
P.O. Box 690, Rockville Centre, NY 11571

Please send me the titles checked above. I enclose _____
Include $1.00 for postage and handling if one book is ordered; 50¢ per book for two or more. California, Illinois, New York and Tennessee residents please add sales tax.

NAME _____

ADDRESS _____

CITY _____ STATE/ZIP _____

(allow six weeks for delivery)   A-9